Jasper Berry:
Out of Time

an **Order of the Time Watchers** adventure

Book 1

Jasper Berry: Out of Time

an **Order of the Time Watchers** adventure

Book 1

David Dubczak

Conjunction Media

For Laura

For my students

And to all those with imagination

For those of you who think time travelers should be able to see things coming, heed this warning.

Warning: this is the way the story happened. It did not happen any other way. Trusting is perilous, and to ask for trust when not prepared is dangerous. But this is the way the story happened, and that is about that.

You cannot go back and change things that happened (unless you're a person who can). But for those normal people like you and me, it's easy to scrutinize, analyze, and ponder, "Why didn't it happen another way?"

Because it happened the way it happened and that is that. If the great creator of the universe willed it to happen another way, it would've happened that way. But it did not; it happened this way.

It would be easy to say, "This did not happen, this *could* not happen," and use the guise of logic to explain why. But that would be wrong, for your brain does not understand the logic it takes to believe the story. It happened this way, and this is the way it happened. It did not happen any other way.

If you can find it in your heart to believe me and trust me, then continue on with the story. But to trust is to risk, and if the risk is too great, you need not read on. But if you do: trust me, this is the way it happened.

Chapter 1

Now

The Rhode Island Boy's Home stank as boys do. Not the kind of stink one remarks about the cruel, rude, and uncivilized behavior often associated with young boys. No, the ever-present stink of the twenty boys who occupy the former Waveland Mansion hidden off the back roads of Rhode Island wafts onto the neighboring farm in such a way that even the pigs plug their noses with mud.

Despite the best efforts of the boys, the Waveland Mansion still stands, as it has since 1837. The large, three-story brick house with tall spires on each side once stood out proudly. But the past two centuries saw the trees grow tall and the vines encroach, brick-by-brick, until the vines consumed the entire home and the trees shielded the structure from view of the road. Where once passers by stopped and gawked at such a splashy display of wealth, they now drive right past, unaware of the boys hidden from view behind the trees and the vines and the brick.

Waveland Mansion has three bathrooms and three showers, though one is reserved for Mr. Moorehouse and Mr. Moorehouse only.

Mr. Moorehouse runs the Boy's Home, and while some are hard-of-hearing or hard-of-seeing, Mr. Moorehouse is hard-of-smelling, making him the perfect director of a group home for boys without any other home. Maybe his height rises above the stench, or maybe his bushy mustache filters it out before it reaches his nose. Or, perhaps, his skinny body simply doesn't have enough room for the smell receptacles owned by all the other people who turn and run away (politely) after merely entering the front foyer of Waveland Mansion.

Nonetheless, the backyard became squishy and flooded if more than six boys showered a night. Thus, stink lived in Waveland Mansion just like an annoying roommate you got used to after a while.

Every morning, Mr. Moorehouse counts the boys. They line up along the second-floor banister overlooking the dining room as Mr. Moorehouse proceeds down the line, tapping each on the shoulder with the tip of his cane as he keeps track of the numbers. He hardly ever misses a number.

Every night, Mr. Moorehouse takes a walk through each of the five bedrooms to ensure he has the same number of boys as he did that morning. If he does, it was a good day, and he rarely did anything else during the day. The boys cooked, and the boys cleaned (but mostly the younger ones, prodded into motion by the older ones).

When a boy turned eighteen, he could leave. Later that day, a new boy appeared. Always twenty, there were. No more, no less.

No boys ever ran away: these were boys without homes, without beds. If one left, he would likely not have a bed when he returned. Always twenty lived in Waveland Mansion; no more, no less.

Twenty, and Mr. Moorehouse.

This was the routine of Jasper Berry for the past five years. At seven, his parents vanished. Within days, two nice but clueless adults who referred to themselves as "The State" had him "relocated" to the Rhode Island Home for Boys.

No one ever came for any of the boys. When one turned eighteen, he simply left. The rest of the boys waited, day after day, year after dreary year, mulling about waiting to turn eighteen.

Many unusual curiosities occupied this town, not the least of which was why the town of Newhaven Bay had no bay?

But that's not why tonight was unusual. It came in the middle of the night, while everyone was asleep.

"Jasper," he heard his name whispered, interrupting his dream. "Jasper!" the whisper interrupted again, this time more urgent.

He opened his brown eyes and brushed his matted blonde hair out of his pale face.

Mr. Moorehouse looked like a ghost, prodding Jasper's shoulder with the tip of his cane. Three blinks, it took, for Jasper to clear the dream from his vision and acknowledge Mr. Moorehouse's very unusual presence in the bedroom.

"Jasper," he whispered, one finger pressing against his bushy gray mustache, "It's very important that you come down with me, quickly and silently."

Day after day and year after year, Mr. Moorehouse always sounded the same. His boring oldness usually induced a drowsy stupor in even the most hyperactive of boys. Now, his sudden urgency unnerved Jasper. Without saying a word, the small tween slid out of his bedsheet and tried to anticipate the squeaks of his bare feet on the old wood floor.

"Leave your things," Mr. Moorehouse whispered a warning. "Come quick." His gray robe sloshed in the breeze behind him as he turned and swiftly pranced out of the room.

Jasper danced around the knots in the floor so as to not make a sound, like Mr. Moorehouse told him. Expertly, he drew not a creak to awaken his four other mates, still sound asleep in this hour past midnight. Gently, he closed the door behind him, and took one last look at George, Barty, Fred, and Calvin.

That would be the last time he left his room at Waveland Mansion.

Jasper was the one the other boys could count on to sneak through the mansion while Mr. Moorehouse slept. The older boys made him swiftly and silently scurry about, gathering up snacks from the pantry. Not enough that Mr. Moorehouse noticed, but also not enough for Jasper to benefit from his deception.

Expertly, Jasper used his well-practiced relationship with gravity to descend the grand staircase from the bedrooms to the foyer. There, at the bottom, Mr. Moorehouse waited with another strange man. The man was tall, though not as old as Mr. Moorehouse; and old, but not as tall as Mr. Moorehouse. And he was big, like a baby elephant smushed itself into a human suit and then stuffed into a sweater and tried to hide it all under a raincoat.

Yet, in the man's eyes, a twinkle of kindness caught Jasper by surprise.

"Jasper," Mr. Moorehouse said softly, "This is Fletcher."

"Is he from 'The State' or something?" Jasper asked. The question made sense. "The State" is the only one who ever visited Waveland Mansion. But usually, they were bringing a boy, not taking one.

"No," Mr. Moorehouse shook his head. "He-"

"I'm a friend of your parents," Fletcher interrupted, his voice deep and old, but soft. "And it's very important that you come with me right now."

Outside the double oak door of Waveland Mansion, Jasper heard the foreboding sound of heavy rain, a running engine, and the beating of windshield wipers.

"Where are we going?" Jasper asked with innocence.

"I'll explain on the way. Here." Fletcher handed him a coat. An already-packed bag occupied Fletcher's other hand.

With a look of confusion and worry, Jasper tilted his eyes up toward Mr. Moorehouse. The old man took a moment to remember what a kind smile looked like, but when he did, gave his best attempt and nodded gently.

Jasper knew from the old man's approving smile that Fletcher was a very convincing liar, or he was telling the truth.

And so, with bare feet stepping carefully on the tile floor, Fletcher gestured for Jasper to follow. For the last time, he walked out of the double oak doors of Waveland Mansion.

His toes splashed in the shallow rain puddles, down the three steps, to the passenger door of Fletcher's running car. The headlights shone through the raindrops like the eyes of a friendly face, inviting Jasper inside.

Fletcher closed the door behind him and ran around the long hood. Without saying a word, he shifted the car into gear and wheeled down the driveway. Jasper never rode in a car this direction down the driveway, but this was faster than he imagined they should be going.

They said nothing to each other as Fletcher raced down the gravel and slung the car to the right onto the long country road away from Waveland Mansion. Neither of them noticed a pair of headlights pull into the driveway behind them.

Jasper looked up at Fletcher, the gray-haired bull of a man who gripped the steering wheel and concentrated on seeing through the raindrops.

"My parents," Jasper queried with morbid curiosity. "You knew them?"

"*Know* them. Present tense."

Jasper's eyes grew wide with astonishment. "They're alive?"

"I presume so."

"Well then, where are they?"

Fletcher shrugged. "I dunno. And don't ask me *when* they are 'cause I don't know that either."

When are they? *What a stupid question*, Jasper thought, now pondering how much to trust this supposed friend of his parents.

It was then that Jasper realized he was cold. Fletcher had a wool sweater and a raincoat. All Jasper had were his pajama pants and a t-shirt. Fletcher took his eyes off the road just long enough to notice and reached into the back seat to retrieve a bag.

"Here," he said, "Warmer clothes and shoes. Put them on."

"While we're driving?"

"Yes, of course, while we're driving. We're certainly not stopping."

It seemed strange that they wouldn't stop. "Are we in danger?" Jasper asked.

Fletcher simply nodded. "Yes. Yes, we are. Very much in danger."

"And what does this have to do with my parents?" he asked, while slipping thick socks over his feet.

Fletcher gripped the steering wheel harder as an oncoming car shone light in his eyes. The wipers continued to thump.

"Has no one ever told you?"

Again with the stupid questions. What is there to tell me? Jasper shook his head and then pulled a sweatshirt over it.

"Jasper, your parents are time travelers."

What? Time travelers? While Waveland Mansion wasn't the most pleasant of places at times, he was at least safe from having to be driven around with lunatics whose muscles never stopped growing. The other boys lied to him but they never lied about his parents, and they certainly never told him a doozy like *your parents are time travelers*.

It wasn't all that much of a stretch for Fletcher to sense his explanation was not all that believable. Fletcher knew, some day, he would have to convince young Jasper to believe the unbelievable. And so, he began his spectacularly absurd spiel.

"Have you ever had dreams, so real and vivid, yet of places you've never seen? Or never been?"

"I haven't been outside of Waveland Mansion in five years," Jasper sniveled.

Fletcher couldn't stop what seemed like a raging delusion. "But, have you? Dreams so real you can read the signs on the buildings and the people look familiar, even though you've never seen them?"

"Doesn't everybody?"

Satisfied that no cars were coming for at least the next few feet, Fletcher looked directly into Jasper's eyes for just a moment.

"No."

They sat in silence for another few moments, with only the sound of the raindrops and the wipers between them. Indeed, Jasper did have vivid dreams. He had told no one lately. Lately being years. Truth was, most of the other boys at Waveland Mansion didn't have patience for his dreams.

He dreamed of frontier towns in the American West, where he felt the burn of the sun on his skin and the dust of sandstorms in his eyes. He knew the horses and the sheriff by name. He knew the heroes and the villains and all the regular folk and they knew him back!

He dreamed of British castles, and pirate ships, where the captains revered Jasper as being so wise, they set their sails in the directions *he* commanded.

He dreamed of the great universities of Morocco and Timbuktu, where scholars from all directions came to hear *him* speak, to learn from *his* knowledge.

But when he tried to tell anyone, the other boys whispered among themselves, barely shielding Jasper from the insults they shared between them. His parents took him to Waveland at the age of seven; by nine, he learned to keep his dreams to himself.

He thought - he *knew* - everybody dreamed. But somewhere inside of him, Fletcher just pressed his truth bone. Very few, if anyone, dreamed the dreams that Jasper dreamed.

Fletcher watched the road, but tried to explain the best he could. "Your parents are time travelers. Not everyone has this gift, but your parents do, and so do you. They're fighting against an evil family who use their time travel abilities to hurt and steal, and have for thousands of years."

The car slowed, and Fletcher turned off the road and through some trees into a hidden clearing. "Tonight, that family is coming for you," Fletcher warned, as he pulled the car to a stop. "Now come on, let's go. There's only one way to keep you safe."

But Jasper wasn't ready to go just yet. "Why me?" he asked.

With one hand on the door handle and the other hand on his bag, ready to leap out of the car, Fletcher simply said, "Because, in the future, *you're* the one who stops them."

Fletcher bounded out of the car and looked back, waving with incredible urgency for Jasper to follow. But he couldn't go, not just yet.

This was the first moment in the past five years he thought of himself as even *having* a future. His future stopped the moment The State dropped him off at Waveland. His future wouldn't continue until his parents came back to get him.

It was supposed to be his parents who gave him a future. Not Fletcher, and not today. But here they were.

Through the thumping windshield wipers, Fletcher waved more and more insistently with a growing look of fear in his eyes. Jasper pulled his coat tight and braved the raindrops, throwing his door open to follow wherever Fletcher was taking him.

They ran to the center of the park. Just like his park back at Waveland, it had no playground equipment nor anything fun to do. To have any fun at Waveland required using your imagination, and the other boys didn't even have that; they just ran about and wrestled, boringly.

Raindrops pelted them and their feet sloshed in the puddles as they reached the center. They stopped, and Fletcher kneeled and reached into his bag.

"What are we doing?" Jasper shouted through the raindrops.

"I'm sending you back in time!"

Fletcher pulled out of his bag a shining crystal - carved with a hundred flat surfaces, like a gem. It glowed a brilliant pattern of green lights that made his hand shine brighter than a lamp. He reached out for Jasper's hand, extended his fingers, and then wrapped his fingers around it until Jasper's hand firmly enclosed the crystal.

"Is it glowing?" Fletcher asked.

"Yeah!" Jasper responded with wonder. Of course it's glowing! How could anyone not see? What's up with all the stupid questions tonight?

"Close your eyes, Jasper, and picture me, as a younger man: black hair and black beard, far fewer wrinkles."

Jasper did as he was told and closed his eyes. His own mind added on to the picture that Fletcher painted. He could see, vividly, a younger Fletcher as if he somehow knew him forty years ago!

It was impossible. He couldn't have known him! But there was young Fletcher, young and strong, kind and smiling. He could see Fletcher's house, an A-frame with a giant picture window nestled on a hillside. He could smell the donut shop on the town square, and hear the jazz music played in the park on Tuesday nights.

"Do you see it?" Fletcher shouted.

"Yeah!"

Then Jasper opened his eyes. A firestorm of green light danced around him. It fully encircled him, like in a storm of enchanted fireflies.

"Do you see the lights?" Fletcher asked, earnestly.

Bewildered and amazed and distracted, Jasper shouted back, "How can you not?"

Then Fletcher's eyes turned sad. "Because I don't have the gift, Jasper. I don't see anything. Your parents gave me that crystal and they had it all set up in case I ever needed to come rescue you."

Jasper blinked and stared back through the enchanted lights. He no longer felt the rain, though he could see it still pelting Fletcher. The trees in the background seemed to grow blurry. The clouds cleared and the stars in the sky left trails behind them as the earth began a rapid swirl.

"You're not going with me?" Jasper cried out.

Fletcher just smiled, in his ever-so-kind Fletcher smile that made Jasper feel bad for thinking he was a madman. "I'll be there when you get there, forty years before now. Just come find me."

The trees vanished. Fletcher became blurry. A final, quick, but important question popped into Jasper's mind and he blurted it out:

"Why now? Why are they coming for me now? Not the day I was born?"

As Fletcher disappeared, the final remnants of his voice carried on and echoed, "Because, Jasper, *tonight* is when your story begins."

Chapter 2

40 Years Ago

Breathing always came naturally to Jasper. It came as easily as it did to everyone save for old Mr. Moorehouse, and his housemate Trent, who had the unfortunate distinction of getting sat on by the other boys when he lost their usual bout of wrestling.

Breathing is impossible underwater, which is where Jasper now found himself. Unprepared and with empty lungs, he thrashed about beneath the twisting surface of a raging river.

He panicked. Up was down, or down was up, or sideways, but this distinction didn't matter while he tumbled around unable to steady himself. His heart raced and his empty lungs screamed for air, with none to be found. He thrashed and kicked, but wouldn't know how to swim in any particular direction even if he knew where to go; swimming was not a skill anyone at Waveland Mansion ever learned.

A normal person would panic. A normal person would scream that this isn't what they signed up for. A normal person would pray to whatever god they prayed to or had adopted in the last few moments. But Jasper had never been normal. He knew where he dreamed he was going, and this wasn't it.

Suddenly, a giant creature he couldn't see grasped his arm. He kicked and thrashed and pushed against it, but the harder he fought, the tighter the creature clenched. It wasn't the suddenness of the creature's appearance that frightened him; it was that this creature didn't fight the water as Jasper did.

Despite Jasper's fruitless fight, the creature gripped his shoulders tightly, and thrust Jasper above the water, and thrust Jasper above the water. His ears popped once freed from the water. He gasped and filled his lungs with the beautiful, fresh air. For a moment, he forgot about the creature still clutching him.

Only for a moment. Water still clogged his eyes, so he kept kicking. But the powerful creature flung him further - through the air - and like a newly caught fish, he now flopped around on the bottom of a boat.

Freed from the creature's grasp, he breathed some more, and wiped his eyes. He relished the stillness of the boat but still couldn't catch his breath for fear of the creature. The puny wooden boat seemed like it would founder under the weight of over three normal-sized people. Surely whatever creature had so firmly thrown him about the water could still splinter this meager craft.

The boat rocked. Jasper looked up along the side rail.

A hand. Giant, meaty fingers of a single hand wrapped themselves around the rail. Had the creature claimed a second victim?

Then a second hand. The boat leaned as the weight of a new stranger heaved himself up, flung his feet over the rail, and then rolled himself in. The instant loss of buoyancy caused the boat's rail to lower nearly to the water's surface.

Instantly, the man came to his knees.

A giant, soaking wet man.

Fletcher.

Just as Jasper had imagined. *Exactly* as Jasper had imagined. Younger, but with muscles just as big. His mustache bushed out jet black, without a hint of the gray to which old men's beards succumb.

Unlike himself, Fletcher was not breathless. He propped himself up on the bench that spanned the center of the boat, water dripping off his white button-up shirt and tan pants.

Had he gone fishing in his best work clothes? Jasper thought, half-surprised Fletcher wasn't wearing a bow tie.

Fletcher cleared his throat, and peered with his own kind eyes into Jasper's. "You should take some swimming lessons. That didn't look like much fun."

It worked. Whatever time travel tale Fletcher told him - *what was it? Just moments ago, really?* - it was true. He wound up where - no, *when* he was supposed to be, if not just a bit off-target distance-wise.

Jasper smiled as he coughed some water from his lungs and propped himself up on his elbows in the boat's front. "Someone should've told me to learn to swim before I took on time travel."

"What?" Fletcher looked confused.

"I saw the town square, and the donut shop-"

"Ed's?" Fletcher interjected.

"Yeah, Ed's. That's where I expected to end up. Not this... this..."

He looked around him. *Lake? River.* He scanned his surroundings. Wind chopped up the top of the water in which the boat now rocked. It seemed wide, with trees all around. But it was hard to tell. He hardly ever left

Waveland Mansion, but he remembered nothing about a *lake* being nearby.

"The current in this part of the lake can get rough," Fletcher warned. "It's no place for a kid."

"Well then, why'd you send me here?"

Fletcher tilted his head like a curious dog.

"Trial by fire?" he suggested.

"More like by drowning! You should've told me you were sending me to a lake," Jasper complained. "Then I would've told you I can't swim."

"You made it pretty far out here for someone who doesn't know how to swim."

"I was dropped, or appeared, or something."

Fletcher picked up the handles of the oars from the bottom of the boat and began rowing toward shore, maybe half a mile away. He smiled, as he rowed the boat slowly through the choppy water. "Like how they dropped you on your head as an infant?"

"What?" This was news to Jasper.

"Well, you would have to be to think it was a good idea to go into the middle of Newhaven Lake without being able to swim." Fletcher looked around, still confused as to exactly *how* Jasper wound up in the *middle* of such a large lake without a boat.

"But really, how *did* you wind up here?"

"*You* sent me here," Jasper reminded him.

A police siren sounded over the surface of the water. Conveniently from the same direction as the sound, a police boat with flashing blue and red lights sped in their direction and pulled up alongside them in moments.

Fletcher saw, painted onto the side of the black hull, "Newhaven Bay Police."

An officer steered the black and white boat from under a canopy, subjecting the presumably much more junior officer to the splash of the waves as he stood with one foot up on the bow. "Storm's comin'," he yelled through a bullhorn. "Want a tow to shore?"

The junior officer looked as though his years on the force gave him too much action behind a desk taste-testing sweets for the other officers. His plump upper body defied gravity's will to toss him over the front of the bow. Something purplish stained the black tie of his blue police uniform.

Then Junior Officer McCrusty-something noticed Jasper. "Hey," he pointed, "Who's the lad?"

"Fletcher was just, um, teaching me to swim," Jasper shouted back.

The officer looked justly confused. "In the middle of a lake? With a storm approaching?"

Fletcher, too, seemed just as puzzled.

"Don't blame him," Jasper replied, "They dropped him on his head as a kid." He winked at Fletcher, who noticeably did not wink back.

Pausing for a moment to contemplate the appropriate look to show on his face, the officer simply stayed blank and held out a rope. "How 'bout a tow, Fletch?"

Fletcher reached out and grabbed the line as the officer threw it. "As long as you don't take the towing fee out of my paycheck," he said, as he tied the line around a hook on the front of the boat.

As certainly as Jasper sniffed the wind in the air, he sensed Fletcher and these officers knew each other.

"Hey," the junior officer shouted to his more comfortable partner in the wheelhouse, "Should we charge Fletcher for the tow?"

In the pilothouse, the older officer's blue police uniform fit nicely, though his scraggly hair was much too long for a man of his age.

"Just get the traffic lights fixed at Fifth and Main," Officer Oldilocks shouted back.

Finished with the line, Fletcher flashed the officers a thumbs up. "Deal," he shouted. "Get us to the dock!"

The police boat gently sped up, and Fletchers dinghy bounced in the waves behind it. Jasper braced himself against the floor and crawled to the bench seat. But Fletcher simply stared at him.

"What?"

Fletcher's bushy mustache scowled and his eyebrows squinted closer together. "How'd you know my name?"

A splash of water hit them in the face as the bow crested a small wave.

"What do you mean?"

"So you *were* dropped on your head as a baby. Such a simple question!"

"How do I know your name?"

"Yeah!"

Jasper broadly gestured at, well, at the world. "You sent me here!"

Fletcher seemed overcome with confusion and pointed to his chest. "*I* sent you here?"

Riiiiight, Jasper thought. It was *Future Fletcher* who sent him here. Of course younger Fletcher would have to be filled in on the plan.

That was the plan, of course. I mean, it had to be, right?

As the police boat motor chopped the waves in front of them, Jasper figured a few of the highlights would be sufficient. "I'm Jasper Berry. Forty years in the future, you pluck me out of my boys' home, tell me my parents are time travelers, some gang in the future is trying to kill me because I'm the one who stops them... I don't know... *eventually* or something. And then you sent me *here* to find *you*."

Fletcher just stared at him as they took another wave to the face. "I sent you to the middle of the lake?"

Jasper smiled and nodded.

"Forty years in the past?"

Another smile and nod. Fletcher seemed to catch on.

"Well, that was pretty dumb of me."

Looking out across the growing waves, Jasper pieced together the next few steps in their elaborate plan of action. "You said it was a plan by my parents, if I was ever in danger, for you to come get me and send me here. So, I think we need to go find my parents, Irma and Marvin Berry."

"Huh," Fletcher sat, dumbfounded.

"Well?"

"Well, I'd say it would help if I knew them."

Jasper's eyes widened as the bow crested a much larger wave and dumped a whole gallon of water in his face. He spat out a mouthful of murky water as he wiped his eyes.

"Sorry 'bout that," Junior Officer McCrusty-something shouted, leaning against the back door of the pilothouse. "We'll have you at the dock in a jiffy."

Fletcher exhaled. "Am I supposed to know them?" he asked with what seemed an earnest desire to help, if not a tantalizing curiosity about the lost boy he just plucked out of the water.

This didn't make any sense to Jasper. He hadn't seen his parents in five years. This marvelous misadventure was supposedly a dream of his parents. Now, he's found Fletcher, but what good is that going to do him? Old Fletcher seemed like the mastermind. *This* Fletcher is clueless...

A dream of his parents...

A dream...

A DREAM!

No, he knew this wasn't a dream. But what was it old Fletcher said? His dreams *meant* something. And then he got...

The crystal.

Oh, no.

He jumped up with dizzying quickness, enough that he nearly fell out of the boat before Fletcher caught him again. He frantically searched his pockets and patted down his clothes, oblivious to the curious gaze of Junior Officer McCrusty-something.

"My crystal!"

"Your crystal?" Fletcher asked, trying to help.

Panicking, Jasper could barely spit out his words. "You gave me a..."

He paused, remembering just how tremendously tricky his life was about to come. "No, not *you* you, the other you, old you, the one who knew what was happening... you gave me a crystal."

His chest spasmed shallow half-breaths as he leaned stretched out over the back of Fletcher's wooden dinghy. "My crystal! You gave it to me. It's what let me travel here! It was all sparkly, and fireflies, and the world started spinning... my parents... my parents set it... they set it so... oh, oh, no!!!!"

Fletcher, not keen on following him into the water for a second time, used his powerful hands to grip Jasper's shoulders just as he had in the water earlier. They were but a few moments from the dock. "Kid," he explained, "if the crystal's in the water, it's gone."

Jasper broke down crying. It couldn't be. It couldn't be! That crystal was central to his parents' plan - whatever this plan was. He didn't know how, and he didn't know why. He didn't even really know his parents, or Fletcher, or Junior Officer McCrusty-Something.

He heaved over and laid down on the wet wooden bottom of the boat, sobbing, Fetcher's hand on the center of his back.

"Everything okay?" Junior Officer McCrusty-something shouted from the dock as he pulled Fletcher's boat to tie-down.

"Eventually," Fletcher shouted back over the waves. "He thinks he failed his swimming test. If you could just help me lift him out of the boat."

Both officers joined Fletcher on the side of the dock. Jasper's sobbing body convulsed as they lifted him out of the boat and plopped him down on the wet dock. Oldilocks and Fletcher did most of the work.

McCrusty looked up while tying rope loops around the bollard. "You shouldn't'a made him take it during a storm," he judgementally concluded.

"What's his name?" Officer Oldilocks asked.

"Um," Fletcher scratched his head. The kid had told him, but an awful lot had happened in the last ten minutes. "Kid, what's your name today?"

The two officers shot him a look as if nothing odd ever happened in this town. "*Today?*" McCrusty asked.

"Yeah, his, um," he brushed his mustache, "his family has a religion where his, um, his parents let him pick a new name every day."

"*Every day?*" questioned Officer Oldilocks.

The trio stared down at the still convulsing Jasper, wet to the core, wailing and beating the wooden deck with his 12-year-old fists.

"Yep," Fletcher pursed his lips and nodded his head. "You know... hippies."

Oldilocks and McCrusty gave each other knowing glances and said, "Ah" in unison.

"You know," McCrusty boasted, "If we weren't such a tolerant community, I'd say that's rather odd."

"J- J- J- Jasper," his syllables came out between spasms.

"You get to pick your own name and you pick *Jasper*?" Officer Oldilocks heckled.

Fletcher shrugged. "You know, try it on, see how it fits. Gotta pick one by the time you're an adult. Can't pick a new name every day when you have a driver's license."

The officers nodded in unison that this explanation made perfect sense, silently thanking his family's hippie religion for conforming to the needs of their legal system.

"He's staying with me while his parents are out of town."

"Ah, well it's a good thing then that you didn't let him drown," McCrusty laughed.

"Well, truth be told, I don't really like his parents," Fletcher stumbled to embellish his story. "They're never... um... in town too much."

Both officers crossed their arms, and looked at him in a *do - we - need - to - get - involved - we - don't - want - to - get - involved - but - we - will - if - we - have - to* tone.

McCrusty-something's face also showed he was overdue for his next pastry.

With a friendly nod and smile, and a wave to indicate he needed no further help from the kind officers, Fletcher picked a still-sobbing Jasper off the pier deck with the same effort as a bag of canned goods. As drops began to fall from the sky, Jasper couldn't help but notice the car toward which Fletcher carried him was the very same car with which he had removed him from Waveland Mansion earlier that day.

He rolled his wet, red eyes. *Earlier that day?* He prayed mercy on anyone who had to listen to him tell the story. For a while, at least, describing time was going to be *very* confusing.

And, once again, he found himself wet, in the front seat of Fletcher's car, driving through rain. He hoped it wouldn't become a habit. He lay, at least, in comfort of knowing that this plan - however foolish or unbelievable - was meant to keep him out of harm's way.

So then, it was probably a good thing he did not know these two facts:

Neither his parents nor Fletcher designed this plan.

And, whoever did, specifically designed it *to* put him in harm's way.

Chapter 3

In the Abrahamic religions, the Serpent tempted Eve with an apple, with the promise that eating it would give her the knowledge of God.

The ancient Greeks know the story of Pandora, entrusted by the gods with a jar filled with forbidden knowledge. Unable to resist the temptation of the jar's secrets, she opened it, revealing evil into the world.

The ancient Egyptians told the story of Setne Khamwas and his obsession with finding a magical, powerful book. No matter the harm that befell him or his family, the temptation of possessing the book's power proved too much to resist.

Attila the Hun conquered a continent with an army he inspired through murderous brutality. Murderous brutality was what people *liked* about Attila the Hun.

Why are the forces of evil always so much louder and more attractive?

Hayalet may have pondered such a question decades ago, but he had little time nor need to now.

He held his green crystal in his hand and watched the night stars swirling behind the crystal's dancing green orbs. Timeshift-induced dizziness went away for him right about the time he stopped pondering the nature of good and evil.

The swirling slowly wound to a stop, and the glow of the green orbs extinguished. The swirling sky gave way to wind and rain, and Hayalet's black trench coat fluttered behind him.

Lightning illuminated his tall, thin silhouette atop the bridge overlooking the Newhaven Bay dam. In front of him, he could see the chopping waves of Newhaven Lake, thrashing in the storm's anger.

The storm before him was nothing like the storm he was about to bring upon Newhaven Bay.

He pocketed his time crystal. He relished the feeling of the rain and the wind on his scarred, bald head. Raindrops bounced off his tall, black, gator skin boots. Despite the wind and the rain, he didn't button his trench coat. The crimson red shirt he wore beneath inspired fear.

He made no attempt to ensure the cuts and bruises his body took over time healed properly. He knew this look. He cultivated this look. It grew on him and he grew into it. It told anyone who came up against him that he could take a beating and survive.

Could *they*?

As lightning rang around him, he feared not being struck. Being struck by lightning would only strengthen him. It would only increase his legend. Just like every other injury that marked his tall, strong, straight body.

He stood tall, his coat still rippling behind him, with clenched fists and an icy stare across what others saw as the *magnificent* Newhaven Lake. But to him, it was nothing but a useful tool.

Time travel isn't magic, as some think. It's science. Science and biology. But not magic. Not that it wasn't useful to have people *think* it's magic, to have people *think* the great Hayalet is an all-powerful sorcerer. But time travel in itself is not magic.

What he seeks tonight *is* magic.

He turned on his heel and began a purposeful march toward the town of Newhaven Bay. The storm would give him the cover he needs to begin.

He chose tonight wisely. Tonight, the object would arrive in Newhaven Bay. But he sought not to steal the object nor to return it to his overseer.

His look inspires fear, but that's not why he wins. He wins because he enters every battle studied and prepared.

He knows this object will bring chaos.

And he knows just how to stoke it.

Chapter 4

It was no ordinary box.

Judged only by looking at the outside, despite a touch of whimsy in its design, it didn't seem that unusual. Important boxes come with locks, this one had none. Important unlocked boxes come with guards, this one had none.

This box, a perfect three foot cube, didn't stand out because of the odd choice of copper siding or the riveted leather edging.

More curious, perhaps, was the hole in the side. One inch was all, in the middle of a single side. Clearly a hole, yes, but one that did not allow a person to look at the contents inside. It was as if the box held a mysterious void. Through this hole, you could see nothing.

But that was just it: normally, you can *see* nothing. Through this hole, you could *not see* nothing the same way you could not see anything. This hole robbed the light from the outside and returned nothing back.

Another clue of unordinaryness is the box's seeming unwillingness to open. No handles, none of Grandma's packaging tape, no buttons nor locks nor codes. A big empty box filled to the brim with nothing.

This foreboding mystery warned all not to approach, go near, nor attempt to open the box. And yet, the very nature of this box made it irresistible in its curiosity.

Jasper found himself drawn to the box. He inched closer, aligning his eyeball with the hole, when suddenly...

BLINDING LIGHT!

Jasper awoke from his dream with the rude flashing of pure sunlight through a crack in the window shade directly on his eyes. "Aaaarrrgggghhh," he groaned, reflexively raising his arm to block the brightness.

Blinking the surprise and sleep out of his eyes, he sat up in the bed. It was a nice bed - a nice bed with comfy blue sheets just big enough for one tucked into the corner of the room. A bedroom, he presumed, seeing as how it was a room with a bed in it. What other rooms have beds in them, save for bedrooms and mattress stores?

Every day for the past five years, Jasper woke up to a cacophony of sounds: his bunkmates tussling through drawers, the other housemates making breakfast, Mr. Moorehouse's cane thumping on the wooden floor of the second-floor hallway of Waveland Mansion.

But now, silence. *Blissful* silence? He wasn't sure yet.

He vaguely remembered Fletcher handing him a stack of dry clothes, and then leaving him alone to collapse on the bed.

Dry clothes... where did these come from? And were they... Jasper examined his super short sleeves and oddly cut neckline. Were they *girl clothes?* Was there a girl in the house somewhere? Had he slept in a girl's bed?

In his first year at Waveland Mansion, an older boy told him that some zoo animals become so accustomed to their cage that they don't want to leave the cage even when granted freedom. "Never be like one of those animals," the boy told Jasper.

Jasper wondered why the boy felt the need to impart such advice. He went to ask him the next day, only to discover the boy had fled in the middle of the night. Ironically, it was Jasper who Mr. Moorehouse charged with stripping down the boy's bed, cleaning the sheets, and preparing it for the arrival of a new boy later that day.

Why would a caged animal refuse to leave when granted freedom? He now began to understand. No, he wouldn't sit in this bed all day. He *would* leave. He *would* figure out what's going on. But that didn't mean he wasn't scared.

The room was typical. A bed. A dresser. But it didn't have that lived-in look of a kid's room. The beige walls were too clean and unscuffed to have been around a kid who wasn't old enough to respect the work their parents put into painting them. The dresser was too pristine for anyone to have used it regularly.

He took his first trepidatious steps off the bed, almost tip-toeing on the plump carpet over to the dresser. Five drawers tall, he opened the middle one. Empty. One by one, he examined the rest of the drawers. They, too, were empty.

So, not a girl's room.

He shut the final drawer so as to not make a banging sound and took another look around the room. It wasn't just to look; it was to study.

What happened yesterday?

Yesterday, Fletcher picked him up from the boy's home. Unusual, Jasper thought, but Mr. Moorehouse didn't stand in his way. That meant Mr. Moorehouse was in on the plan.

Did that mean Fletcher was a good guy? Not necessarily. Mr. Moorehouse and Fletcher could be criminal co-conspirators! He could be in grave danger! He could be in danger of being kidnapped, thrown into a lake, and have to be rescued by…

Fletcher.

Who is Fletcher?

The unremarkable framed paintings on the walls gave no clue. No pictures of Fletcher, no family. Most of the paintings displayed ships or boats, and tranquil port side towns. In the largest, under the rays of a rising sun, a fleet of sailing ships with stowed sails lay still, docked in "Liverpool, 1750." Staring at that painting for a moment, it was almost as if he could see the residents of Liverpool going about their daily work.

Fortunately, the residents of Liverpool, 1750 didn't need his help right now. His attention moved on, to a bookshelf below the painting. The collection didn't show any particular interests. Old books, like Dickens, to coffee-table photo albums. Even one he recognized: <u>Paddlewheelers of the Mighty Mississippi</u>. He recalled flipping through an old copy of this one by his bedside at Waveland Mansion, and the story in the middle that captivated him - the sternwheeler *Natoma*. He flipped to the page showing passengers ascending the gangway to the majestic vessel on her last voyage. They claimed it was a boiler explosion that sank her outside St. Louis, but others weren't so certain.

Carefully, he replaced the book, moved on to the bedroom door and carefully poked his head out. The door didn't open to a hallway, as he expected. His room was on the second floor of a large house, and all four bedrooms on the second floor opened to a central foyer, with a large window in the house's front, overlooking the lake.

The house actually seemed about as grand as Waveland Mansion, but better taken care of. The overhang on which he now stood stretched out over the main floor of the house. Below him, a kitchen, dining, room, and a living room with a fireplace at the base of the grand window.

Jasper thought he could stand and look out at the lake all day! He had never seen such a sight! Now that the storm was over, the sky was a perfect blue and the waves had gone away to reflect the trees perfectly in the water's gentle ripples.

"Hello?" he called out over the railing. "Hello? Fletcher?"

No response.

"Anyone?"

His voice echoed through the house, but no other voice rang out in reply. No Fletcher. No girl.

He wasn't ready to check the other rooms on the second floor - not yet. He cautiously kept tiptoeing down the staircase that wound along the side of the house. "I'm awake!" he called out.

At the bottom level, he continued his search for clues into his mysterious rescuer, captor, or combination of the two. Above the fireplace mantle, where people normally put pictures of their family...

Jasper suddenly felt weak. He stopped and braced himself on the corner of a couch. The thought of a *family - his* family - his parents used to keep their picture on the fireplace mantle. He hadn't thought of that since going to Waveland.

He had to take a few deep breaths and push through. He didn't know what to expect, and he didn't like that feeling. *Keep going*, he thought.

The mantle stood empty, with no pictures of Fletcher nor a family. More tasteful yet unimpressive paintings decorated the bottom level - paintings of beaches, sunsets, farm life - but nothing that gave him any insight into Fletcher.

Maybe Fletcher rented this house, for all he knew.

But then he noticed something on the dining room table - a note, folded in half to stand on its edge. *"Jasper"* it read on the front of the note.

Grateful he could take a moment to conserve brain power and not have to worry about whether he should read the contents of the note, he picked it up and read.

Jasper

I hope you slept well. Sorry about the clothes. They belong to my niece. They're all I had.

I had some business to attend to in town this morning. There's cereal and milk in the refrigerator. I should be home by lunch.

Make yourself comfortable. We'll try to figure this whole thing out when I get home.

Fletcher

He put down the note and nodded. *That explains the clothes*, he thought.

BANG BANG BANG BANG!!!!

The swift antsy pounding on the front door rattled the door frame as much as it did Jasper's heart rate. He jumped and dropped the note back on the table. The house's front door stood on the other end from the large picture window overlooking the lake. Through the heavy wooden door's window... a girl!

Older than him, by the look of it, the dark-skinned girl's spring-loaded hair bounced atop her head as she kept pounding the door. Her bright eyes locked on to Jasper intently, and she pounded harder.

"Jasper!" she shouted. "Jasper!"

What? Who was this witch that knew his name? A witch was the only explanation. Nobody here but Fletcher knew him, and even barely so. The cops he met yesterday think "Jasper" is yesterday's news. No, he had to be wrong. She wasn't shouting...

"JAAASPEER!"

She was.

Wide-eyed and in disbelief, he just stared at the door and pointed to himself in doe-eyed stupidity. *Me?* He signaled.

"Yes, you!" the girl's muffled shouts made their way to him. "Open this door!"

If Jasper had truly thought about it, he wouldn't have appreciated how open to suggestion people are. Here, a stranger he doesn't know stands at the door of a stranger he doesn't know and demands to be let into the house of the stranger he doesn't know. And, yet, not because it was a good idea but because of her sheer insistence... he did it.

He unlocked the door. The girl swiftly pushed it open, slipped inside with all the energy of a nervous capuchin monkey, slammed the door shut behind her and quickly bolted not one, but both locks.

Her bright eyes darted around the ground floor, scanning, jumping about from corner to corner before landing on Jasper's forehead.

"Is Fletcher here?" she quietly demanded, a hint of suspicion in her voice.

Jasper performed a swift series of calculations in his head. He could either tell her the truth, he could say that Fletcher's upstairs, or just had to step out for a bit, or...

"He's not here," she jumped in and interrupted his thinking. "If he were here, the door wouldn't've been locked."

She marched into the living room, sucking Jasper behind her with the wind vortex spun up by her quickness. "I got a lot to catch you up on. We better get started."

Jasper shook his head. "What?" he asked, once again disappointed by how little his answers reflected the amount of thinking he was doing.

The girl spun back around with nearly enough intensity to cause a hurricane right there in the living room. "My name's Ertha, by the way. Fletcher's my uncle, and yes, those are my clothes. They don't fit anymore, you're welcome to keep them. We got a lot we got to work through, so sit down on the couch and get comfortable."

But he did not sit down on the couch. His feet - through no decision of his own - remained firmly planted in the kitchen. His face stared blankly, yet another disappointingly poor representation of what was happening in his mind.

Sensing Jasper's frustration, Ertha took a breath, and slowed her tempo half a beat.

"My name's Ertha. I'm an archeologist. A time archeologist. I'm the reason you're here."

Chapter 5

The most powerful person in Newhaven Bay isn't the mayor, Shelly Nygaard. It's the President of the Newhaven Bay Boater's Group, or the "Yacht Club," as they called it, in perhaps one of the most ill-named groups of all time.

Does one need to be a boater to join the Yacht Club? Not by a nautical mile! At one point, yes. But then, the group grew to include any businesses that supported the boaters, and then any businesses that supported those businesses, and then anyone related to anyone who worked at those businesses.

Today, just about everyone who lives in Newhaven Bay is a member of the Yacht Club! Except for the mayor, who by the provision set forth in town bylaw 102.66(a)(c), must resign from the Yacht Club upon being elected mayor.

And, yet, as president of the Yacht Club, Fletcher wasn't exactly sure what he did. Or why, today, he was called out to Fisherman's Park at sunrise. Well, he knew *why*. He just wasn't sure what anyone expected him to actually *do*.

Newhaven Bay first popped up on the map one hundred fifty years ago, when a group of European settlers tried to form a fishing town around a lake the native tribes had long given up on. There were no fish in Newhaven Bay, until Broderick Lillenthall had the bright idea to plant fish in the lake the same way farmers plant corn.

That didn't work very well, and it was his ten-year-old daughter Lillian who suggested they should just allow the fish to swim around instead of being planted into the lakebed tails up.

Now that fish actually lived in the lake, the natives made another go at rebuilding their settlement on the opposite side of the lake as the new town of Newhaven Bay.

Planting fish attracted fishermen, and pretty soon they found themselves with bigger boats, needing a bigger lake. So they built a dam. The dam swelled the lake to quadruple its size, flooding the native settlement and causing them to give up for a second time.

Today, Newhaven Bay finds itself a town of two thousand, tucked away between the east side of the lake and the bottom of a small range of hills.

Fletcher stood, arms crossed in his brown woolen sweater and khaki work pants. Fisherman's Park stood in the town's very center, and the Fisherman's Memorial Statue stood in the very center of the park.

Or at least, it used to, until sometime last night when a vandal toppled the bronze statue of a single angler holding a fish to the ground. There had been some controversy about the statue in recent years. The whole town erupted into an uproar when eight-year-old Timmy, for a school project, measured the trout at the end of the fisherman's pole and found it too short to catch and keep according to the town's regulations.

(Mostly, though, the town was upset with the teacher who assigned Timmy the project, and an angry mob ran her out for having the audacity to question their cultural history).

Flanking Fletcher, officers Oldilocks and McCrusty-something stood next to him. Fortunately, Fletcher knew Oldilocks as "Sergeant Pierce," and he knew McCrusty as "Deputy Street."

Pierce's freshly brushed hair did little to calm its straggles, but Street's new tie gave him at least a slightly improved image. They crossed their arms and stared at the toppled statue.

More specifically, they stared at the unusual copper box in its place on the concrete pedestal.

Customarily, when you don't know what to say, you say nothing. Deputy Street hadn't yet learned this lesson. "What is it?" he asked.

"What does it look like to you?" Pierce chipped.

Street shrugged. "I dunno. A box?"

"So then why did you feel like you needed to ask?"

"To make sure you know, I guess?"

"I know what a box is, thank you," Pierce fired back, smartly.

Fletcher held his arms out, as if to separate the two officers who hadn't yet moved closer to each other. "Fellas," he said, "have you tried taking it back to the station?"

Pierce cleared his old throat. "Actually, that's the thing, Fletch: we can't lift it off the pedestal."

"Yeah," Street chimed in, "it's good and stuck."

Fletcher cautiously stepped up and nuzzled the three-foot cube with his foot. "Stuck? Or heavy?"

"What's the difference?" asked Pierce.

"Well, *stuck* means, well, *stuck*," Fletcher explained. "Conversely, *heavy* isn't stuck, it's just, um…"

"*Heavy*," Street happily contributed.

Fletcher found himself thankful in that moment that crime was a relative rarity in Newhaven Bay.

Before he could say anything, the screeching of car tires dragging over concrete by a carelessly parked car interrupted the picturesque scene of the slightly defaced park.

The officers lowered their heads and stared at the ground. "That's Mayor Nygaard," Pierce complained with a touch of guilt.

Street commiserated, "She's gonna be mad that we called you first."

Mayor Shelly Nygaard didn't step out of the car. She *rose* through the open door the way steam exits a boiling kettle. Appropriate, they thought, because ten minutes in the car with Mayor Nygaard is enough to make you *feel* like you're in a boiling kettle.

Tall, with wispy-red hair and lightly freckled skin that had avoided sunlight as much as possible, the mayor covered her delicate features with a silky-white outfit, headscarf, cartoonishly-large sunglasses, and heels. Though she hid her eyes, her look of contempt shone through them.

With swift gracefulness, she danced toward them with purpose, sauntering across the picturesque trees toward the pedestal.

She met them and pulled her sunglasses down slightly. "Good morning, gentlemen," she carefully exercised her acting skills to cover her disdain for them. "And I see Mr. Fletcher is here as well, how lovely," she lied.

"Mayor," Fletcher greeted her nicely. His continual niceness toward her was one of the many things that irritated her about him.

"What have we here?" she asked, beginning a slow walk to investigate the object.

The three men stumbled over themselves to stupidly explain how they arrived at the conclusion that *they don't know*, and that they can't figure out how to move it.

"Have we looked inside?" asked the mayor.

Again, the three men shook their heads, with Fletcher a bit miffed for how stupid he always seemed when he was with these two.

"You did notice that hole, did you not?"

Again, the men shook their heads.

The mayor carefully leaned down, removed her sunglasses, and pressed her eye up to the hole in the side. Her white silk summer scarf fluttered in the breeze.

"Veeeerrrryyy curious," she awed, "Very curious."

"What do you see?" asked a very curious Deputy Street.

She studied for another moment. "Nothing."

"Nothing?" asked Fletcher.

"Well, no. Not exactly. I can't see anything, but I also can't see that it's nothing."

She moved aside to let the gentlemen have a look, and they came back up to agree that, at this point, they were no further than they were ten minutes ago. A giant, unmovable box of *maybe* nothing.

Fletcher, the problem-solver, was the first to suggest a solution. "I think we should get a truck out here," he offered. "Tie a tow rope to it and try to pull it away. Take it to the police station, and then we can figure out what to do with it there."

But the mayor just shook her head, shaking faster and more intently the longer Fletcher talked. "Oh, no, no, NO!" she insisted. "Whatever that is, I don't want to run the risk of breaking it and letting whatever's inside there out. I think it's time we call a town meeting."

Fletcher's eyes shot wide. "Mayor, no! That'll never..."

But the mayor gently pressed her index finger into his chest and silenced him with gentle authority. "Oh, no, Mr. Fletcher. I can't just make decisions like this like you can at the Yacht Club. This is a democracy. We must allow the town to have a *voice* in this decision."

Then, she donned her sunglasses, and patted Sargeant Pierce on the shoulder. "Not to worry, dear, I'll get everything arranged!"

As she whisked herself away, the three men remained staring at the object. "Boys," Fletcher warned, "You better beef up your security. Whatever this thing is, it's about to cause trouble."

***

From a nearby hillside, Hayalet looked through a long looking glass at the site of the object. As he pulled the looking glass away from his eye, he smiled.

The object has arrived. He has work to do.

Chapter 6

The clothes Jasper wore belonged to Ertha, the girl who now sat on the living room couch across from him. At least, they used to. Jasper figured her to be about six or seven years older than him, and so the clothes no longer fit.

And, for the bedroom, at least she wasn't the current occupant. When she came into the house, she only asked if *Fletcher* was home, not anybody else. Fletcher lives here, in this giant, modern, brightly lit window-filled hillside home overlooking the lake, all by himself.

Did that make Fletcher lonely? Only time would tell.

And this girl, Ertha, knows who he is and is his... *archeologist?* Very curious.

"What does it mean, you're an archeologist?" Jasper asked, interrupting a stream of ramblings that he hadn't really been paying attention to.

Ertha stopped mid-stream and gawked at him. "You really *don't* know anything, do you?" She said with utter surprise. "Wow... okay..."

She stood up and bounced around like she was warming up for a tennis match. "Well, here we go, we'll start at the beginning." Jasper could see her mental calculations as she tried to determine just what part of the story was the beginning. "Time travelers need research. You can't just go to any particular place in time. You need accurate information in order to build a mental picture of where you're going. You need to know the buildings, the people, the geography. If you don't have a clear dream of what the place you're going to looks like, you'll never get there.

"And, when you do get there, you need to know how to act, how to behave, how to fit in." She leaned forward and looked him square in the eye. "Ever heard of medieval witch burnings?"

"Yeah," he nodded, "where people were falsely accused of being witches in medieval Europe and burned alive?"

"They weren't witches. They were time travelers. They knew things that the time-natives weren't ready to understand. The only way the time-natives could explain how they knew all that was to consider them witches." Ertha looked at the ground with a hint of regret. "A lot of good time travelers died before they wisened up and started working with archeologists."

That answered a major question. He decided to skip the entire history of time travel and asked the more important question:

"Who's trying to kill me?"

Ertha scratched the back of her neck through her bouncy black, curly hair. "Um," she paused, "I don't *completely* know the answer to that."

Jasper jumped up from his seat! "What?!" he shouted. "What do you mean?"

"Now, calm down, I know a little. I just don't know the entire story because it happens in the future and I'm a time-native to here. Sit, please?"

Reluctantly, Jasper sat. But he folded his arms and plopped back down on the couch.

"The Krylios Family runs all the time travelers. Time travelers all over were in danger - being burned at the stake as witches, arrested for trespassing when they wound up on somebody's property during their jump, arrested for being cult leaders when they're just trying to warn people about the future.

"Krylios the First realized what was going on. He tracked down time travelers - just a few - and offered them protection, for a price."

"What kind of protection?"

"He would monitor the news and the history books. If they got in trouble, he would know, and make arrangements to help."

Jasper gulped. "And what kind of price?"

Ertha sat down slowly, leaned forward, and wrapped her arms around the back of her neck. She said nothing.

Jasper leaned in. "What kind of price, Ertha?"

Again, she said nothing. She wasn't ready. "So, Krylios is trying to kill me?" Jasper pushed the conversation along.

Ertha sat back up. "Krylios IV, his great-great-grandson. But it's not just him. He's not the one who does the dirty work. He has an enforcer. He's a tough, evil monster. One of them is trying to find you."

"And this evil monster? Does he have a name?"

Ertha shuddered as she spoke. "Hayalet."

Jasper felt the spirit of the room darken. It was the most mind-bogglingly strange sensation. He wasn't sure how, and he wasn't sure why, and there was no way this could be possible, but he *knew* that name: *Hayalet*. The moment Ertha breathed the name into the room, Jasper was instantly aware: of all the evils in the world, Hayalet was likely an instigator of a great deal of them.

And with that knowledge, came the memory of what Old Fletcher told him in the car last night. Somehow, in the future, it's Jasper himself who stops them. But how? He knew it had something to do with the unanswered question still between them.

"Ertha," he leaned in, insistently. "How does Krylios protect the time travelers? What's the price?"

A sound from outside broke Ertha's focus. She spun toward the kitchen window, and her eyes widened when she looked outside. "Fletcher's home!" she gasped. Her eyes darted about, quickly calculating an exit strategy. A sliding door below the grand picture window seemed like her target.

She jumped and pranced to the lakeside door. "I'll have to tell you later."

"But-" Jasper protested.

"Stay safe!"

"But-"

"I'll pop in next time you're alone!"

Jasper tried to run, but he couldn't catch her. "But what's the price!"

Ertha started to push the sliding door closed. "They don't know you're here, which is good." She turned to run, but then spun back and shouted through the glass, "And don't tell Fletcher I'm in town!"

The sound of keys opening the front latch distracted Jasper for a single moment. By the time he turned back, Ertha was gone.

Fletcher opened the front door and took a moment to relish the solidarity of his grand lakeside home before he spotted Jasper in the living room.

"Ah, you're awake. Good. Now we can figure out what's going on."

Chapter 7

The crystal is the key to everything. As far as he was concerned, Jasper had three options: die trying to find it, get in big trouble returning Fletcher's stolen rowboat empty-handed, or come back with some answers. Of the three, he greatly preferred the last.

Rowing Fletcher's stolen rowboat across the quiet lake in the middle of the night, Jasper reviewed his evidence: Ertha told him *dreams* enabled time travel. Time travelers built detailed dreams of where they wanted to go. Earlier, when Fletcher rescued him, it was putting the crystal in his hand that started the time travel process. Ergo, dream plus crystal equals time travel.

What happened between Fletcher and Ertha?

Jasper shook his head to shake out such intrusive thoughts. He didn't have time for this right now. He stole Fletcher's boat in the middle of the night. It was his only option, really, for Newhaven Bay's elite police task force already knew he couldn't swim, and he doubted Fletcher would allow him to simply take the boat.

When Fletcher rescued him, he could see the crystal glowing and Fletcher could not. If that were still the case, the blackness of night is the best time for Jasper to retrieve the crystal from the lake's bottom.

Maneuvering the rowboats oars came quickly to him, as if he had been a boater his entire life. The paddles swished through the water in rhythm, steady enough a talented musician could have built a song around it.

Swish. Swish. Swish.

Under the moon with the dim lights of Newhaven Bay growing dimmer in the distance, Jasper tried to remember where he had arrived in the lake in the first place. There wasn't much to go on. He was under a bit of shock and stress at the time, so it wasn't exactly like he plotted his coordinates. The best he could figure was to start in the exact center...

And hope the crystal shone brightly.

He dragged the paddles in the water, disrupting the rhythm but easing the boat to a stop. With no wind, only Jasper's movements rocked the boat.

Not being able to swim might have been a problem for a lesser mind, but Jasper worked out a solution: the boat's rope and anchor. He checked the rope again, and made sure it was coiled cleanly on the boat's floor.

While waiting for Fletcher to fall asleep earlier that night, Jasper timed himself holding his breath. Two minutes, if he focused, before his body overrode his own wishes and forced himself to breathe again. To play it safe, he would stay on the lakebed only thirty seconds, no more.

He flipped his legs over the side of the boat and then, with the anchor in both hands, he took a deep breath and slipped off the side into the water. The sounds of the world gave way only to the pressure of water against his ear. The weight of the anchor in his hands pulled him swiftly to the bottom.

Moments later, his feet hit the squishy silt of the lakebed.

One. Two. Three.

He opened his eyes and looked around. Only blackness.

He reached down and pat the ground.

Seven. Eight. Nine.

He felt a rock. It fumbled through his fingers before he could grasp it enough to bring it up to his eyes. The water blurred his vision, but it didn't glow. It was just a rock.

Thirteen, fourteen, fifteen.

Clutching the anchor rope, he meandered along the bottom; the water resisting his movements.

Twenty-one, twenty-two, twenty-three.

He looked left. He looked right. He looked down, but certainly not up.

Glow. Please, glow. Please!

Twenty-five, twenty-six, twenty-seven.

And then, two arm-lengths away, partially covered in silt, a dull green light pulsated on the floor. He reached out.

Twenty-eight. Twenty-nine.

Too far. He needed his arm to be twice as long.

Thirty. Time's up.

Clutching the rope and being careful not to move the anchor from the lakebed, he climbed up the rope and inhaled the deep breath of life as his head broke the water's surface.

So close, he thought. *But it's down there.* And he didn't move the anchor. He can climb back down the rope and get back to it. He hung off the side of the boat, feet dangling in the water while he caught his breath.

Looking toward the shore, everything still seemed clear. No lights shining in his direction, no shouts, no other boats. Fletcher and his bumbling badge brigade seemed to have entirely missed his escape under the cover of night.

Almost like escaping from a pirate cove, Jasper thought. He pictured a great pirate ship, sails reefed while the ship sat in port. He smiled as he imagined himself commandeering the dinghy tied up to the back of a ship, a ship from a storybook he once owned called the *Rogue Wave.* The crew aboard, lazy and weepy from celebrating their spoils, lay asleep, swinging from their cots or generally strewn about the deck.

No matter the most difficult moments back at Waveland Mansion, Jasper could always conjure such scenes as a mental refuge, a place of his own to go amidst the chaos of nineteen other unruly boys.

His breathing slowed, and he readied himself to go back down. Firmly grasping the anchor rope, he took one more deep breath, held it, and made himself as thin and straight and rigid as possible. He climbed down the rope, again as though repelling off the side of a pirate ship, until his feet hit the soft mud of the bottom.

One. Two. Three.

He knew where to look. Off to his right, two arm lengths away, glowing under a fine layer of silt lay his crystal. He reached.

Too far.

Seven. Eight. Nine.

He looked back toward his rope. Under the blackness of the water, though he felt the rope in his hand, he couldn't see it. He knew what he had to do. He just had to make himself do it. Normally such an act would require taking an apprehensive breath, but that would prove fatal in his current environment.

Eleven. Twelve. Thirteen.

He chided himself for wasting time. He knew what to do. He just needed to do it.

He let go of the rope and took a step toward the crystal. He reached forward, keeping his feet planted and... *got it!*

With the glowing green crystal firmly clenched in his hand, he took a step backward to climb the rope back to the boat. He reached out and... nothing.

Nineteen. Twenty. Twenty-One.

He flailed. The rope had to be there somewhere. He reached and grasped and twisted, but in the blackness of the deep water where no light reached, the rope was as good as gone.

Twenty-Four. Twenty-Five. Twenty-Six.

With no other options left, he squatted down, charged his legs, and thrust upwards with as much force as his legs could muster. He shot from the lakebed to the surface, making sure he held his crystal so as to not repeat the same mistakes as last time.

His face erupted from beneath the water's surface and his lungs gasped and sucked in a deep, desperate breath. He kept his feet kicking. He wouldn't drown. Not now. He had to get back to his boat. It wasn't in front of him.

He spun himself around, and the sight robbed him of his precious fresh breath.

Where he expected to find his boat was now a solid wall of wood. He felt his heart rate rising as panic set in, but the sound of a heavy rope plopping in the water next to him soon distracted him.

"Grab hold!" a gruff voice shouted from somewhere above him. Instinctively and without forethought, Jasper shoved his crystal into his pocket and firmly clutched the rope. The rope jerked, and he clung to it as it pulled him from the water.

He dangled and swayed as he went up and up. Finally, his hands reached an ornate wooden railing, and two men grabbed his forearms and hurled him over the side. His body collapsed on the wooden deck.

A wooden pegged leg stomped down next to his face. He rolled over and looked up.

"Ahoy," scowled the leg's owner, gruff and bearded and unkempt. "Welcome aboard the *Rogue Wave.*"

Chapter 8

200 Years Ago

The shining tip of a sword rested against the wet underside of Jasper's chin. "Stand," a gruff voice commanded, high above where Jasper could see. Slowly, his wet jeans weighing him down and soaked socks pressed firm into the deck, he stood.

The moonlight shone from behind the strange sailor, illuminating the sword's blade but keeping his face in shadow. The moon's rays bounced among the scraggly long beard that grew from the stranger's face.

Jasper clutched his crystal and tried to hide it from view and then stood straight. Inside, his heart throbbed, part from fear, and part from sheer giddiness that his plan was working! Finding the *Rogue Wave* was no accident.

Imagination plus the time crystal? Perfect.

"Take me to your captain," Jasper stated.

The blade pushed ever so much harder against his chin. "I'm the captain," the man responded. "We've taken you prisoner aboard the..."

"Yes, the *Rogue Wave*, I know..." Jasper stopped abruptly, mid-sentence. "Wait, *prisoner?*"

"Aye," replied the captain, "for swimming over from the *Crimson Kraken* to plant an explosive on the bottom of ye ship, sinkin' us to the bottom."

Jasper furrowed his brow. "Why would I want to sink the ship *before* plundering the treasure?"

The captain clearly didn't like being upstaged. He pressed the blade further, and Jasper leaned backwards. "Yer think yer smart, then, eh?"

Jasper nodded, but only with his eyes, lest he dig his chin into the sword. "Yes. Yes, I do."

The captain withdrew the sword, but reached out and pulled Jasper close to him. Unable to escape the grasp of the strong, calloused hand on his shoulder, he could now smell the stench of an accumulated week's worth of body odor, sea salt, and stale jerked meats. The wrinkled details of his face barely popped through the darkness.

"And what treasure be we be carryin'?" The captain's words hung on the odor particles in his breath.

"What?"

The captain asked again. "And what treasure be we be carryin'?"

Jasper smiled. "Oh, I just wanted to be sure you said 'be we be' the first time."

"You swam from the *Crimson Kraken* to insult me grammar?"

Around the captain, Jasper saw the moonlit silhouettes of a dozen crew members crowding around and inching closer. *Tread lightly*, he thought, but he had confidence. He did, after all, have his time crystal. If things got dangerous, all he needed was to close his eyes and imagine being back home - or at Fletcher's house, or something.

Escape should be easy.

Should be.

The story of the *Rogue Wave* was one Jasper read over and over again, as it was one of the few books so uninteresting that the other boys at Waveland Mansion had not bothered to destroy it.

The *Rogue Wave* was not a pirate ship. It left England carrying a treasure, though the exact treasure was lost to history. Why? None of the crew survived to tell the tale.

A single rowboat of three survivors of the *Crimson Kraken* landed in America to tell the tale. Somewhere off the shores of England, the *Kraken* intercepted the *Rogue Wave*, boarded the crew, and took over. They supposedly allowed the original crew to get away on their rowboat, but it succumbed to the waves before reaching shore. No one ever heard from the crew again.

The *Kraken* split her own crew, and a detachment of sailors took over piloting the *Rogue Wave*. But the new captain of the *Rogue Wave*, Arnold Moxie, decided he and his crew should take the treasure for themselves.

Determining that their new ship would be faster, the crew ran up the sails and sped away from the *Kraken*. The *Kraken*, out of cannon range, followed, but fell further and further behind in the weeks-long journey across the Atlantic.

But then, both ships hit a spot of dead air within sight of the coast of Maine. With both ships dead in the water, and no wind to power the sails, the battle was on.

The three surviving crew members suffered injuries that robbed them of the memory of any details: what happened, where it happened, or what the treasure was. All anybody knew was, off the coast of Maine lie the wreck of the *Rogue Wave*, and still locked in its hold, a treasure.

A wreck that many had tried - and all had failed - to find over the next two centuries.

Jasper still grinned, excited to watch the battle play out, and return home once he learned about the treasure and the location of the sunken ship.

"I don't recognize ye," the captain squeezed his shoulder. "How'd ye get aboard the *Kraken*?"

But Jasper didn't care to explain. What was he going to say? *I'm a time traveler?* They wouldn't understand that. No, he didn't want to change history. He didn't want to warn them of the impending attack. He just wanted to watch, learn, and escape.

He clinched his crystal.

"We have better food aboard the *Kraken* that keeps our memory intact, Captain Moxie. No one over there is forgetting who people are."

The crew shuddered. The captain, still in Jasper's face, grimaced. He bared his few remaining teeth, and nearly growled. "What did you call me?"

"Vitamin C deficiency," Jasper replied. "That's what happened to your teeth."

"Scurvy's what happened to me teeth."

"Yeah... a vitamin C deficiency."

From the line of crew surrounding them, one called out, "He called him 'Captain Moxie!'"

As if that was some sort of surprise. As if Jasper was wrong.

Was he?

Suddenly, the eyes of the man in front of him went blank and rolled backwards into his head. Jasper's senses fell behind, and he only now processed the sound of a sword plunging into the man's back. The pirate collapsed on the ground, and the moonlight revealed another tall, strong, younger sailor pulling his own sword out of the man's back. The entire crew sported scraggly, filthy beards. But this sailor's was close-cut and clean, accentuating his chiseled face and dark eyes.

"Feed Captain Willis to the sharks," the sailor ordered, addressing his crew and raising his sword up high. "*I'm* the captain now." He then turned around and looked Jasper directly in the eye.

"Captain Moxie."

He then thrust the bloody blade of his sword against Jasper's clenched hand. "And what is this you're holding?" the tall, new captain asked, Jasper noting his perfect grammar.

Jasper recoiled. "Nothing," he shook his head, his demeanor changing and fear growing.

"Gentlemen, take it," he ordered his men. A crowd rushed Jasper and, as much as he fought, he found himself powerless to fight back against a crew of seasoned pirates.

With Jasper flat on his back and pinned against the deck, one of the stinky men pried his hand open and plucked out the time crystal. "Looks like some sort of diamond," the crewman said, handing it over to the captain.

The captain held it up to the moonlight, and the moon shone green through the translucent crystal.

"When we make it to our cove, I'll have it cut up and made into diamond rings." He then pointed his sword at Jasper and gestured, "Lock him in the brig."

Jasper struggled against the crewmen as they dragged him across the deck, but it was no use.

He couldn't leave.

It was then the first sound of cannon fire rang out.

Chapter 9

The iron door rattled as it slammed shut behind Jasper. The roll of the ship in the ocean helped him tumble across the floor, along with the awesome force of a strange pirate's push. With nary a word, the pirate locked the gate and scurried atop the deck, leaving Jasper alone.

Alone with nothing but the sound of another cannon firing in the distance, and the pattering of the crew's feet on the deck above his head to prepare their response.

Alone without his time crystal. His escape plan.

A miscalculation. A hapless happenstance of madness. Never in any of Jasper's reading had he ever read of a captain other than Captain Moxie.

Was this even a mistake? It wasn't even his fault! But it didn't matter. The result was the same.

Locked in the brig. Trapped.

Another cannon shot rang out across the water. It didn't echo. Nothing echoes on the water because there's nothing to bounce the sound back.

And Jasper had not even a window through which to peer out and observe the battle. He wanted to go home. But the bigger problem right now was how not to go down with the sinking ship. Any thoughts of finding the mysterious treasure of the *Rogue Wave* sank like the ship itself was about to sink.

Suddenly, a glimmer of the candlelit deck shone through as a hatch opened in the deck above him. Captain Moxie swiftly ran down the stairs, his trench coat flowing behind him. He slid a wood crate across the floor and sat, revealing Jasper's time crystal from his pocket, holding it tauntingly before the gate.

His dark eyes peered into Jasper's. "How do you know Hayalet?" Moxie demanded.

Jasper winced. He remembered his conversation with Ertha. She struggled to even say his name! Even as she said it - *Hayalet* - Jasper knew, somehow he knew, that Hayalet was a bringer of evil.

Jasper sat up, focused, but cautious. "How do *you* know Hayalet?"

The captain stood and paced. "How does anyone?" his gruff voice angrily shot back, tossing his coattails behind him. He turned back, his angry dark eyes begging for an answer. "Have you more information? A buyer for the treasure?"

Jasper tried to hide the puzzled look in his face. The captain's questions made for him an opportunity; an opportunity to learn the treasure, learn the vessel's fate, and get away before he joins the *Rogue Wave* on the ocean floor. But only if he made his next moves in the most calculated manner.

But before Jasper could respond, the Captain again marched up to the brig bars. "I can't pay," he said, matter-of-factly as if Jasper would know what he was talking about.

"I *will* pay, but we're stuck in dead air. We can't move until we catch some wind. And I can't find a buyer until we disappear."

"As soon as we catch wind, we'll sink the *Kraken,* and then send two of our men to shore to claim we were lost as well. With all of Maine believing we sunk off the coast, we'll sail to Africa and sell the treasure. *Then* I'll pay Hayalet. In fact, I'll pay him double!"

Was that why no one had ever found the wreck of the *Rogue Wave?* Because there was no wreck of the *Rogue Wave?*

But what was the treasure? And Hayalet... Jasper couldn't help but wonder... had the captain made some sort of deal with Hayalet? Of course he had. And that was Jasper's ticket to freedom.

"Give me my crystal back," Jasper demanded with hand outstretched. "I'm here to inspect the treasure."

But the captain wouldn't yet oblige. He held the crystal, delicately shuffling it between his fingers. "You do work with him, this much is obvious." He held the crystal up, studying it in the dim candlelight rays. "Do you *all* have the same crystal?"

It wasn't just a question. This was a test. Answer wrong, and the captain would see his lie. The captain clearly knew the answer.

And Jasper did not.

His heart fluttered. It was sink or swim and he knew not how to swim. And yet his answer, correct or not, came to him instinctively.

"Hayalet and I share a connection, and so we share a crystal."

Satisfied, at least for now, the captain passed the crystal through the bars and moved to unlock the gate.

"Tell him we will have the money as soon as we catch wind and make it to Africa."

The gate creaked as Captain Moxie swung it open. But then, suddenly, an explosion of splintered wood burst inward from the ship's side. A half beat later, the sound of cannon fire rang out.

Both startled, the captain ran toward the upper hatch. "We're in range of the cannons!" he shouted. "The treasure's in the aft hold. Tell Hayalet our plan! We *will* pay him once we get to Africa."

The ship swung as the crew ran about on the top deck, readying cannons. Jasper tried to keep his balance, but his sea legs were still unsteady. Swerving, he ran toward the door closing off the aft cargo hold.

Locked, with a padlock.

He looked around. In the darkness, he couldn't see a key. The ship lurched as the *Rogue Wave's* own cannons fired off a shot, and Jasper fell.

His arm landed on a pile of cannonballs. He could use one to smash the lock, he thought, but then decided against it. He didn't want to fail and render the lock completely unable to open.

Get the treasure and then get outta here.

He fumbled and stumbled his way through the hold, looking for something - anything - he could use to pry open the lock.

Again, cannon fire sounded and another section of wall erupted in splinters and shrapnel. The ship jerked back and forth, absorbing the impact, and knocking Jasper back to the floor and landing him in a pile of debris.

Getting up, his hand landed on something sharp, and the pain pierced through his body. He screamed! But then, wincing, suppressed his voice back into his gut. His hand wasn't cut badly, but it was cut, and bleeding. But it worked.

But more importantly, Jasper found the long metallic object that sliced his hand.

Holding it carefully, he held it above the padlock on the aft hold door, and reached out for a cannonball. Gripping the cannonball and carefully placing the tip of the metal rod, he smashed the rod, directing the force into the padlock.

One, two, three bangs it took before the padlock flew off.

The ship lurched again, blasting shots toward the *Kraken*. Jasper steadied himself against the wooden wall and, in the dark, grasped the door handle and ripped the door open.

The aft hold had more windows, and thus more light. Moonlight from the outside gently lit the room in a blue hue. Inside, barrels. A dozen, maybe twenty wooden barrels.

And a girl, a bit older than him, with black hair and a black dress, chained to the wall. Her head rose at Jasper's entrance, though grogginess remained.

He stopped. What was this? And where was the treasure?

"Which one is it?" he shouted to the girl. But the girl only moaned and mumbled. He couldn't understand.

He ran to the first barrel and pried open the lid. Gunpowder.

The second: jerked meat.

The third: dried biscuits.

He looked back at the girl. Her head drooped back down and she no longer watched him. Should he free her? What could he do with her? Could he help at all?

In this whole encounter, Jasper's mind stayed one step behind every occurrence. Every event, every encounter, and every moment kept him guessing. He knew he needed to stay ahead of things in order to be successful, even to stay alive. But he couldn't get there; he just fell more and more behind.

Especially when the aft hold illuminated in a green flash.

He knew that flash.

Another time traveler had just boarded the *Rogue Wave*.

Chapter 10

Jasper ran from the aft hold, leaving the girl and the treasure behind. He bounded up the stairs, still in darkness, but stopped before reaching the top deck. He stepped up only enough to peer his curious face above the floor.

What he saw startled him. Captain Moxie's boots floated a foot above the ground, his neck firmly grasped in the hand of another powerful man.

The man towered over Captain Moxie, who already towered over most everyone else. In the candlelight, briefly lit more by the flash of an exploding cannon, Jasper could tell the bald man wore his scars proudly.

Just looking at the man's scars inspired fear in Jasper's gut. And with that feeling, Jasper knew, that's what they were meant to do.

And he also knew - somewhere, it was like his *soul* knew - the identity of this brute: *Hayalet*.

Hayalet shook the captain, and Jasper could hear him as he spied from the floor. "I *told* you how to evade the *Crimson Kraken*, and you couldn't even do *that!*" Hayalet shook the captain like he was wringing water out of a rag.

"We… caught… dead… air," the captain croaked back, forcing air through Hayalet's grasp on his throat.

"You told me you were going to Africa!" Hayalet scowled, low and rhythmic, his tone designed to intimidate.

"I… am…!"

Hayalet squeezed harder. "Then why are you in *Maine*?" The surrounding crew continued to man their cannons.

Moxie squeaked through struggled breaths, "Everything… is going… according… to plan… the plans… I told… your agent! Ask him!"

Jasper's eyes widened. This was not good.

Hayalet squinted. "What… agent?"

In an act that jolted all of Jasper's nerves all at once causing what he was sure was lightning bolts jumping out of his ears, the captain reached out and, with a single outstretched finger, pointed to the hatch through which Jasper now peered.

"Him."

Hayalet's face slowly turned, and they locked eyes. In a single, swift motion, Hayalet dropped the captain to the floor and flew toward the hatch.

Without thinking, Jasper ran down the steps and toward the aft cargo hold, grasping for the crystal in his pocket. He slammed the hold's hatch shut, and shoved a broom through the handle.

It wouldn't hold long. He needed it to hold long enough. With his crystal in one hand, he grabbed the limp hand of the girl, who still barely acknowledged his presence.

"Where's the treasure?" he asked one more time, desperate. She didn't answer, nor even respond at all.

Hayalet banged at the door, and a crack formed down the length of the broom's handle.

Jasper took a deep breath, unsure this would even work. Clutching the girl's hand, he closed his eyes, and imagined Fletcher's boat right where he left it on Newhaven Bay. Through closed eyelids, he saw green flashes and heard the sound of splintering wood.

But then, everything changed. The green flashes gave way to a gentle amber hue. Clearly, like he was watching photographs from an old book come to life, he saw a room.

The room had no windows, only sterile white walls and stainless-steel shelves and countertops. They glowed a dreamy glow of bright amber waves, flickering. It was a laboratory. Beakers and flasks and jars. Medical equipment: needles and tubes and monitors. As he looked around more, a disturbing image became more clear: most of the equipment was broken, shattered, and strewn about the room.

And in the corner, the single unscientific object: a picture frame. And in the picture, Jasper recognized the subject: himself, in the loving arms of his parents.

It's not magic, he remembers Ertha explaining. *It's science. Science and biology.* Is that what his parents were doing? Is this their lab? What were they working on?

What happened?

But then, a pair of arms reached into his vision and picked up the picture frame. Jasper's view widened. It was a monster, a monster he knew: *Hayalet.*

The sound of his heartbeat thundered, and the dreamy, amber vision blurred with each thump until it vanished completely.

Then, silence. Only the sound of gently lapping water against the hull of a wooden rowboat under the warm glow of a sunrise.

He opened his eyes, only to see Fletcher standing over him.

"Welcome back," Fletcher smiled, curiously. "Who's the girl?"

Chapter 11

"You must remove that box!" Jasper heard the mumbled voice of an angry woman through his cracked bedroom door. His eyes opened, and he found himself lying on the floor, which had become a much more frequent occurrence over the past few days.

In the glimmer of the morning's light, he saw the girl he rescued from the *Rogue Wave* napping soundly in his bed - or Fletcher's bed - or Ertha's bed - whatever. The bed in his bedroom. No, the bed in *this* bedroom.

Slowly, Jasper slipped his fingers into the open space between the door and the frame and pulled the door open just wide enough to slide his body out without making a noise.

"Now, Gladdys, I have strict instructions from the mayor not to remove, nor touch, nor disport with that box," Fletcher replied, from the dining room.

"Really?" the old, angry voice of Gladdys replied.

"She was very specific with her use of the word 'disport,'" a snide Ertha remarked from under the balcony on which Jasper now stood. He could sense her smile in her response.

"Thanks, Ertha, for your contribution to this civil conversation," Fletcher replied.

"Any time, Uncle Fletcher."

"How do you purport to protect us from the evil contained in that box?" Gladdys continued, pointedly.

Fletcher shrugged. "I think that's the mayor's job."

"The mayor said it was *your* job."

"Of course she did," Jasper sensed Fletcher roll his eyes while Ertha hid her smile behind a sip of coffee.

Gladdys pressed on. "Because you're the president of the…"

"…the Yacht Club, yes," Fletcher finished her sentence. "Ready the cannons and run up the sails, the British are coming!"

Ertha chimed in. "Ready to plunder our village with their dreadnaught, sailing from far across our landlocked man-made lake."

Ertha pounded the table. "Mister Fletcher! That is no way to respond to a crisis."

"No Gladdys, it's not. So it's a good thing we have no crisis."

"Evil has arrived in Newhaven Bay!"

"In a box?"

"Precisely!"

"Trust her, Fletcher," Ertha quipped, "She is an expert on all things evil."

"Indeed, I am!" Gladdys replied, not getting the joke.

"Would it help you, Gladdys, if I offered not to *open* the box?" Fletcher offered, neglecting to tell her they couldn't figure out *how* to open it.

"Get rid of it, Mister Fletcher," she warned. "It's already poisoning the well of our humanity."

Ertha chuckled. "So that's why my coffee has a hint of demon blood this morning."

"Mister Fletcher!" Gladdys shouted. "I don't think you're taking this seriously!"

Fletcher gestured to defend himself. "I didn't say anything!"

"The bridge club will hear about this!" she continued.

"Only if they turn their hearing aids up," Ertha mumbled.

"What?"

"Exactly!"

Gladdys attempted to storm out of the house, but the effect was lost on them as she could only muster a slow shuffle. Still, she enhanced the rhythmic pulsing of pushing her walker forward every two steps by doing so as angrily as possible.

"Shall I slam the door shut for her?" Ertha asked, as Gladdys left the door wide open behind her in her own unique form of protest.

Interesting, Jasper thought. Ertha asked me not to tell Fletcher that she's here, but they seem to get along just fine.

"What do you think of the box?" Jasper heard Ertha ask, but it seemed strange, like she was interrogating Fletcher.

Fletcher sat back down at the table. "Strangest box I've ever seen."

"Does it seem in any way... *extra-dimensional* to you?"

"Don't start with this, Ertha!" Fletcher snapped. Jasper ducked a bit lower, and pressed himself into the back wall, wanting to listen, but definitely not wanting to be seen.

"Where did the boy tell you he came from?" Ertha pressed on. But Fletcher remained silent.

"Oh, come on!" Ertha continued. "I've been trying to show you evidence of time travel for years! And now when one appears in the middle of your lake, you don't believe me?"

"A runaway juvenile floating in the middle of the lake is not evidence of time travel."

"And the girl?"

"*Two* runaway juveniles are not evidence of time travel."

"Well then, it sounds like there's a plague of runaways determined to swim to the middle of your lake. You better do something about this."

Fletcher stood up. "I will!"

Silence stirred between them, the silence of a sword fight, of two duelists teasing out their next move. It was Ertha who made the next jab.

"Why did you cover for him with your cops?"

But Fletcher said nothing. All Jasper heard was the sound of Fletcher and all his muscles plopping back into his chair, and Ertha carefully shuffling closer.

"You *want* it to be true, don't you, Fletcher?"

Again, Fletcher replied only with a stiff silence that Ertha worked to soften. She allowed the silence to waiver, just for a few moments.

"He knew your name right away."

Fletcher shook his head. "I'm one of the most recognizable people in town."

"To businessmen," Ertha argued, "not twelve-year-olds."

At that point, Jasper couldn't take it anymore. He rose to his feet and popped his head over the banister. "I am from the future!" his kind but insistent voice shouted down.

He trotted down the stairs as he spoke. "I saw you! I know you! You were older, but something about you just told me I could trust you. *You* sent me here... to *you!*"

"The box, Jasper, the girl..." Ertha gestured broadly, silently begging Fletcher to accept the connection.

Fletcher simply stood up and strolled to the window overlooking the lake. It seemed Fletcher was the kind of man who didn't like to think aloud, but he did like to think, and to think for considerably long lengths of time. An annoyingly long amount of time.

"Do we know anything about the girl?" Fletcher asked, still staring out the window. "Is she awake yet?"

"All I know is I found her, tied up below decks on a ship," Jasper answered. "On the *Rogue Wave.*"

Ertha's focus snapped around to Jasper. Her eyes opened wide, and her tone changed. "You were on the *Rogue Wave?*" Ertha quickly replied, stunned.

"Yeah... does that mean something?" Clearly it did. One doesn't suddenly pop their eyes out of their head for statements that mean nothing.

Ertha furrowed her brow. "Perhaps. I don't know yet."

Fletcher turned around. "Ertha, pretend for a minute I'll believe everything you say."

"Well, gee, I'm not sure I can," Ertha quipped.

"Ertha..."

"It's just such an unusual occurrence..."

"Ertha..."

"I never thought you... you're blowing my mind right now!"

"Ertha!"

"Alright, fine!" Ertha gave in. "What?"

Fletcher continued. "Pretend I'll believe everything you say. What's going on?"

Ertha exhaled. "I don't know. But there's something about *here* and *now*. That box isn't from here, that much is for sure. There's something deeper to it, and it doesn't belong here. It being here is no accident. Whatever it's doing here, Jasper's here for the same reason."

"And the girl?" Fletcher asked.

Jasper interrupted. "I think that's an accident. I was being stupid."

Ertha turned to him and smiled. "I'd like you to stop doing that."

Jasper chuckled. "I'll try."

Fletcher, his face deep in thought, moved back to his couch. "So, why then? If it's no accident, why?"

Ertha hesitated. She grasped the sides of her head, pushing down her springy black hair. Jasper saw her scrunch her face in a multitude of expressions before she inhaled deeply.

"I don't know, but..."

Suddenly, a voice interrupted them. From overhead, overlooking them from the balcony and leaning over the banister, the girl Jasper rescued from the *Rogue Wave*, still wearing the same dirty colonial dress from the belly of the ship, all innocent, sweet, and blonde. Gripping the banister, she simply said,

"It was Hayalet, wasn't it?"

Chapter 12

"This is *niiice*," the girl exclaimed, walking down the stairs while looking everywhere but. The once beautiful remnants of her tattered black dress flowed with her as she descended. About Ertha's age, her mangled and dirt black hair fell past her shoulders, but didn't look like it took all that much care to keep clean. Jasper watched her brown eyes dart from corner to corner with focus and intent - studying.

"Mid-century American A-frame?" she asked, a slight Spanish accent coming through. She pointed to the bare wood ceiling. "You should install some fans and have them blow down in the winter," she explained, while gesturing with her fingers. "You'll get quite a bit of warm air stuck up there, and blowing it down will help you save on your heating bill."

That was a curious statement, Jasper thought. Didn't he rescue her off a ship from the 1700s or something? How would a pirate - or pirate mistress - or pirate captive - or pirat*ess* - or, perhaps, princess of the non-pirate variety possibly know how fans and heating bills work?

"But anyway," she continued, her bare feet shuffling across the wood floor to join them at the table, "Nice place. It'll age well." She scanned the faces around the room. "So which one of you is on the hook for something from Hayalet?"

She locked eyes with Jasper. Through her eyes, he could feel a sudden change in her own brain cells. Her quizzical, "*Do I know you?*" became the most important question of that moment.

Seconds, perhaps whole minutes passed before Jasper realized he hadn't answered. "Um, well," his mouth struggled to cooperate with his failing brain, "I rescued you from the *Rogue Wave*," he finally spat out, too dumbly for her to believe he was capable of such an act.

"Ah," she replied, her tone showing Jasper was right. "Well, thank you, then. I lost my crystal trying to free that ship from Hayalet's deal."

Ertha wasn't much for standing by and idly observing a conversation. "So you're a time traveler," she stated. "I'm an archeologist with the Time Traveler's Order."

"Ah, yes, the Union," the girl said, with no one realizing they still didn't know her name. But she pointed at Jasper, and warned him, "Don't join the Union."

Whatever this "Union" was, such a notion sure seemed to upset Ertha! She leapt out of her chair. "The Union is what keeps time travelers safe!" she shouted.

But the girl, unnerved, remained seated. "The Union is subservient to Krylios and Hayalet. *I'm* independent."

"They would never have taken a Union member prisoner aboard a pirate ship."

"I wasn't a prisoner," the girl smiled.

"Then why were you tied up and unconscious?" Jasper asked.

"Was I?"

"Yes!"

"Oh. I would've figured something out."

"Who are you?" Fletcher jumped in, putting an end to the argument with what to him seemed like probably the most important question. Jasper and Ertha stopped, wondering why they hadn't thought to ask for such a basic detail.

"My name's Catalina Rodriguez, but most people call me Cat. I'm also an engineer, mechanic, builder..." her voice trailed off as though she could go on and on. "In my time, people use the word 'savant.'"

Ertha eyed Fletcher with half a smile. "That means *very smart.*"

"I'm aware, thank you," Fletcher replied. "Cat, when you came out of the bedroom, we were talking about a mysterious box, and you seemed to think this *'Hayalet'* has something to do with it."

She nodded. "I'm pretty sure I know what it's for, but I need to see it before I say anything?"

"Why?" Fletcher asked.

"When I'm wrong, people die," Cat explained flatly and matter-of-factly. "I won't pass judgment until I know for sure." Another moment passed as she looked around the room. She pursed her lips, debating her next move.

She pointed at Jasper. "Since you... what's your name?"

"Jasper." Somehow, Cat's eyes betrayed her, like she already knew.

"Since you, Jasper, are new, I presume," then she pointed at Ertha. "And you..."

"Ertha."

"And you, Ertha, are too dependent on Krylios and his so-called *union* to know any better..."

Before Ertha could spew the protest that was surely forming in her vocal cords, Cat pointed at Fletcher. "And because they unwillingly roped you into all of this...

"My name's Fletcher, by the way. And his parents sent him to me!" He exclaimed, pointing at Jasper.

"Of course they did," Cat barely acknowledged his statement. "Anyway, because of all that, here's what I can tell you:

"The Krylios family has spent four generations looking for one thing in particular. When they find it, they won't need any of *you* anymore," she explained, nodding in Ertha's direction. "But they've spent four generations using people like you, and probably him and his parents, to find it," she continued, of course gesturing to Jasper.

"What are they using my parents for?" Jasper asked.

Cat simply rested her arms on the table. "The box first," she said. "When I'm wrong, people die. Let me see the box."

Chapter 13

Windows full of pricey new appliances lined the charming brick storefronts of Newhaven Bay's lone commercial street. Shoppers hoped that the mere purchasing of these appliances could give them the same gleaming smiles of the people who sold them. Cars hummed down the lane at a sporty twenty-seven miles per hour.

Washing machines, televisions, radios, dishwashers, and even new cars filled the residents of Newhaven Bay with joy from sunup to sundown, but not any earlier nor any later. A few restaurants and diners, about one on each block, filled their spirits in places where vacuum cleaners could not.

West of Main Street, nestled into the side of a hill, a church with a preacher competed with cars, cooktops, and cakes to fill the souls of Newhaven Bay. He liked to note that his church could not fit all the residents of Newhaven Bay, which he failed to realize was the reason none of the churchgoers ever invited the non-churchgoers.

Four layers made up Newhaven Bay. First, the bay, of course, and the street alongside that brought cars, boats, and bicycles to the shore. Then Main Street, lined on both sides with bricks that blocked the view of both the bay to the east and the hills to the west, so as to not distract the shoppers from their quests.

The third layer, moving further west and alongside the church, contained the city parks, in case frolicking beside the beach was unappealing to you. Two schools on one end, and the police and fire station on the other, indicated that the firemen were far too trusting of the adolescent boys inhabiting the school. This is the second fire station; the first burned down when boys from the school launched an illegally produced rocket that hit the fire station while the firemen were away fighting a fire elsewhere.

Finally, nestled in the hills, a few small factories produced boats and boating goods, furniture and cabinetry, and a small building that produced printer's ink. Rumor had it, the printer who owned that factory sold this ink, only to use the profits to purchase far superior Dutch ink to use in his own printing.

Newhaven Bay was not in a place anybody ever simply passed through. The bay itself was not big enough to be a destination, and the boats produced in town were largely sailed down the river to other towns. Trucks sometimes came to the furniture factory, picked up loads, and left. Likewise, trucks often came to the appliance stores, dropped off loads, and left.

The charm of this quaint town was contagious. It appeared all the men, women, and children flourished under their web of connectedness. In fact, the people of Newhaven Bay had only one true problem:

They had never been tested.

The crowd that gathered in the park ignored the toppled statue of the boy fisherman and formed a semicircle ten rows deep around the mysterious box that stood in its place. Officer Pierce's long gray hair fluttered in the breeze, and Deputy Street relished the opportunity to use his size to his advantage to hold back the crowd.

From their vantage point as Fletcher's car pulled up to the back of the park, the crowd energy was rising quickly. Each individual slowly made their way around each other, as two distinctive sides formed: one side in favor of moving, opening, and/or destroying the box, and the other determined to let it sit for all eternity.

"I just need to see the box," Cat told them. "If I'm right, I know what's happening."

Fletcher and Ertha slid out of the front seat, and Jasper and Cat jumped out from the back. The morning dampness had given way to the gently rising summer heat, and Fletcher removed his wool sport coat. He rushed to the front of the crowd with such speed that his salmon-colored polyester polo shirt rippled in the breeze.

It surprised those who knew them that their energy didn't vaporize Fletcher's shirt when he arrived at the front of the crowd at the same time as Mayor Nygaard. The mayor's Hollywood sunglasses rested on the tip of her nose and she peered through them, down at the crowd before her with perfect posture.

"People of Newhaven Bay," cried out the mayor, beating Fletcher and thus gaining the upper hand, "you will have a voice! You should have a voice! You will, very soon, vote on what to do with this box!"

That was, at least, one thing the crowd could agree was a good thing. They cheered! The mayor, believing this as a personal sign of approval for her, continued on.

"Until then, we won't be taking any chances. I've commissioned the boat factory to build a very strong boat hull, which we will then install upside down on top of the box to use as a containment vessel."

Fletcher interrupted the once-again cheering crowd by waiving his hands. "Now, now, folks: we need more information! We can run tests on it..."

"Tests?" a woman in the front row shouted, "I don't need no stinkin' test to know that's pure evil inside that thing!"

"They're going to vote, Fletcher," the mayor reminded him.

Fletcher shook his head. "Voting doesn't matter if all they have is bad choices to vote on."

Mayor Nygaard puffed herself out to address the crowd, broadly gesturing with outstretched arms, "You hear that, people of Newhaven Bay? Mister Fletcher says your vote doesn't matter!" Which is in fact precisely *not* what Fletcher said.

But it didn't stop the polite residents of Newhaven Bay from erupting with a ferocious chorus of angry *booos* and insults. A few of the louder men in back seemed to believe that the size of Fletcher's long-dead mother had something to do with their current predicament. It was clear to Jasper, Cat, and Ertha, standing in the back, that it was Fletcher who grew the crowd from a mild disturbance to an angry mob.

A few residents even gestured with their weapons of choice, including the chef standing right in front of Cat, angrily waving two metal spatulas in the air. Cat pointed them out to Jasper, and simply rolled her eyes.

"What do you think is happening?" Jasper pressed Cat.

"I want to tell you, Jasper," she replied, "but not until I get a good look at that box."

The angry mob kept shouting, but Fletcher still had more to say. "No, no, no!" he shouted. "You need to have good information! What if it's all harmless? Just an empty box?"

Amid another series of *booos*, another angry woman in the front shouted back, "Who on Earth would make an unopenable box full of nothing?"

"Yes, Fletcher," the mayor mocked, "And how do you propose to 'test' this oddity if we don't even know how to open it?"

"Some archeologists and historians use X-Rays to look inside ancient clay jars before they try to open them."

In the back of the crowd, Cat whispered to Jasper, "I just need to see it! Even with today's camera technology, I could probably make a borescope. All I need is the tools to shape a lens just a half-centimeter! Then maybe a diamond-tipped drill could make a small hole…"

But, once again, the nice people of Newhaven Bay drowned out Cat's well-thought-out idea. They all seemed to agree with the lady in the middle who shouted, "Evil spirits wouldn't show up on an x-ray!"

"That settles it," the mayor announced, clearly believing that ability to decide what "settles something" resides solely with her. "We will vote on whether to move it. But first, we will entomb it!"

Mayor Nygaard couldn't have made a more chant-ready phrase if she tried. The crowd immediately erupted into chants of, "Remove it or entomb it! Remove it or entomb it!" It didn't take long before one side started shouting only, "Remove it!" and the other only, "Entomb it!"

Amid the chaos, the shouting, and the fighting, a small, barely noticed, but very much intentional event occurred that would change the entire future of the town.

Someone bumped into Ertha. She felt a small prick in her shoulder. Not enough to be alarmed, and she merely scratched the itch away without another thought.

Ertha, Cat, and Jasper watched as Fletcher lost total control of the crowd, and a puff of wind blew out Mayor Nygaard's hair at just the right moment as she crossed her arms and signaled triumph.

"She's not trying to solve the problem," Cat said to Jasper. "She's just trying to one-up Fletcher. Isn't that right, Ertha?"

But suddenly, Ertha seemed pale. Cat and Jasper rushed to her side as her eyes rolled back and supported her collapse to the ground.

"Help!" Jasper shouted. "Help!"

The crowd hushed, and backed up to form an empty circle around Ertha, now unconscious on the ground. Officer Pierce and Deputy Street pushed their way through the crowd, with Fletcher and the mayor trailing closely behind. Officer Pierce kneeled down beside her and put his ear to her mouth.

"She's not breathing!" he announced.

Fletcher rushed to her side. "No, no, Ertha, wake up, come on!" He started slapping her cheeks, trying to stir her.

"No pulse!" Officer Pierce continued.

"Is there a doctor? Anyone?" Shouted Deputy Street, scanning the crowd for any raised hands.

Cat rushed in and felt Ertha's forearm, only for a few moments before being forced away by Deputy Street. "Get away, we need a doctor!" he barked at her. But no doctor made themselves known.

"It's thready," she told Jasper. "She's fibrillating. She's alive, but not for long."

"Fibrillating?"

"Her heart's not beating. It's just..." She tried to find the right word. She found a hand motion to demonstrate. "It's just quivering."

"Do you know what to do?" Jasper asked, wide-eyed.

Cat winced. "I shouldn't."

"Cat!" Jasper insisted. "You know what to do, don't you?"

"I shouldn't!" Cat resisted. "They're not ready."

Jasper grabbed Cat by the shoulders. "Cat, she's gonna die!"

With a look of determination and a bit of regret for going against her better judgment, Cat pushed Jasper aside and rushed toward Ertha. She placed her hands on the center of her chest and pushed up and down. Officer Pierce was about to push her away when Fletcher stopped her.

"Cardiopulmonary resuscitation," Cat said. "I need someone to keep doing this. It's easy. Just up and down."

"Are you a doctor?" Officer Pierce sneered.

"You'll break her ribs!" Deputy Street warned.

"No, she's young," Cat replied, still pulsing. She gestured toward Officer Pierce, "It would break yours though."

With no one jumping in to help, she implored again. "Just up and down. That's all we need." Finally, Fletcher jumped beside her and took over.

"You know what to do?" Fletcher pleaded.

"Jasper," Cat pointed at him, "Go get Fletcher's car!"

Jasper jumped into motion, desperately wanting to help and eager to get to figure out how to drive for the first time.

Cat then pointed into the crowd. "Where's the chef? Who wanted to kill Fletcher with the spatulas?"

Someone pushed the chef through the crowd to her. "Give me those!" she shouted.

"You gonna roast her?" the chef asked back.

"Maybe, but hopefully not."

Moments later, the crowd gave way for Fletcher's car, as Jasper brought it to a stop right by Ertha's side. Fletcher continued to pump.

"Pop the hood," Cat instructed, as she ran to Fletcher's trunk and removed a set of jumper cables.

The next few moments, the crowd watched in awe as Cat jumped into action. She quickly attached one end of the jumper cables to the car's battery, connected the other end to the two metal spatulas, and then hovered over Ertha.

"Stand back," Cat demanded. "Don't touch her." Fletcher stopped pumping and took a step back.

Then, the crowd gasped as Cat slowly brought the flat ends of the spatulas to Ertha's chest. Cat grimaced, moving with caution mixed with a bit of fear, and touched the paddles to Ertha's chest.

The lights on Fletcher's car dimmed and flickered, and Ertha's entire body tensed up. Cat only held the paddles to her chest for a second, then pointed to Officer Pierce. "Check for a pulse!"

Nervous and unsure, Pierce put his ear to Ertha's chest. After a few moments, he sat up. "Nothing."

"Stand back again," Cat said, and again touched the spatulas to Ertha's chest. Again, Ertha tensed up, and the crowd gasped. Cat nodded to Pierce, who again checked for a pulse.

His eyes grew wide. He slowly sat up, dazed and amazed. "There's a pulse," he announced as though he didn't quite believe it himself. He leaned back in and put his ear to her mouth. "And she's breathing!"

The crowd gasped again. Sure enough, they could see the slow rises and falls of her chest. The once-angry mob stood stunned and silent. Cat, instead of being relieved and triumphant, scanned the crowd with worried eyes.

"Jasper," she said with a cautious tone, "Unhook the cables."

In silence, Jasper unhooked the jumper cables from the car's battery and shut it off.

One more time, the crowd gasped, as Ertha opened her eyes and sat up. "What happened?" she asked, feeling her chest. "And why is my skin burning?"

From the tense, silent crowd, a man a few rows back shouted, "She was dead!"

A murmur grew from the crowd. Jasper couldn't make out what they were saying, but they certainly were not congratulating Cat the hero.

"I saw it with my own eyes!" exclaimed a woman in the front row. "She wasn't breathing, and she had no pulse!"

Officer Pierce and Deputy Street couldn't refute that statement, so they casually shrugged and nodded.

And then, the next shout made Jasper shudder. Instead of being grateful for saving a life, as people usually are after seeing a life saved, Jasper knew Cat was in for a lot of trouble.

"What kind of magic is this???"

The crowd erupted into chaos. Jasper remembered Ertha's warning, the warning of people from the future showing people from the past things they weren't ready to see. Stories of well-intentioned time travelers burned as witches.

Cat ran up to Jasper. "Jasper!" she shook him, fear and panic in her eyes. "Jasper! I don't need to see the box. I know what's happening!"

But before she could say anything, two men grabbed her and yanked her away. They pushed their way through the crowd. Jasper tried to press through, to follow, but the crowd engulfed them and he lost sight of Cat and her captors.

He kept pushing and shoving. The crowd shouted chants, something about ridding the town of the evil contained in that girl. He couldn't hear them clearly and he didn't care. He kept pushing and shoving.

He made it through to the other side. Once clear of the crowd, he looked around.

Nothing.

Cat was gone.

****

From a small clearing in the wooded hill overlooking the park, Hayalet observed the crowd through a spyglass, and smiled a half smile. Only a half smile because the boy bothered him. Contemplatively, he removed the spyglass from his eye and collapsed it, then turned back toward the abandoned cabin he had commandeered.

He had sewn the seeds of chaos in Newhaven Bay. The next part wasn't his doing, but he knew it was no coincidence that Cat and the boy were both here, in the same place, at the same time. They would prove even more useful.

Newhaven Bay did not know how important it was in the Order of Time.

Chapter 14

Fletcher refused to sit when he, Jasper, and Ertha rushed into his spacious living room overlooking the lake. The lake was calm, in stark contrast to the hurricane Fletcher had inadvertently conjured in town earlier. He just paced nervously back and forth behind the couch. That wasn't much better than what Jasper was doing, which was hiding his face under a pillow.

"I made her do it!" Jasper's muffled voice screamed from below the pillow. "She didn't want to, and I made her anyway!"

"Just one more in the long line of time travelers mistook as witches," Ertha grumbled, rubbing her shoulder where a strange man injected poison just an hour earlier. "This is why we prepare you; this is why you don't show people from the past future technology."

"She saved your life," Fletcher reminded her, still pacing.

"Well, there's that," Ertha quipped. She looked at Jasper. "Thank you."

Jasper didn't see her. He still buried his face under the pillow. He wanted to suffocate himself with the pillow. He wanted to wake up to find one of his bunkmates at Waveland Mansion had tackled him and smashed his face into a pillow. He had never gotten beat up at Waveland, but he tried to imagine what that was like because apparently his imagination could make things happen.

He rescued Catalina Rodriguez from the brig of a pirate ship, from being kidnapped, only to get her kidnapped again. Who even was this girl, and why was Jasper so intent on ruining her life? Despite smashing his face into the pillow so hard his eyeballs nearly popped, all he could see was the fear in Cat's eyes when she told him she knew what was happening with the box.

Fear.

He decided in that moment his parents were clearly not as smart as he had always thought they were. Who in their right mind would devise a rescue plan that involved the supposed "rescuer" not knowing who he is? What sane person would send him for safekeeping in a town so inept at getting to know strangers that they would skip a lot of very reasonable questions and jump straight to "witch"?

Jasper wasn't from this era of Newhaven Bay. He should probably hide the fact that he knows their lake is going to disappear. Otherwise, when it does, they'll probably blame him. Then they'll rebuild the lake and stock it with alligators just to throw him in it.

Unless Hayalet kills him first, which is still a thing nobody in this house is talking about.

"Uncle Fletcher, I thought this town liked you?" Ertha wondered aloud.

"They like me to get businesses to work together to get them deals on stuff," he replied, still pacing. "I'm good at that. I guess I'm not good at..." he sighed, "...see reason and think with their brains."

His legs finally couldn't take the nonstop pacing, and he let gravity plop himself down on the couch next to Ertha. With a deep sigh, he continued, "I mean, it's a box. How harmful could it be?"

"It's not just a box," Jasper interrupted, finally uncovering his face. They both looked at him, puzzled. He realized they hadn't heard what Cat told him - Ertha had only recently become conscious and was still discharging static electricity, and Fletcher was too busy losing his next election to notice.

"I mean, it could be just a box, but there's a bigger picture we're not seeing," he explained.

They looked at him, expecting more. And so, he came up with the best, most intelligent, well-reasoned, fully thought-out explanation based on all the available information he had:

"Something bad."

The way Fletcher slapped his knee, stood up, and bounded to the window to ponder his future in front of the lake told Jasper that wasn't enough information.

I know what's happening, Jasper remembered Cat telling him. She didn't need to see the box. She *knew*. Based on what?

The reaction of the crowd. *They weren't ready for what she showed them.* Why? Why did she show them? Because she had to save Ertha's life.

And why did she have to save Ertha's life? Jasper stared at the floor, only more intently than a moment ago. Why did she have to save Ertha's life?

He looked up and saw Ertha rub her shoulder again. Someone injected her with something. *On purpose!* Why?

Someone knew Cat was there. Someone knew Cat's skills. Someone knew, if they induced... what was the word... *fibrillation* in Ertha, Cat couldn't help herself but save her. And that would cause...

Somebody picked Newhaven Bay either because of the town's collective lack of critical thinking skills or their propensity to believe anything at all unusual is a harbinger of evil. Somebody wants to sow chaos and, based on Jasper's brief but extreme experience with the people here, Newhaven Bay is the perfect place to do it.

"The chaos is intentional," Jasper told the group. "I don't know what the box is, but the box isn't the point. The chaos is the point."

"Why?" asked Ertha.

"You with the Union, or whatever it is," Jasper said. "Do they have anything to do with it?"

Ertha shook her head. "I'm just a researcher. I have no way of knowing what Krylios is up to."

Jasper knew the only way of finding the truth was to get Cat back. They didn't know where the stranger took her, but that didn't matter. Jasper knew where she was going to be.

Or, rather, where she *had been*.

If only the others could see the inside of his magnificent mind, they would understand the wonderfully complex thought that just sparked and ignited all his brain matter. The one thing that Jasper truly knew for sure on this journey is that he *grows up* to be the one who defeats Hayalet and Krylios. But now, it occurred to him: armed with this knowledge, he can do it *now*. He doesn't have to wait to *grow up*. He didn't know how many decades he waited, but he can stop all that suffering *now*. To get started, he needs Catalina Rodriguez. He didn't know where Hayalet had taken her, but he knows her exact whereabouts in at least one time and place in history.

Impulsively, he ran back upstairs to the bedroom to grab his time crystal and take one quick glimpse at a particular painting on the wall.

Chapter 15

Back at Waveland Mansion, Jasper was always the most independent of the other nineteen boys. He didn't like to wrestle in the yard and he didn't like stickball, knucklebones, or whip and top. For this reason, none of the other boys particularly liked him.

What he loved most of all was reading stories of wit and cunning. And, when he ran out of those stories, he particularly enjoyed creating his own. His stories were detective stories, with a twist: his hero was never an actual *detective*, but someone like him, with a big problem, and finding clues just as a detective might.

His favorite story involved the fictional disappearance of Mr. Moorehouse. In this story, when he and the other boys awoke to find Mr. Moorehouse missing, they rejoiced, until they realized it was Mr. Moorehouse who provided them with their food. They resolved it would be Jasper who bravely trekked away from Waveland Mansion into the great unknown of Newhaven Bay, the New England Town without a bay (nor a body of water of any kind), on a mission to find their absent caretaker.

Jasper located the elderly caretaker by sitting in a bush, observing the comers and goers from the local pharmacy. It would take a young person, Jasper thought, to move Mr. Moorehouse from place to place. Yet the aging warden would require medications and other types of care goods on a frequent basis.

So, Jasper waited, in the bush, taking note of everyone who visited the pharmacy. He paid particular attention for an annoyed-looking younger person coming every day. Once he found such a person and followed him back to his snake den (yes, of course there was a snake den. This story was Jasper's to imagine and there was no reason it couldn't have a snake den), he rescued Mr. Moorehouse, became the pride and joy of Waveland Mansion, and earned his own bedroom.

That was the prize in each of his stories. Earning his own bedroom.

No one ever *actually* kidnapped Mr. Moorehouse. Yet, Jasper hoped his vivid imagination wasn't just for his own entertainment, but served as some sort of practice. At the very least, they kept him sharp enough to outwit the other boys, who were blissfully unaware of how Jasper played them against each other to avoid chores for himself.

As the green sparks faded from his vision, his practice was finally about to pay off. Armed with nothing but his brain, that was all he needed. If he got in trouble, he could clutch his time crystal, which for some reason always tried to drown him in Newhaven Bay, though he was getting a lot better at swimming.

The first thing Jasper noticed was the smell. He didn't expect the putrid smell. Self-hygiene was a rather modern concept and, when the shower had yet to be invented, you just got used to the smell, apparently. He wasn't sure he could do that.

His next sense honed in on the *clomping* of horse hooves on the cobblestone streets. As he looked around, the scenery was exactly as he imagined.

From his limited experience with the Order of Time Travelers (which is what Jasper decided this mysterious group would be called), it seemed that each time traveler had an archeologist to help them imagine their destination and keep track of history. Fortunately, Fletcher's painting of "Liverpool, 1750" in his bedroom helped him keep this mission a secret from Ertha. It was Liverpool from which the vessel *Rogue Wave* departed... with Catalina Rodriguez in its cargo hold.

Liverpool wasn't too different from Newhaven Bay - hills in the background a little way away from the bay. Tall ships with stowed sails floated, tied up to long wooden piers. A smattering of one and two-story brick buildings lined the cobblestone streets. In the distance, a church with a tall steeple was the tallest building in town.

He couldn't help but gaze at the repetitive swirling of the seagull flock floating in the breeze overhead. But, as he took in the wind, a breath distracted his survey - a rapid, wet breath. It seems a dog, curiously attracted to Jasper, made a seat at his feet.

He looked down at the dog. It had a luscious, brown, white, and gray coat. Its bared teeth would be threatening if not for the kind, blue eyes that stared directly into Jasper's own. An Australian shepherd, by the looks of it. It curiously looked at Jasper as though they were already friends.

But more curious than the look in the dog's eyes was its collar and tag. Was this typical of the 1750s? Was it even typical to have an *Australian* breed in Liverpool of all places? Slowly, Jasper reached down to examine the metal tag. A machine clearly engraved the blue metallic tag. Bone-shaped, it said one word:

Gizmo.

"Is that your name, bud?" Jasper asked the dog. "Gizmo?"

The dog's smile grew, and his tail flipped quickly on the ground. *Gizmo* it is. With the tag still in his hand, Jasper rubbed his thumb over the engraved name and asked, "You're not from here, are you?"

Without warning, Gizmo suddenly sneezed directly in his face! Jasper recoiled and wiped his eyes clean with a groan. "Eeeuuuccchhh!"

Gizmo just sat there. Once Jasper could see again, he asked, "Does that mean no?"

Gizmo smiled. Jasper was right. Like himself, Gizmo was a stranger to the 1750s. Then he wondered how Gizmo found *him*, so easily and so suddenly.

It made sense once he took stock of his clothes. It was strange his green t-shirt, jeans, and sneakers hadn't attracted more attention! He had no way of knowing whether Liverpool was a very accepting community, but if knowing science could get you instantly branded a witch, these clothes could get him branded an alien. He doubted the old English had a word for "hipster."

Suddenly, Gizmo barked, and ran away! "Wait!" Jasper called. "Gizmo! Where you going?"

Foolishly thinking the two brick buildings to each side protected him, he paused too long pondering his next move. He stepped out to give chase to Gizmo but, before he could make a move, he suddenly felt two firm hands grab him on his shoulders, pull him into the alley, and hold him up against a wall!

"What's all this rags ye've got draped about ye?" Jasper immediately noticed the stench of the short, burly, slightly bearded hulk pinning him against the brick. His gravelly voice continued, "See those bright hues? He thinks he a king!"

His partner, a woman of even more impressive a stench, laughed back, "A king of rats, perhaps!"

But the man seemed not to understand the joke! With a straight, dumbfounded face, he replied, "Can't make heads or tales at yer jab, can I?"

"What d'ye mean? I'm a real riot, ain't I?" The filthy woman insisted she was funny.

The man took one hand off Jasper to scratch his head. "But the lad hath no whiskers?"

"Nooo, ye daft nave!" The woman slapped him, "'cause he's pint-sized, that's why!"

Jasper felt like explaining to the woman the perils of having to explain a joke, but the man was doing a good enough job showing that the joke wasn't funny.

"Can rats really stitch together such flashy threads?"

The woman slapped him again, this time perilously close to Jasper's own face. He winced.

"Just shake him for shekels!" she shouted.

Jasper's eyes widened at the realization he was being robbed. So much for blending in, and so much for Gizmo being a guard dog! And he knew, he didn't have money - neither dollars from Newhaven Bay nor shekels from old England. But he did have a giant green diamond that would be the envy of any petty thief in any era of time.

Languages, currencies, and national borders come and go, but diamonds are forever! Did legitimate time travelers have this much trouble hanging on to their crystals? Save that question for Ertha, if he gets out of this predicament.

He thought quickly, and as clear-headed as he could while in the middle of a mugging. He also needed to quickly translate into Old English. He didn't think it would be that hard: Replace *have* with *hath*, *you* with *ye*, *do* with *dost*, and *any* with *nary*. Add *-eth* to the end of as many words as possible. When given two possible words, always choose the bigger. Anything else he'd figure out later.

"I hath nein shekels!" Jasper cried.

"Nine?" the woman replied. "That's good enough. Hand'em over!"

"No, sorry, that was German," Jasper covered, unaware that Germany didn't exist as a country in 1750. "I hath *nary a* shekel? That better?"

The man's face turned angry. "That's the blarney they all spout!"

Jasper didn't know what the man meant, but his face said he didn't like that answer. Of course he didn't like that answer! What robber *does* like hearing that the person he's robbing doesn't have any money? Everyone wants to be paid at the end of a long day's work, including robbers.

But there's one thing Jasper *does* like about robbers: they're scrappy, resourceful, and able to move in the shadows. He didn't want to escape this dangerous duo; he wanted to use them.

He reached into his pocket and withdrew his time crystal, continuing his mediocre attempt at translating into Shakespearian. "I dost hath here an item of envy..."

Something was off. As his new criminal friends' eyes gazed longingly at the shiny, invaluable diamond in his hand, Jasper held back a gasp for a different reason. To the robbers, nothing was off. But to Jasper, the crystal wasn't its usual green luster, but clear as glass. He could see why the robbers gawked - to them, it was a proper diamond. But to Jasper, he knew something was terribly, terribly wrong.

He swallowed. He had to continue. He would have to figure this out later. And his likely plan for "figuring it out" would probably be just to pray it would work like normal when he needed it to.

"I doth hath here an item of envy, but it hath nary a value now when to taketh it would mean to forsaketh a heftier prize." The English tutor who visited Waveland Mansion would be proud of that one.

The woman gestured with her head for the man to let him go. "A heftier prize, eh?" she asked. "Pay tell."

It was here he knew he had a problem. Deciding to use these thugs to sneak his way onto the docks where the *Rogue Wave* lay was easy. Thugs want treasure, the *Rogue Wave* has treasure, therefore, thugs go to *Rogue Wave*. But, they would want to know *what* the treasure was. Aside from Cat, all he had time to see on his last venture aboard the vessel was barrels full of food. Could he use nothing but his natural charm to convince them to chase after a treasure without knowing what the treasure is?

Confidence. Sell his story with confidence. Complete confidence. Hide his hesitation and banish any uncertainty. Only complete confidence would convince these criminals of his crooked plan.

He smiled. "Ye can see from my clothes..." he paused, remembering the words they used earlier, "...er, *rags* that I be not from here... um, from this land."

"Sorry I feel for yer countrymen," the woman sorrowed for him, "for the pitiful speaking skills ye all must have."

"Yes," Jasper played along, "'tis tragic how bad ye all speak."

"Stop interruptin' him!" the man barked. "Needs he all his brain to make the words to tell us of this treasure."

"Poor thing," said the woman. "Ye must've already forgotten. Ye were speaking of treasure."

Wondering how he could be both simultaneously smart enough to scheme to steal a treasure *and* dumb enough to know all the words needed to explain his plan, he suddenly felt defensive! He jumped to explain himself, not using many words and doing so without thinking, just like a dumb person would.

"I'm no thick-headed fool!" he insisted, harshly. "I speaketh different words than you speaketh."

"'*Treasure*' be somethin' gold or as worth as gold," the man tried to help him.

Jasper angrily snapped back, "Yes, I know what treasure is!" He paused. "Sorry, in my land, that be how we say, "Yea, I kin what treasure be."

"The lad kin what treasure be," said the woman.

"Yea," replied the man. "Speaketh more."

Finally, Jasper got to explain his plan. "I sailedeth here aboardeth the vessel *Krimson Kraken*, whereth the crew planeth to becometh pirates, and pillage the vessel *Rogue Wave* for its treasure. I knoweth for certain the *Kraken* and the *Rogue Wave* beith in this here harbor."

The man leaned in closer, and the stench oozing from his rotten teeth nearly made Jasper pass out. "Dost thou know what be in the treasure?"

Here now was the moment of truth. Could Jasper get them on his team without knowing what the treasure was, exactly? Instinctively, he knew he couldn't say, "no." Enticing the goons with promises of wealth was his only way forward.

"Something valuable enough for the crew of the *Kraken* to mutiny against their own captain." As Jasper saw them look at each other with raised eyebrows, he added, "And I know how to endear you to the new captain, so he makes you his best mates."

He tried to hide how he held his breath, waiting for them to accept his answer. Was his mystery compelling enough to cause them to join his quest? All he needed, really, was access to the docks. He could find Cat and rescue her again before the *Rogue Wave* departed Liverpool for

Maine. Whatever was happening in Newhaven Bay, Cat was the answer.

The plan worked. The criminal couple, who now identified themselves as "Jane" and "Henry," excitedly agreed to find him appropriate clothes and take him to the docks, so long as he could introduce them to the soon-to-be captain of the *Rogue Wave*, who Jasper remembered as "Captain Moxie."

Getting down to the docks was easier than he thought. Jane and Henry, instead of trying to pummel him, now protected him, their key to gaining the mysterious treasure of the *Rogue Wave*. All he needed to do was find Moxie, reveal the plan that Jasper already knows, and drop off his new friends to join the crew. He may even suggest they join the crew of the *Rogue Wave* instead of the *Kraken*, placing them onboard as mutineers ahead of Moxie's arrival.

But, as they walked down the wooden planks of the Liverpool docks and approached the *Kraken*, somebody was already aboard, talking to Moxie, that made Jasper shudder.

Hayalet.

A confrontation seemed to be growing unavoidable. Here he is, mere *feet* away. Maybe he can take care of this now, while Hayalet doesn't see him coming.

Chapter 16

"He'll be back," Ertha reassured Fletcher, after they noticed his absence from the house. Standing in the empty bedroom, Fletcher was lost. This was a side of Fletcher that Ertha had never seen. He was always in control, *large and in charge,* they used to joke.

Used to. Back when things were good between them. Ignoring that tension seemed to satisfy Fletcher for now, while he figured things out. There was too much tension elsewhere for him to resolve things with Ertha. Right now just isn't the right time.

At least that's what he told himself.

"Where did he go?" Fletcher asked, staring off into space as if Jasper had vaporized and floated into the heavens.

Ertha's eyes scanned the room and locked in on the painting, *Liverpool, 1750*. She pointed. "My guess is, here."

"Into a painting?"

Ertha shook her head. "Time travelers need to construct a perfect representation in their mind of the time where they want to travel. A *perfect* representation. That's where I come in. I'm usually the one who does the research so they can make the picture."

She gently caressed the golden plaque, *Liverpool, 1750*. "Unless they already have a picture."

Deep in thought, Fletcher sat down on Jasper's bed. The bed that used to be Ertha's. "How does this magic work?" he asked.

Ertha wandered around the room, trying not to be distracted by memories of spending her summers at the lake with Uncle Fletcher. "It's not magic. It's science, just a science we don't yet fully understand.

"Einstein called time the 'Fourth Dimension.' You and I can perceive depth, width, and height. But people like Jasper can perceive that 'Fourth Dimension.' It's something in their brain. And their crystal lets them move along it."

By now, Fletcher sat in the *thinking man* pose, his head resting on his hands as he sat on the bed. Without looking at Ertha, he asked, "Did I lose out on the last few years with you because I didn't believe you?"

Ertha glanced at a small picture, sitting in a frame on a shelf. A picture of young Ertha, frizzy black hair going all over the place, laughter exploding off her face as Fletcher stood in the water rocking her small wooden boat back and forth. Together, now, in her old bedroom, she could almost forgive him for thinking, "I've joined a group of time travelers," sounded too much like, "I've joined a cult of crazy people."

She put down the picture and sat down on the bed next to him and exhaled thoughtfully. "I think our experience this morning shows how easily people become afraid of things they don't understand."

That answer didn't comfort him. He had always considered himself better than that. His intelligence put him above jumping to quick conclusions. A man like Fletcher was always right, and he was right about trying to keep Ertha from joining that time travel cult.

Pride is often the biggest barrier to seeing the truth, even when that truth is sitting on her childhood bed right next to you.

"We have to save Cat," he decided.

Ertha shook her head. "The Time Travelers' Order will handle Cat. You have to keep the town together. That's your role in this."

"This... *Hayalet*... can you, or your people, see the future? Know what his next move is?"

"No," Ertha explained. "It's impossible to travel into your own future. The future is always in motion, always evolving... at least that's what they tell me. The best we can do is use the past to inform our future.

"Chaos is his goal," she continued. "I don't know why. But the best way you can fight him right now is to hold this town together."

"Somehow," Fletcher sighed. "And Jasper?"

Ertha smiled. "You leave him to me."

Chapter 17

Liverpool, 1750

From a distance, Jasper stared at the deck of the *Krimson Kraken*, at the villain about whom he knew precious little. Ertha seemed afraid of him, yet Cat not so. At least, not until she deduced what Hayalet was up to in Newhaven Bay.

Hayalet is out to kill Jasper, and Jasper has run into him at every step of his journey. He knows - or was told - that *he* will defeat Hayalet and the Krylios clan. But should this give him comfort? Does this make him invincible as he confronts this mysterious villain? Or is he capable of making a wrong move, imperiling humanity by causing an untimely death to its hero?

Does it even matter? Would his parents have dropped him off at Waveland Mansion if he mattered in this story?

Of course he mattered. Hayalet is out to kill *him*, after all. But the very act of being dropped off so unceremoniously at a group home without an ounce of love within its walls will always get to him.

Water sloshed against the surrounding posts, and a pair of seagulls landed on the deck nearby. His heavy wool clothes retained the smell of their previous occupants, a number that is certainly more than one. At what point did *smell good* become a human right?

One end of the pier led to an assortment of large sailing ships. The other end seemed to be where the smaller, single-person row boats and fishing boats tied up. And somehow, jumping from boat to boat, and keeping a careful watch on Jasper - *Gizmo*. Most certainly, Gizmo followed them.

Approaching the docks, Jasper held out his arms and stopped Jane and Henry.

"What ho?" exclaimed Jane, stumbling to a stop with Henry behind.

Jasper looked around. Everyone on the docks was doing something. Workers carried baggage and carted crates. Sailors scrubbed their decks and tied down ropes. Passengers ordered around the workers and the sailors. Jasper, Henry, and Jane, with their dress, couldn't possibly pass for a passenger.

Furthermore, guards patrolled the docks. Gizmo had gotten past them, but these were guards charged with keeping out people exactly like Jasper, Henry, and Jane. Guards on the lookout for people who weren't supposed to be there. Every ship that sailed into Liverpool and tied up to the docks owed a fee. But, on the horizon, no new ships seemed to make their way into the harbor, and thus, no security was about to become preoccupied with collecting a docking fee.

They had to busy themselves with something, but every crate already had a carrier. And it appeared one guard was paying particular attention to ensuring everyone who walked toward the *Kraken* had a purpose for being there.

While still hiding behind pillars, Jasper turned around to Jane. "Do you..." he cleared his throat, "*ahem*, dost thou still havest my clothes of olde?"

"Yes, I havest them in my stachell!"

"Good. I'm just gonna speak like I do in my country. Do you understand me?"

Both Jane and Henry nodded. Then Jasper smiled, and gave them both a thumbs up. "This is how you say you understand," he coyly explained.

Jane and Henry, smiling as though Jasper taught them something valuable, grinned and nodded back to him.

"Good," Jasper continued, "Give me my clothes back. I have an idea."

He checked over his shoulder before he explained his idea. Sure enough, Gizmo sat at the end of the pier, watching.

***

Wearing a burlap sash across his chest adorned with dry leaves over his green t-shirt, jeans, and sneakers, Jasper held his head high as he led Jane and Henry down the Liverpool docks. He walked with purpose and intent. They belonged there, or so he told himself.

The portly guard with the tricorn cap swayed in his leather boots as Jasper and crew marched down the wooden planks toward their ship. Their show of confidence *almost* snuck them past the guard, but only when they had fully and completely passed him did he realize something both seemed out of the ordinary *and* that he should do something about it.

"Excuse me!" he totted toward them, one hand raised with urgency. "Excuse me!" His voice whined and strained as if the lack of exercise that affected his body also extended to his voice. His leather boots pattered down the wood planks. "Excuse me!"

They stopped. Jasper turned on his heel, arms crossed behind him and chin held high. His voice said nothing, but his presence said, "How dare you speak to me."

The guard cleared his throat, a move that vibrated a collar of fat that lived beneath his chin. "Do you have a pass to be on this dock?" he asked.

Jasper rolled his eyes and nodded toward Jane, who stepped forward to handle this. "Why, *this* is the crown prince of Oaklandia. How dare you suggest his presence is disallowed, nay unwanted!"

The guard leaned forward with suspicion. "The crown prince of... *Oaklandia?*"

"Yeah!" Henry barked. "Can't ye see he's a wearin' a sash?" Jasper tugged at his burlap sash, proudly.

"It's burlap," noted the guard, still with suspicion.

Henry and Jane parted to move aside for Jasper, who stepped through with all the air of an aristocrat, hands still folded behind him. "Clearly," he announced, "the commonfolk here in England still have much to learn about Oaklandia. Yes, it is I, Prince Fernindand, son of King Olaf the Seventh, the ruler of divine right so as such that to question him is to question God."

The guard scrunched his forehead. "How old are you? Twelve?"

Jasper smiled, shrugging off the man's impoliteness as a cultural difference. "I'm legally an adult in Oaklandia. By our religion, I've been an adult for four years, but Oaklandia has a strict separation of church and state, and so the state didn't recognize my adulthood until last year."

The guard scratched his head harder. "How does your father rule with divine right if Oaklandia has a strict separation of church and state?"

Now, Jasper cleared his throat, not expecting to get into a philosophical discussion on government legitimacy with a dock guard. "My father, through his divine right, has the authority to create a separation of church and state."

"So you're saying that God made your father king, only for your father to turn around and say that God has no voice in the government?"

Jasper was taken aback! "Well, he is about to die," he tried to cover. Bringing up death is a tactic that should have ended the conversation quickly, but didn't.

"Probably because he lost God's favor by using God just to become King."

"No, he didn't *use* God. God speaks *through* my father."

"Then how do you have a separation of church and state?"

Now, Jasper scrambled. "Um, well... that's only for everybody else!"

Now, the guard seemed to understand. He relaxed, clasped his hands, and exhaled. "Ah, yes. Royalty."

"Exactly," Jasper replied, glad they had come to an understanding.

An understanding that the guard quickly shattered. "Because the Royals are inherently better than everyone else."

Jasper stirred inside, frustrated both that he couldn't make any progress with the guard *and* that the guard would have the audacity to question his fictional royal lineage. It was the brilliant Henry that came to his rescue.

"Of course they are!" Henry insisted, grabbing Jasper's burlap sash. "You think mere commoners can wear material such as this?"

The guard sighed and pointed to Henry and Jane's own outfits. "You are literally wearing a burlap sack right now."

The guard's powers of reason proved too much for Henry, who backed away. Jasper decided it was time to switch tactics.

"Can you swim?" he asked the guard.

"No."

And with that, Jasper promptly and without warning shoved the guard off the deck, who landed in the water with a splash proportional to his ample size.

"Run!" Jasper shouted to Jane and Henry. "Climb aboard the *Kraken* like you're already crew. I'll square you away with Moxie."

He was lying, of course, but with a smile and a thumbs up, Henry and Jane were already running down the pier.

***

Water gently sloshed against the side of the wooden tall ship as Jasper crept alongside on the pier's edge. The ship's rudder poked out the stern. Ropes hung off the top decks, as if they were used to tie the ship to the dock, until the lazy crewman was fired before he had time to not tie them up.

From the end of the pier, Gizmo watched Jasper slip himself off the dock, into the water, and to one of these ropes. Then, he climbed. Without knowing how he knew to do this, he wrapped his foot around the rope and squeezed it between his knees, using his legs to climb. Quietly, up and up he went.

Right above the stylish, blood-red letters *Krimson Kraken* that emblazoned the stern, the windows of the captain's stateroom hung open. Jasper's rope swayed right between the *m* and *s*, conveniently above these windows. As he was about to climb in, a sudden noise from within gave him pause.

He heard the sound of a door opening and two distinct pairs of footsteps entering the captain's stateroom. "Captain Moxie," the voice announced with authority. This voice's distinct chord stunned Jasper. Carefully, he lowered himself just an inch, enough to peer in through the window's side. There, he saw him. It was unmistakable. He towered over Moxie. His leather boots and trench coat inspired fear, almost as much fear as the scars on his bald head.

Hayalet.

"I'm not the captain," Moxie replied.

Marching back and forth, Hayalet smiled. "You will be," he said. "You will be the captain of the *Rogue Wave*."

Moxie said nothing, though the sound of a deep inhale showed unease with the situation. Seeing an opportunity, Hayalet continued. "You're starting to believe me."

Moxie wasn't a navy captain, and he didn't wear the sparkling, bright blues of a sailor in command. His coat was gray, his pants brown. Average height, nothing particularly striking about his strength. But he kept a neat beard, and his eyes showed ambition.

Ambition being tested by a deal with the devil. With Hayalet.

"Everything you've told me has come true," Moxie reluctantly admitted. "I don't know how you do it..."

"I see your future," Hayalet interrupted, ominously. "We've discussed this. Who foresaw that the doctor that would save your son's life would stay nearby your house last week?"

"You did," Moxie admitted.

"And when did I tell you this?" Hayalet leaned in.

With an exhale, Moxie nodded. "Before I even knew I would have a son."

Hayalet turned and continued his march. "Your son will die within the next year..."

"NO!" Moxie shouted.

"Shhhhh!" Hayalet continued, calming Moxie with his energy. "I will stop this, *if* you do something for me."

Jasper nearly dropped off the rope. Hayalet's game just became obvious. How did he inspire fear? He earned the trust of his victims by predicting a series of innocuous events in their lives. Then, *WHAM!* Drop on them the news of a devastating fate that he, of course, would help them avoid... for a price. Jasper continued to listen.

How he wished he had a weapon, any weapon, of any kind. He scanned the area within reach of the window. Hayalet stands, mere feet away. How small the room seemed, how tiny the distance he needed to change history, for the better.

"There's a girl being held captive and taken prisoner aboard the *Rogue Wave*."

"A girl?" Moxie questioned.

"This girl is more valuable than any treasure," Hayalet pressed into him. "You will see to it that she is delivered to the coast of Lagos, in West Africa."

"But how?" asked Moxie.

"You will commandeer the *Rogue Wave* and become the captain. Here's how..."

Suddenly, Jasper slipped! In an ill-advised moment of panic and instinct, he reached out and grabbed the bottom of the windowsill. His still-falling legs swung freely, and he wrestled his other arm over the ledge.

Did he scream? Shout? Grunt? Not for him to remember. How does one remember such details in a panic? No matter, his sudden battle against gravity caught Hayalet's attention. He quickly found himself face-to-face with this villain.

They both paused. They both caught the look in each other's eyes, inches from each other's face. Staring beyond the battle scars that decorated Hayalet's bald head, Jasper lingered, captivated. He saw more than anger, more than fear. It was almost a... *curiosity?* And the look Hayalet returned showed he, too, seemed struck by something about Jasper. Hayalet was used to being someone in complete control, not accustomed to being caught off-guard.

For both of them, a moment of profound disturbance. A mountain of mystery compressed into just a single second.

But the second passed, and Hayalet leaned and scowled, "You!"

Jasper's options seemed limited. Without thinking, he let go of the ledge and plummeted backside first down into the water below. He seemed to fall in slow motion, with Hayalet slowly leaning further out the window and reaching out to grab the escaping Jasper.

Jasper flailed, and Hayalet failed. As Jasper hit the water, he reached into his pocket, grasped his time crystal, and built in his mind the most detailed picture of Newhaven Bay he could conjure. He held his breath and waited for Fletcher to yank him from the water once again.

It didn't come. His breath ran low. His heart raced. He opened his eyes underwater and found no green sparks. The blurry form of the crystal in his hand seemed... white.

He looked around. Something was wrong, but he couldn't solve this issue underwater. He kicked toward the surface.

After taking a deep breath and clearing the water from his eyes, he looked at the ship. Though few crewmen were aboard, he heard the muffled, unclear shouting of some sort of commotion. The sight of his new friend Henry being thrown in the air and plummeting to the water below must have meant he got in Hayalet's way.

Escape.

Gizmo started barking from the end of the pier. So much for not attracting attention.

Escape was the only thing on Jasper's mind now. With his time crystal flushed white and not working, he had to find a hiding spot.

"Jasper!"

He heard a voice call his name. He pushed his hands through the water to turn toward the voice.

"Jasper!"

Under the dock, a man, skin so dark he couldn't see the features of his face in the pier's shadow. "Jasper, swim to me!" the man called, his voice deep and accented. Not knowing what to do but not having any better options, Jasper figured the only man in Liverpool who could possibly know his name *might* be safe.

Still getting a hang of this swimming thing, he laid on his back and kicked toward the man, not sure how best to use his arms.

"Kick, boy, kick!" the man shouted. "He is coming."

But Jasper couldn't move that fast. His body still didn't know how to use the water. Progress was slow. "Come get me!" Jasper shouted.

"I can't rescue you if Hayalet sees me," the man shouted. "Just kick harder! Use your arms!"

But Jasper didn't know how to use his arms! When he lifted an arm, his face immediately sank under water. He lowered his arm back down and just kicked as hard as he could possibly kick toward the direction of the man he hoped was there to rescue him.

From the ship, he saw Hayalet's tall figure slip out of the hull and on to the gangway. Instead of running down the gangway, he removed his jacket, threw off his boots, and dove into the water!

"Kick, boy!"

Jasper's legs thrashed. The man was just feet away, his arm outstretched, reaching as far as he could.

A new splashing sound joined him. Hayalet surfaced and swam quickly in Jasper's direction. Tall and strong, the villain could swim.

From the other end of the pier, unseen by Jasper, Gizmo ran. He ran and ran, swiftly sprinting toward Jasper. Then, he leaped off the pier, landing with a splash right next to Jasper!

Hayalet's rhythmic paddling grew closer and closer! Jasper's arms flailed uselessly in the water, but Gizmo bit down hard on Jasper's shirt and pulled him toward the man hiding under the dock.

Finally, they reached the man's outstretched hand. With a firm grasp, the man pulled Jasper close, out of the water, and a shower of green sparks flew around the two of them. At the last second, Jasper instinctively reached out and grabbed Gizmo's collar.

Liverpool swirled and evaporated. Hayalet closed in, and Jasper could barely make out the frustrated disappointment in his face as he watched his target escape.

The wet, dampness of Georgian-era Liverpool vanished. When his world stopped spinning, Jasper and this man lay in sand, under the dry, scorching sun.

Gizmo woke Jasper from his daze, standing up and shaking a spray of water from his coat.

Buildings of limestone and sandstone brick, with decorated spires, lined the distance. The sounds of a vibrant, lively market emanated from inside the walled city, decorated with palm trees.

Now, under the sunlight, Jasper saw the man. African, his brightly colored clothes sported rich blues and golds. It seemed fun, almost festive.

"Jasper," the man's deep, friendly voice boomed, "My name's Idrissi Hassan."

Still catching his breath from his swimming adventure, Jasper sat up. "Thanks," he said. "How do you know who I am?"

Hassan smiled, revealing huge, perfectly white teeth. "Ertha sent me. I've been watching you since you arrived in Liverpool."

He was a rescuer. And Ertha was connected. Though she wasn't a time traveler herself, she certainly was resourceful. And, like he could read Jasper's mind, Hassan filled in the rest of the blanks.

"We're in Lagos, in west Africa," he explained. "This is where your treasure is about to arrive."

The treasure, of course, being Catalina Rodriguez, prisoner aboard Captain Moxie's *Rogue Wave*.

Jasper pulled his flush-white crystal out of his pocket. Hassan couldn't help but notice.

"Ah," Hassan said, "you wore out your crystal."

Worn out? Clearly, there was more to this whole time travel thing that Jasper had to learn.

"And, I have to say," Hassan continued, "I didn't expect a dog."

Gizmo smiled.

Chapter 18

Newhaven Bay

"We've already had three men try to drag the box away with their truck in the middle of the night last night," Officer Pierce reported to Fletcher.

The Newhaven Bay Boater's Supply Store held much more than boating supplies. In fact, just about everything one needed sat lining the shelves of the boater's store. The deepest building on Main Street, with the most elegant brick facade, the boater's store showed where Newhaven Bay's priorities lay.

Between the deep red brick walls and beneath the wooden rafters of the ceiling, Officer Pierce followed Fletcher through racks of flannel shirts and blue jeans. "I've never seen anything like this in my life, Fletcher," he continued, as Fletcher moved a light around a newly placed canoe that cast a rack of clothes in shadow. "After the incident in the park the other day, the people in this town who want the box removed... well, they won't even talk to the ones who want it entombed."

"That'll make church interesting on Sunday," Fletcher replied, marking off inventory on his clipboard.

"I hear there'll be two services now," Pierce said.

Over the top of his clipboard, Fletcher just stared at Pierce, who added, "With separate preachers."

Fletcher shook his head and turned toward the back of the store. Behind a sliding, unfinished wood barn door, Fletcher's magnificent office and a conference room joined the back of the building. Pictures of the beautiful landscape around Newhaven Bay adorned the brick walls of the conference room around its long table.

Pierce followed Fletcher through into his office - an equally majestic brick monstrosity, with shelves adorning model ships and antique navigation equipment he didn't pretend to know how to use.

"People listen to you, Fletcher," Pierce said as Fletcher sat down behind his desk. "What can you do?"

Fletcher shrugged. "What about the girl who saved Ertha?"

"No word," Pierce shook his head.

"Pierce, you saw how quickly the mayor turned people around on me. I tried to calm things, and she just… it was like her very breath set the town on fire!" Fletcher sighed. *"I don't know* that people will listen to me."

Pierce sat down opposite Fletcher. "What do *you* want done with the box?"

"I want it gone, but that doesn't appear to be an option."

They shared an uncomfortable moment of tension, the type of moment shared between two people not used to not knowing what to do when truly stumped.

"How are my two delinquents?" Pierce changed the subject.

Fletcher checked his wristwatch. "Late," he replied.

With unnaturally good timing, two ten-year-olds burst through the door. A boy and a girl, slightly disheveled, hair unkempt, they ran together to Fletcher's desk.

"What's he doing here?" the boy asked about Officer Pierce.

"Making sure you didn't rob anything on the way here," Pierce replied, only slightly sarcastic.

Gus and Lilly, as the town's two delinquents, occupied a great deal of Officer Pierce's time. Fortunately, he had the time to deal with their rash of petty thefts. This was also fortunate, because Fletcher wasn't sure larger crimes were really in Pierce's wheelhouse.

"What's first, mister Fletcher?" Lilly asked, as sweet as can be.

Fletcher handed each of them a clipboard. "Inventory the storeroom," he instructed, "then wash the windows up front."

As the two children ran out, Pierce noted, "They didn't ask you to count their hours."

"They stopped asking me two weeks ago," Fletcher replied. "I don't think they want to leave."

"I haven't had any reports that they've been getting into trouble. You must be doing something right."

Fletcher just shrugged. "Let's hope we don't go through a town crisis or anything."

Pierce chuckled.

Bursting through the door at that moment, Ertha just about tripped over the threshold, barely able to contain her excitement, her energy seeming to sizzle out of her bouncy hair.

"You alright, Ertha?" Fletcher's concern wasn't so much concern as it was a sarcastic comment on her energy.

"Yeah, yeah, yeah," she stammered, her brain moving faster than her mouth could keep up. "I ran through here so fast your cashier probably thinks I'm mad at you, which is a good thing."

Pierce characteristically seemed a mental step behind them.

"I figured out a plan!" Ertha nearly shouted. Both Fletcher's and Pierce's eyebrows shot up. But Ertha, clearly proud of her scheme, smiled as she spewed forth her plan.

"Things aren't good between us, right? Like, *everybody* here knows I haven't talked to you in forever."

Fletcher nodded, and Pierce's eyes suddenly understood why he thought it strange Ertha was even there in the first place.

"Alright," she continued. "This town's split into two sides, and we need to keep tabs on each of them. So, here's what I'm thinking," she wildly flailed her hands as she kept explaining.

Hassan puckered his lips in thought. "Does he know what you're after?"

Jasper replayed the story, of his own rescue, of his first rescue of Cat, of Cat's kidnapping in Newhaven Bay, and of his journey to Liverpool to rescue Cat a second time. Most importantly, how Hayalet was there each time.

Hassan nodded. "Then it's likely he knows where you're headed, whether or not he saw me. In fact, he may already be here."

Gizmo's ears popped up, and his eyes suddenly focused with attention. He left Jasper's side and began a slow walk around the two of them, carefully monitoring their surroundings.

"Idrissi..." Jasper started. Hassan stopped him.

"Call me Hassan," he explained. "Your name is Jasper Berry. To me, *Idrissi* is like *Berry*. My name is *Hassan*."

"Your last name comes first?" Jasper asked, confused.

"No, *your* last name comes first," Hassan said, smiling. "We're in my country. You're the weird one here!" He then pointed to Jasper's t-shirt and jeans. "Good thing it's not unusual for Africans to see people dressed different from them."

"Hassan!" Jasper interrupted, taking his guardian by surprise. "Newhaven Bay is under attack of some sort, and Cat knows what's happening. I need to rescue her!"

Hassan nodded and crossed his arms contemplatively. "Let me ask you this, Berry Jasper: you are now the past, which means the events you will witness have already taken place. Are you sure you want to go about changing them?"

Jasper thought about this for a moment while Gizmo continued to circle. It seemed simple enough. If the events continue to go on as they were meant to, uninterrupted, Hayalet and Krylios will continue to hunt him forever. The only way to change his own future is to change the future of Newhaven Bay.

Besides, why does Newhaven Bay not have a bay in Jasper's own time? This has something to do with it.

"Yes," Jasper said. "Otherwise, what good is time travel?"

That statement changed Hassan. He put his hands on his hips and stared, unblinking, at Jasper for a few moments. A slight breeze rippled Hassan's beaded blue robe. Even Gizmo paused to look back at him.

Jasper felt a change in the mood. "What?" he asked.

Hassan felt it, too, and changed the mood back. His bright smile returned, and he spoke with a deep, booming laugh under his voice. The sleeves of his robe hung off his arms as he pointed in the distance. "Well then, Berry Jasper, we best be on our way. An historical document recalls that a ship matching the description of the *Rogue Wave* arrives here in Lagos nine days from now. We have that much time to replenish your crystal so you can rescue your girl and get back to Newhaven Bay."

He took off walking, and motioned for Jasper to follow. "Dog," he instructed, "walk ahead of us and look for Hayalet. I have a place in town overlooking the port. We'll be safe there, as long as Hayalet didn't see that it was I who rescued you from Liverpool."

Jasper squinted. "And if he did?"

"Then it's probably the end for me," Hassan said, not breaking his step to check Jasper's reaction, nor giving any sort of mention to Jasper's future fate.

Chapter 20

Newhaven Bay

People hardly ever argued in Newhaven Bay. Yes, the box arriving in town was something new and different that caused years of pent-up disputes to come flowing out all at once, like when you eat a mouth full of vegetables you don't like and are just holding it in until your guest isn't watching. Except in this case, they waited to spit it out until *everyone* was watching.

Still, apart from the skirmish at the park, hardly anyone ever argued. Even if you told a friend something silly and ill-advised, like you were naming your baby "Quasimodo" or "Satan," your friend would politely nod and tell you how wonderful of an idea that seemed. Judgment was to be done behind one's back, not to their face.

One hundred years prior, one of the most popular forms of entertainment in the world was to go out to the town square and watch criminals be hanged. This made sense, because a hanging was usually shorter than a play, and didn't require the audience to grapple with ambiguity or suspension of disbelief. It also had a very certain ending: the justly served suspension of a criminal from a rope. (This may have gone out of style for the same reason nobody watches westerns anymore - "They're all the same.")

So it made sense, then, when Fletcher and Ertha burst through the front door of the Fisherman's Supply Store shouting at the top of their lungs, nobody was too proud to drop everything they were doing to watch.

Neither Ertha nor Fletcher were ever trained in the literary arts. No one had ever given them advice such as, "Avoid too much exposition," or "Show, don't tell." But, the art of eloquent insults was something nobody had to teach them.

Bursting forth with her usual energy sizzling from the tips or her hair, she screamed toward Fletcher standing in the doorway, "Spending any more time with you is like watching a marathon of paint drying competitions!"

Fletcher shouted back, "If you leave again, who's going to keep the cobwebs from taking over the house?"

"Usually, an old worm emerges from its cocoon a butterfly, but you'd turn into a mop!"

"That doesn't make any sense!" Fletcher stepped onto the sidewalk to shout back. "How can a worm turn into a mop?"

"I don't know!" Ertha threw up her arms and made sure the crowd was watching. "Maybe it just fossilized while waiting for you to try something new!"

As if she were a conductor stirring the orchestra through a marvelous crescendo, the gathering crowd all chanted, "*ooooohhhhh*" right on her cue. All their heads at once turned toward Fletcher to see his response.

"I thought I was raising a free-spirited bird, not a foul-mouthed parrot perched on a pirate's shoulder."

Around town, the sounds of pots and pans dropping to the floor echoed around with the sounds of tires screeching to a stop. People from blocks away came running. Just seeing Fletcher angry was enough to cause people to join the crowd before someone started charging admission.

"How do you know how to raise a bird, Fletcher, when you're a mole-rat with its bum burrowed underground?"

And again, heads snapped toward Fletcher.

"Thanks for not calling me a *naked* mole-rat," Fletcher said.

"You're welcome," Ertha replied with consternation, crossing her arms. "We need... to open.. that box."

Fletcher took deliberate steps to walk up to Ertha, using his height over her to his advantage. A good two heads taller than her, he looked down and pointed for emphasis. "I will *not* put this town at risk."

"It is *already* at risk."

"I find your sudden care for this town suspicious, after you so unceremoniously left me without a word three years ago."

This left Ertha, for a moment, without an instant reply. The look in Fletcher's eye showed her he wasn't acting with that one. Fletcher still hurt, no matter how much Ertha explained.

But, this was not the time for making up. She needed to have the final word, and storm off in a huff. That was the only way for her plan to work, for both sides of the town to rally around each of them. In the moment, without forethought or care for the consequences, she went to a place she knew Fletcher didn't want her to go.

"If I hadn't left, my mind would have wasted away and my soul died of starvation."

The crowd hushed with her truth, but she wasn't done yet. With dagger-sharp words pointed directly at Fletcher's own soul, she simply said, "You're not some wise elder, Fletcher; you're a blind old mule who can't see beyond his own doorstep. People trust you because you're predictable."

With Fletcher looking on, knowing that Ertha had responded to his truth with her own truth. Their fake fight, perhaps unavoidably, became real. Her rant seemed vaguely rehearsed, and he feared those were the words she said about him as she fell asleep at night.

He stared at her longingly as Ertha walked away. Just as she predicted, the gathered crowd, which had somehow all earned time off to watch their street spat, split in two. Half chased after Ertha, and he watched the leaders push their way to the front to have her ear.

Fletcher's half seemed familiar. People like him, that he talked to over coffee or at the drugstore. Everyone in the crowd reassured him with variations of the same two phrases:

"That box is better left unopened."

"Let's go figure out what to do next."

But the phrases blurred and muffled as he watched Ertha walk away again. His young little niece had indeed become confident and smart. Would she have, if she had followed Fletcher's advice and stayed in town?

For the first time in his life, Fletcher questioned the wisdom of his own instincts.

Chapter 21

Lagos, 1750

Past the market and up a tree-lined hill overlooking the port, Gizmo led Hassan and Jasper to a two-story adobe building nestled among the branches. The orange building stood square, but ornamented with arched doorways and windows. A clay dome covered the roof. Lightly colored geometric patterns decorated the orange walls. Even tiny pointed spires poked out from the corners of the rooftop.

"My home," Hassan said as they approached.

"By yourself?" Jasper asked. It seemed strange to him. At this point in history, people didn't have time, nor money, nor effort to waste on building such an elaborate home just for themselves. People depended on each other, and several generations of the same family shared a single living space out of necessity. Around the world, grandparents cared for grandchildren while the parents worked to provide for all.

A look of sadness grew on Hassan's face. He led them to the door and pushed the door open without a lock of any sort. Inside, sunlight shone through the glassless windows. The floor was red brick, and a table sat in the middle of the room. The inside walls matched the outside.

Along one wall, a firepit lay beneath a chimney, still smoldering. On the opposite wall, a wooden staircase led upstairs. Jasper noticed, unlike the homes with which he was familiar, the walls of this home had no photographs of family. This was the 1750s, after all.

Most strange of all, the house smelled of... fresh stew?

Hassan poked the fire and stirred the pot hanging above it. He took a long sniff. "Ahhh," he said. "Efo riro. Vegetable soup. I just made it this morning." He scooped a ladle-full into a bowl and handed it to Jasper.

"This morning?" Jasper said. "This morning you were saving me in Liverpool."

Hassan winked, a momentary distraction from sadness. "Time travel," he reminded Jasper. He then gazed out the window. Jasper sensed he didn't much care for sadness.

"In your time, you call this place 'Lagos,'" Hassan explained, distracting himself with cleaning to hide his grief. "We call it 'Eko.' It's the Portuguese colonialists who call it 'Lagos.' And, history being what it is, it's not the people of Eko that write the maps that the rest of the world uses."

It didn't seem possible for Hassan's normally bright face to sink any lower, but it did. His eyes became distant. "Traders forcibly took my family, loaded onto ships, and sent across the sea for labor."

Jasper shuddered with a startling realization that someone kidnapped and enslaved Hassan's family. Studying that era of history was always abstract, impersonal, and disconnected. Though he knew deep inside that real people encountered these horrors, it was hard to connect it to real life.

But he couldn't avoid it now, not while sitting in Hassan's nearly empty family home. "Why not you?" he asked.

"Because I can time travel," Hassan explained, "Krylios saved me... for a price."

For a price. That's the same thing Ertha said back in Fletcher's house. Krylios helps people *for a price.* "What price?" Jasper asked.

Hassan stood below a window, and ripped a few pieces of jerked beef from a clay jar, placed them on a plate, and set it on the floor. Gizmo took one last, careful look out the front door before trotting to the plate for his meal. Hassan pet Gizmo's head as he ate.

"I'd rather not talk about that right now," he answered, "but I'm planning to rescue my family just as I imagine you're planning to rescue yours?"

He hadn't shared that detail with Hassan. But, he didn't need to. All the time travelers he's met seem to share a connection of some sort - Cat, Hayalet, and now Hassan. He knew without Jasper having to say anything.

Hassan pointed out the window overlooking the sand dunes, and the wide rivers coming in from the Atlantic Ocean. "Your ship comes in nine days," he said. "We need to replenish your crystal. Take it out."

From his pocket, Jasper removed his now-clear crystal and placed it on the table. "What happened to it?" he asked.

Hassan picked up the crystal and held it to one eye, studying it. "This crystal, Jasper, is no simple rock. It is a *living* rock. If you ask more of it than it can give you, it will wear out. Just like if you ask the soil for more than it can grow, it will wear out. Or if you ask a horse to run more than it can run, it will wear out. Even a man's labor, if you ask more of him than he can give you, he will wear out. A person's labor is valuable, but exploiting it will damage them."

"Like the soil," Jasper thought aloud, "it needs... *fertilizer?*"

Hassan placed it back on the table. "Yes, fertilizer, that's a good way to put it."

"Well, how do I fertilize it?"

With an all-knowing smile, Hassan said, "Blow on it."

That's it? Blow on it? Confused, but trusting, Jasper held the crystal up to his mouth, inhaled, and as though he were blowing out the candles on the birthday cakes he never got, blew on the crystal.

And then nothing happened! Nothing, except Hassan erupting into laughter! A great, bellowed laugh so hard he nearly fell out of his chair!

"That always works for me, but I guess you're not full of hot air like old Hassan, are you?" He squeezed his words out between his laughs.

Jasper slammed the crystal down on the table in frustration, and Hassan's face instantly changed. "Oye, be careful!" he warned sternly, with a finger outstretched. "It can feel that."

Jasper sighed in frustration. "Then how *do* I replenish it?"

Hassan's laugh returned. Then, much to Jasper's dismay, he simply shrugged! "I don't know!" he bellowed. "That's a mystery!"

"What?" Jasper popped out of his chair in anger, partly at Ertha for sending him this buffoon. "What do you mean you don't know?"

Hassan smiled and shrugged again. "It's *your* crystal!"

"Yeah, but I don't know anything about it!"

"Ah ha!" Hassan pointed at him. "That is problem number one!"

Jasper twitched, not knowing what words to spit out. "Well, Fletcher - old Fletcher - just gave it to me. It... it didn't come with instructions! I certainly didn't know it could *wear out!*"

"You said you do not know your crystal," Hassan interrupted. "Does your crystal know you?"

What? The look of confusion that crossed Jasper's face was clearly obvious to Hassan.

Hassan reached out and grabbed Jasper's hand, placed the crystal inside, and folded his fingers around it. "This crystal is your *partner*," he explained. "It doesn't want to be a passive tool you only use when you need it. It wants to be a part of *you*. It wants to be *one* with you, to be a part of your life.

"What rejuvenates you, what gives you *purpose*, will rejuvenate the crystal and give it purpose." Then, he paused, only briefly, and looked Jasper directly in the eye.

"What keeps *you* going will keep your crystal going."

Jasper signed again. "That doesn't make any sense," he complained, not trying to be rude but genuinely confused. "*Partners?*"

"Like any good partner," Hassan explained, "you will learn to listen to it as it will learn to listen to you."

Jasper sat back down, trying to think and sincerely trying to take Hassan at his word. "Okay," he said, "how do I learn to listen to it?"

Hassan sat as well. "Ertha told me about you. She told me you're a problem-solver. You like to get your hands dirty and figure things out."

Jasper couldn't argue with that. That *was* why he was here in the first place. Rescuing Cat from the *Rogue Wave*, and then going back to Liverpool to find her again was his solution to trying to figure out what exactly threatened Newhaven Bay. He did these things without waiting, and without asking. And he liked it.

"I have a problem for you to solve," Hassan announced. "While you solve it, pay attention to what feels good, and pay attention to your crystal. *Listen* to it."

"Listen to it?"

"I can't explain it, but you'll understand when it happens. Are you ready?"

Jasper nodded.

"This girl - Catalina Rodriguez - Hayalet is having her brought here for a reason. Find out why."

Gizmo looked up from his plate and whimpered. Jasper knew how he felt.

Chapter 22

Newhaven Bay

As the sun moved across the sky, it reached a point that the rays of sun poked through a narrow opening and illuminated a cave on the outskirts of Newhaven Bay. Catalina Rodriguez sat against the damp limestone wall and stared at the bald giant of a man standing watch over the cave's entrance. Right on cue, his trench coat fluttered in a gust of wind.

Almost no one knew of this cave. The trees on the hilltop obscured vision of the cave from the town. The path up to the cave was not normally accessible by hikers. When Cat started messing around with his plan for the town, this cave was the perfect place for Hayalet to stow her away.

Unfortunately, how exactly Hayalet knew of this cave was not a question Cat thought to ask. This was unusual for her, because normally Cat was pretty smart. But being tied against a wall in a cave has its way of distracting you.

"I bet you thought Jasper Berry was smart to come looking for you?" Hayalet said, as he turned around to face her. "But, I assure you, it was nothing more than an accident. He was chasing a pirate's loot. Not you." A certain menace in his voice gave Cat goosebumps.

Shaking her head to get her hair out of her face, she looked up at Hayalet. "I know what you're doing," she said, fearlessly, looking directly into his scarred, evil eyes.

"Causing a rift in time in a place where this rift otherwise wouldn't belong?" Hayalet answered. "Sewing chaos, in a place where historians have always known there was none?"

He took a step closer to her. "Historians and time travelers will have a good, hard look at what happens here, won't they? The question though is, why?"

Cat knew why. "Because that's what Krylios wants. And you're the one who gets Krylios everything he wants."

Hayalet huffed. "Not everything. Do you know what he wants?"

Money. That's why he does everything. That's why Cat, despite the guarantees to her safety, despite the threats to her family, and despite the freedom that comes from a steady income, declined to join the Krylios network. For a time traveler *not* to join Krylios was nearly unheard of. But Cat couldn't bring herself to do his bidding, no matter what sort of "protection" he offered. She wasn't trying to fight him directly - that would be stupid - but she kept track of him, his movements, and his desires.

She kept track of Hayalet. She hadn't yet determined where he came from, but now wasn't the best time to find out.

Like a spurned lover, he probably kept track of her as well. It wasn't often a time traveler declined to join Krylios. That would at least explain why he seemed to know her so well, here in this cave.

But no amount of money nor protection could entice Cat to allow herself to exploit vulnerable, innocent people. And anyone who did was a monster, including the one who stood in front of her. Cat was better off rogue, independent, on her own.

"It's not money," Hayalet explained, returning to the entryway. "There is only one thing that Krylios truly wants."

"Power?" Cat surmised.

Hayalet chuckled. "Of sorts."

"Why were you sending me to Africa?" she asked.

"To resolve a dispute."

"In Krylios' favor?"

Hayalet didn't answer. This, of course, meant, "Yes."

She contemplated her situation. A strange fact seemed just out of reach, like a word on the tip of your tongue or when one can't remember another person's name and has to act like it's not a problem. It was unsettling, unnerving. It bothered her in the back of her mind, which is especially problematic because the back of her mind is usually quite good at working things out.

As Hayalet stood in the entryway, hands clasped behind his back like the captain of a ship, she mulled over her situation. At the very least, she's alive. Hayalet wins his battles through careful study and preparation. That she's alive is...

Wait.

I'm alive.

That's what bothered her. She's alive, and she shouldn't be. Hayalet's entry into town was part of a carefully scripted, prepared, multi-step plan that accounted for every eventuality *except her.*

There is no reason to keep her alive. Hayalet doesn't need her. His plan - whatever it is - will continue on without her. In fact, keeping her in this cave adds another wrinkle in the plan that he shouldn't have to deal with. The best, most logical course of action is to kill her.

So why hasn't he?

"You're planning to kill me, aren't you?" she inquired.

No reply.

Not that she isn't grateful! Despite the horrible conditions of the cave, she would much rather not be dead. This is a win so far. But it still makes little sense.

Maybe he's forgotten?

No, he hasn't forgotten. But nonetheless, it's best not to draw attention to it. He won't talk about his plans for Newhaven Bay - and she already knows as much as she needs: sow division and chaos in order to attract the attention of another time traveler.

How to get him to talk about Africa?

I know.

While Hayalet still faced away, she smiled. "The Africa plan probably wasn't gonna work, anyway. It's a good thing Jasper brought me here."

Hayalet instantly turned around, a move that revealed to Cat her tactic worked. "It was most definitely going to work," he barked.

She shrugged. "But I don't know anything about Africa!"

"You didn't need to know anything about Africa."

"See," she replied snidely, "that's why it wasn't going to work. You assumed I didn't need to know anything. What's their culture like?"

"It doesn't matter."

"What language do they speak?"

"It doesn't matter."

"Who's in charge?"

"Whoever purchased you."

Bought. Cat raised her eyebrows. "Ah, so they were bidding for me." She made a show of doing mental calculations so Hayalet could see her thinking. "Still, wouldn't work."

She laid back against the wall, confident in her answer, and more confident it would draw the information she needed out of Hayalet. Hayalet's plans *always* worked, and he knows it.

Hayalet seethed in anger. Who was this mere girl to question his plotting? His carefully assembled plan? He didn't get to where he is by *failing*. He pointed a single finger at her face, nearly touching her as he towered above.

"It would work," he scowled.

Cat shrugged again. "We both know success as a time traveler depends on our homework. So, unless you can convince me, me going in blind is-"

He interrupted forcefully, nearly yelling. "Two clans constantly battle each other over a single source of fresh water. Whoever purchased you would use you to design a system to harvest that water for themselves. Then they would win."

He stood straight and then withdrew back to the entrance. "It doesn't matter who wins, as long as one of them does. Whoever wins gets control over the area and owes favors to Krylios for giving them you."

He looked back at her, hands again crossed behind his back. "Happy now?"

Cat furrowed her brow to think for a moment. "Why me?" she asked.

"They've killed every outsider who tries to talk to them. But your knowledge is your protection. They'd kill each other over you before they killed you."

Cat nodded. Now she understood. Krylios planned gradually to gain control over the entire world by gaining the allegiance of one clan, one culture, one nation, one town at a time. The scrappiness and resourcefulness that came with being an independent time traveler made her more useful than a time traveler in Krylios' network... and so, being in his network or not, Krylios used her anyway.

For a moment, though she knew nothing of these two warring clans, she felt sorry for any outsiders who had the unfortunate call to interact with them.

Like Jasper is about to do.

Chapter 23

Eko, 1750

It didn't take long for Jasper to get into trouble. Jasper had never tried paddling upstream or running up a down escalator, but this journey into the trading port outside Eko made him long for the peaceful bliss of tumbling inside a tornado.

Even Gizmo, as good a guard dog as he is, couldn't overcome the crowd that captured the two of them.

Most importantly, after all of that, Jasper's crystal is still white. Escape is impossible.

***

"What do I do now?" is usually not a question Jasper asked out loud, though Gizmo could tell that's what he was thinking. To Jasper, every plan his young mind hatched was brilliant, even when it wasn't. This is especially problematic when there's no one around to tell him.

Gizmo wished he could speak Jasper's language, to say something like, "Jasper, your fool scheme sounds like you pulled it out of the butt of a borzoi," which was the dumbest dog breed Gizmo could think of. Nonetheless, all Gizmo could do was stay by Jasper's side and try to nudge him out of harm's way while he ran full tilt toward it. Being nudged a single inch extended out over time can add up to a great deal.

Alongside the sea inlet, rows of tiny fishing boats made their way toward the beach. Crews of two or three unloaded nets teeming with fish, as crowds from the villages nearby made their way down, empty baskets in hand, ready to pick up that afternoon's supper.

In a way, Jasper's plan made sense to him. He knew Cat's skills as a scientist and engineer. If she were being brought here to Eko as a prisoner, and Captain Moxie were looking for a buyer, someone needed her talent. Thus, finding *who* would buy her seemed like an easy ordeal.

Gizmo rolled his eyes as Jasper climbed atop a wooden crate on the dock, but sat next to him, on guard, anyway.

"In a few days," Jasper shouted from atop a crate in the middle of the port, "a ship will arrive carrying a very special cargo: a woman of science who can solve your most difficult problems."

Gizmo whined at Jasper's feet as a crowd grew around him. A hundred men and women, some with baskets full of still-flopping fish, encircled him, listening to his proclamation. Seeing this, Jasper smiled, and continued.

"Does anybody know this already?" he asked the crowd. When nobody said anything, he sighed in relief.

"Whew, good. Okay then. Well, she's a woman of science, as I said. She can create energy out of nothing! She can build incredible tools to ease the burden of your work! If you want to purchase…" He thought for a moment. *What's the best way to say this?* "…her services, come speak to me!"

With the crowd still waiting to hear what he had to say next, and Jasper having nothing more to say, he simply said, "That is all," and dismounted the crate. He grabbed hold of Gizmo's collar and walked through the crowd, which parted around them.

"See, Gizmo," he said, "Now, whoever wants Cat will come to me."

He reached into his pocket and looked at his crystal. Sensing his disappointment at seeing the crystal still flush white without a hint of green, Gizmo stood on his hind legs and put his paws on Jasper's chest to draw his attention away from the crystal and toward a very pleasant smell in the distance.

Not far from shore, a small group of people gathered around a fire pit, roasting fish on skewers. From a distance, Jasper noticed the skewers seemed free for the taking - anyone who needed a fish could come take one. He led Gizmo to the pit, took two skewers, and slid the fish off its long, wooden stick. He easily tore a bite-sized chunk of fish meat and, after savoring the smell, nearly swallowed it whole. When Gizmo put a paw on Jasper's knee, he tore off another piece and fed it to his companion.

"Don't worry, one of these is for you," he reassured Gizmo. "We'll take turns."

Mid-bite, Gizmo regretted becoming distracted by the aroma of freshly cooked fish. A small crowd of seven men, all dressed as festive as Hassan, and strong enough-looking to make anyone second-guess fighting with them, covered Jasper and Gizmo in their shadow.

"Adekunle would like to see you," one man said in such a way as to convey that seeing this Adekunle was not a choice.

"Can he wait until we're done eating?" Jasper asked.

That was stupid, Gizmo thought.

But they didn't have enough time to reply before another group of men, also seven strong, joined from the opposite direction.

"Oladipo would like to hear about this woman of science," their leader announced..

Taking another bite of fish, Jasper talked with his mouth partly full. "You'll have to wait. Sounds like Adekunle wants me first."

Jasper may as well have insulted their grandmothers, for before he knew it, all fourteen men engaged themselves in a fierce fistfight, tumbling and throwing each other around, as Jasper and Gizmo ate their fish and watched.

So engaged in watching the fight, they were, they didn't notice the two men sneak up from behind them, grab Jasper under the shoulders, and drag him away. Had Gizmo reacted a half second earlier, he may have been able to bite their ankles, but a third man in their group picked him up and carried him - which is impressive given Gizmo's size and strength. But the man was stronger.

Their captors carried them, and their attempts to fight back seemed to them like nothing more than the playful flailing of an infant. Nothing stopped their ascent up the hills, away from the port, and into a tiny village hidden among the trees. Without a pause nor even a hint of struggle from their captors, not from the hills, nor the brush, nor the distance slowed them.

Plopped down under the thatched straw roof of an open-walled hut, Gizmo sat down beside Jasper, on guard. Though he was powerless to stop the kidnappers, he still bared his teeth any time someone dared come near Jasper, including to the two who held spear tips to the back of their heads.

The captors stood guard around the outside of the hut, and slowly, a crowd of men, women, and children, gathered around. In front of them, the crowd parted.

An older man, bald, with a shirt and skirt of bright beads, carrying a tall staff, walked through with ease and sat down in front of Jasper and Gizmo. Jasper heard "*Adekunle*" whispered among those gathered.

"You will bring this woman to us when she arrives," he instructed, with a soft voice that seemed to calm one's nerves despite his obvious threat.

Jasper quickly thought through possible responses. Learning from this interaction was more important than escaping.

"Why?" he asked. "What do you need from her?"

"You say she is a woman of science?" asked Adekunle.

"Yes."

"We will tell her when she gets here. When does she arrive?"

Jasper kept thinking. *He needs more information, but he lacks power or influence.*

"I know what she's capable of! So, if you tell me what you want her to do, I can make sure you have everything she'll need when she arrives!"

Adekunle nodded. "Does she know anything about wells?"

"For water?" Jasper asked.

Adekunle grunted as he stood and used his staff to point to a hill in the distance. "Beyond that hill is a well used by the clan of Oladipo. An underground river feeds it. I want the water from that river redirected here."

"But then how will *they* get water?" Jasper wondered aloud, though Adekunle took it as a threat.

"That is for them to figure out," he explained. Jasper looked around as Adekunle studied the people gathered around the hut. They all seemed... *tired... thirsty.* "For me, I need to bring water to my people. For that, you will bring me your woman of science."

As Adekunle stood and walked away, Jasper stood up. "Cat!" he shouted.

Adekunle stopped and turned back around to face Jasper.

Feeling the spear pressed into the back of his neck, Jasper grimaced, but stood tall. "Her name is Cat." He took another breath for courage. "I'm Jasper, and this is Gizmo. Call us by our names."

The pause may well have been hours as the clan leader stared back at Jasper. "I'm Adekunle. Call me by mine." Then, he pointed out toward the crowd. "Tell them what Cat needs. They'll have it ready when she arrives."

With that, Adekunle retreated to his hut. With a deep breath, Jasper snuck a peek at the crystal still in his pocket.

Still white.

Chapter 24

Newhaven Bay

Fletcher about had enough. The Fisherman's Supply Store was, in fact, a store, not the city council chambers nor a public meeting space. But, with a crowd of 50 or so all with the energy of having double dosed their morning coffee but with the anger of having skipped it, Fletcher just sat behind the register on his stool and let events play out.

For his trouble, he hoped people would buy a few lures on their way out. But for now, Fletcher's status as a town leader was considerably more valuable than anything for sale in his store.

The discussion went on, led by Henry Hoffner, a dashing black-haired, square-jawed, chiseled man of 30. He lost his election to the city council last year and still hadn't come to grips with how anyone could possibly have *not* voted for someone whose first words as a baby were, "I approved this message." He emerged as the leader, playing the crowd as a conductor commands an orchestra. The crowd's eyes latched onto the movement of his arms, and their mood flowed with the tone of his voice. Henry's very presence was entrancing, mesmerizing even.

Fletcher couldn't help but wonder: did Henry Hoffner actually believe this message? Or was he an opportunistic leader who stepped in front of a group of followers that seemed free for the taking?

"The outside world *hates* Newhaven Bay," Hoffner shouted to the crowd, his arms gesturing like a Broadway villain. "They hate your slow, unhurried pace; they hate that you wave at cars even when you don't know who's inside; they hate your quaint traditions..."

"Booooo!" a voice from the back of the crowd shouted.

Hoffner continued. "Your love of maple syrup, the annual Squirrel Days carnival," and then he turned behind him and gestured to Fletcher, "They hate this store, that Fletcher can sell whatever he wishes!"

The crowd cheered along with their new leader, and Fletcher gave a good fake half-smile to show that he appreciated the mention. Yet, try as he might, he failed to recall a single person on his many out-of-town business trips who was as bitterly infatuated with Newhaven Bay as Hoffner claimed the entire outside world seemed to be. Furthermore, Fletcher couldn't just sell *anything in his* store - he was beholden to what his customers would want to buy; he couldn't sell raisins, for instance, because no one in Newhaven Bay liked those.

(Legend has it that, during a fishing competition, a kindly old woman made a batch of oatmeal raisin cookies for the competitors. Those men, unfortunately, mistook them for chocolate chip, and were bitterly disappointed. When one was asked how he liked the cookie, he said, "You don't mind getting the silver medal, but it's never what you actually want." Since then, raisins rarely appeared in Newhaven Bay.)

Because, in a town meeting like this, anyone could speak at any time, a woman from the middle of the crowd shouted back, "You ever heard of Pandora's Box?"

The crowd nodded and murmured a few "mmm-hmms" and "yeps," as if that's what they were *all* thinking before someone was brave enough to say it.

"We have a literal Pandora's Box sitting in the park and *they* want us to *open* it?" She emphasized the *they* as though Newhaven Bay were being occupied by a band of unruly Vikings. *They* were, in fact, the friends and neighbors to everyone in the room.

"Exactly," Hoffner latched onto the commend and expanded on it. "And who knows what's inside that it could unleash. The box could be a gateway to a parallel universe, a transmitter for aliens, or worse: a swarm of hyper-intelligent bees bred to swarm all your doorknobs and lock you out of our houses."

The rest of the meeting flew by to Fletcher, who put a pleasant smile on his face once his brain became unable to absorb any more of Hoffner's insanity. He sat in the back, wondering what kind of nonsense Ertha might be dealing with on her end. He also wondered if he and Ertha may be stoned to death if seen together again in public after their respective meetings.

Hoffner used his newfound power to deputize "agents" from the crowd to stand guard over the box and ensure it wasn't opened by the evildoers on the other side, some of whom had served them breakfast not twenty-four hours earlier. Then, they made plans to meet again tomorrow evening, and dispersed from the store.

Nobody bought anything.

With a sigh, Fletcher locked the front door. The sun outside lowered toward the horizon, and there wasn't much business left to do, anyway. From behind the counter, he grabbed his broom, and began sweeping in sweet, sweet silence.

Only to be startled and interrupted by Gus and Lilly, his two deviant juveniles he thought had gone home for the evening.

"Sorry, Mr. Fletcher," sweet Lilly said, her haphazard blonde pigtails flopping. She had obviously tried to do them herself. "We should be doing that."

"Don't hurt her!" Gus popped out from behind a clothes rack and jumped in front of his friend.

Fletcher sighed, calmly. "Gus, when have I ever seemed to be even the slightest bit upset with her... or you?"

Gus dropped his freckled face toward the ground, and his red hair blended in with his flannel shirt. "Sorry," he said, "I guess I'm on edge from that meeting."

"Me too," said Fletcher, placing the broom back behind the counter.

"That stuff the guy said about the box," Lilly asked, "Is it true?"

Fletcher shook his head. "No."

"But everyone believed him!"

Street kids, Fletcher thought. Their instincts knew danger. Their instincts knew when someone was leading them toward trouble. Fletcher thought it his job to protect them, to guide them. And he wondered if he was up to the task. He sat back down on his stool and looked them in the eye.

"Something doesn't need to be true for a leader with bad intentions to say it and have people believe it."

"But why?" asked Gus, after thinking for a moment. "What's the point?"

Fletcher sighed and answered truthfully. "I don't know."

Chapter 25

Eko, 1750

This was all too much work, and too much waiting, for Jasper's crystal to still be bleach white.

Waiting was never Jasper's strong suit, and having his crystal made it even worse. For nine days, he waited for the *Rogue Wave* to arrive in Eko. Had his crystal been working, he would have just jumped forward nine days. Actually, he'd probably just jump home...

A sudden thought caught him off-guard. *Home.* When he thought of "home," he pictured Newhaven Bay.

For nine days, he stalled. He wouldn't know what Cat needed to help Adekunle's clan redirect their underground river, nor did he care that much. His plan was to wait for Cat and the *Rogue Wave* to arrive - which should be any day now - and then escape.

Except his crystal was still white. But rescuing Cat would rejuvenate his crystal. He was sure of it!

"Listen to your crystal," Hassan told him, what seemed like forever ago. He was trying, for sure, but it hadn't told him anything yet! What did it sound like? What was he listening for? Was Hassan crazy?

Like every day for the past nine days, he sat on a rocky cliff overlooking Eko's port. Gizmo laid next to him, clearly bored but not wanting to make a fuss. Besides, with the way the heat from the sun balanced the cool breeze from the ocean, their predicament could have been worse.

Adekunle's clan offered Jasper clothes that helped him fit in better with the rest of the tribe, and the wind now tussled the beads woven into the silky blue fabric of his tunic. So helpful these people were that they even gave him a small leather sack to wear as a necklace, a place of safekeeping for his crystal.

Like every day for the past nine days, three guards from Adekunle waited behind Jasper and Gizmo. Adekunle afforded Jasper the freedom to do just about anything he wanted - anything, that is, except run away. At the end of the day, they reported back to Adekunle Jasper and Gizmo's every movement.

Back at the camp, the rest of the clan were engaged in brickmaking, at Jasper's direction. He once read in a book how the ancient Egyptians made bricks of mud and straw, baked in clay forms. He couldn't tell if he was teaching them something new, or if they politely listened while secretly annoyed that Jasper didn't think they knew how to make something as simple as a brick. Nonetheless, they seemed to trust Jasper that his friend the scientist would need bricks, so they made as many as they could.

Pulling his knees to his chest as he watched out at the ocean's horizon, he held his white crystal close to his mouth.

"What should I do?" he whispered.

He heard nothing. He saw no soft green glow grow in the crystal's center. He felt no warmth, no connection.

Could a time crystal die? Could his be the first? Could he be the first time traveler to have killed his crystal?

"What am I looking for, Gizmo?" he asked the dog out of frustration. "What am I doing wrong?"

Gizmo just raised his head and looked at him, his tongue hanging out of the side of his mouth.

"You need water, don't you?" Jasper looked at the poor dog's panting. Tied to his waist, Jasper carried a small canteen given to him by Adekunle. In a village short of water, giving a canteen to a stranger was a sign of their trust in him.

He found a low point in the rock, a small dip that served as a useful bowl. After blowing out a small cloud of dust, he rubbed it clean, and then poured a few sips of water for his friend.

Watching Gizmo slurp, Jasper wondered aloud, "We have to come through for them. When Cat gets here... we have to come through." Never before had actual lives depended on Jasper's actions.

The sun shone directly overhead, but the ocean's breeze kept the heat away. He dropped his crystal into his other hand in order to pet Gizmo's fuzzy brown head as he drank. The crystal barely crossed his vision, but it did so just enough in that one moment that Jasper saw something different.

Quickly, he snatched it back up and held it up to the sun. What did he see but... a tiny hint of green!

Green!

It's alive! Or something. It wasn't the deep, pure, emerald green that glistened in his hand at first. This green was faint, as if it were a clear diamond discarded for a slight impurity.

For the first time in nine days, he had hope.

Gizmo nuzzled back up to him, noticing that Jasper was shaking before Jasper even did.

And, just beyond his gaze, at the ocean's horizon, a set of tall masts rose into view. The *Rogue Wave* and her crew were making toward Eko.

Jasper smiled that things finally seemed to go his way.

"Hey!" he stood and shouted to the guards, pointing toward the ship in the distance. "There it is."

The guards approached the edge of the rock. These were the same men that kidnapped him from the beach earlier. Part of him wanted to push them off the cliff, but their imposing height and strength made Jasper reconsider due to the fact that they could probably just bounce off the land below unharmed, and then jump the thirty feet back up to impale him with their spears before he and Gizmo had a chance to run away.

Or, Jasper himself would just bounce off of them backward on the ground at the mere attempt at securing his freedom. Killing was just not in the cards today.

"You're sure that's your ship?" the lead guard asked, studying the sails on the horizon.

"It could be any ship," another said.

"This ship has haunted my dreams for years," replied Jasper, which was true. "And I've been aboard before."

The third guard stood behind them. "If we leave now, we'll be at the harbor well before they arrive."

With no need for prompting, Gizmo stood up and looked back to Jasper, waiting for him to start their journey toward Eko harbor. Jasper pocketed his slightly greened crystal. *Tell me if you have any ideas*, he thought, as he pulled the satchel shut.

Jasper was so sure of what awaited him at the port, so sure his plan would work, so sure he had thought through every detail, that he failed to imagine any scenario in which he could possibly be wrong.

Hassan, too, had blessed his plan - even gave him the idea! But Hassan, like anyone and especially like Jasper, could be wrong.

And they were. They had both overlooked one key detail. Once Jasper met the *Rogue Wave* in Eko Harbor, no element of his plan could be saved.

Chapter 26

Newhaven Bay

When Officer Pierce called Fletcher at the store to tell him Gus and Lilly had broken into the Carp Cafe, he wasn't sure how to react.

"Tell me they're in jail," Fletcher implored, his frustrated first thought, followed by a long, awkward pause on the phone. "Pierce?" Fletcher asked.

"Well, um… okay, well, they're in jail," Pierce stumbled over his words.

Fletcher sighed. "They're not actually in jail, are they?"

"Just sayin' what you wanted me to say, Fletch."

Fletcher shook his head as if Pierce could see him. "Where are they?"

"They're outside, in my car."

"Why aren't they in jail?"

In Pierce's voice, Fletcher heard signs of weariness. "Jail's full, Fletcher. There've been fights down at the park all week long."

"And their social worker?" Fletcher asked.

This time, Fletcher could almost see Pierce shaking his head through the phone. "She won't come into town. Says it's too dangerous."

Fletcher lived in Newhaven Bay all his life. He always loved the people here. But now, he couldn't help but wonder if it were better to just let this town extinguish itself and start over. What kind of mad corruption had infected them? Was there a small-town equivalent of mad cow disease?

"I think you should just throw them in a jail cell with the baddest thug down there," Fletcher said, "See if they want to commit petty theft after a few days of that."

"I dunno, Fletch," Pierce replied, "Looking at our crowd, Gus may be the baddest thug down here. I'll bring 'em by." He hung up without giving Fletcher a chance to reply.

A week had passed since he and Ertha's public fight. Their fight was supposed to be an intelligence-gathering mission. He was supposed to see Ertha more, and learn what she knew. If they were conspiring together, why hadn't he seen her in a week? Instead of seeing Ertha, Fletcher found himself immersed in a garden of exotic plants that smelled revolting and looked like his neighbors.

Cat was still missing. Ertha wasn't talking to him. Gus and Lilly were turning back into hardened criminals. Jasper was in the 1750s. Newhaven Bay's residents were practically building battle trenches down Main Street. Fletcher's new life hit him with all the pleasantness of diarrhea.

The phone rang.

"Fisherman's Supply, Fletcher here," he answered.

"Fletcher…" It was Ertha. But something was off. She whispered. Ertha wasn't the whispering type. She was born projecting her voice to the back of an auditorium.

"Ertha!"

"Shhhh!" She interrupted. "I'm going to rob you in ten minutes. Don't be alarmed. Call the cops and make sure they show up in exactly eleven minutes."

The line went dead. *Eleven minutes?* If he wanted the cops to show up in eleven minutes, he should have called them thirty minutes ago. He checked his watch.

10:17.

An engine shuddered to a stop outside his storefront window. Officer Pierce stepped out of the driver's seat, walked around to the back, and opened the door for Gus and Lilly. Their eyes sunk, and they avoided looking at Fletcher through the window as Pierce led them into the store.

Stepping in front of Fletcher's counter, they said nothing.

"I'll take them from here," Fletcher said. "Hey, what time do you have?"

Pierce checked his watch. "Ten eighteen."

"Can you be back here at exactly ten twenty-eight?"

"Why?"

"Ertha called..."

"Oh, good! You finally heard from her?"

"...She's going to rob me."

Pierce's face twisted as if it was necessary in order to think through the confusion that swirled within his head. "And you want me to... stop it... presumably?"

Fletcher shrugged. "Between ramming your squad car through the front window and coming in guns-a-blazin', and making waffles on the sidewalk, you're free to do whatever you want. Just show up."

Pierce rubbed his stomach. "Now, a waffle I could get behind."

"As long as you're back at ten twenty-eight, I'll buy you the waffle myself."

Pierce nodded, replied with a smile, "Ten twenty-eight," and then walked out and drove off. Fletcher turned his attention to the two miscreants standing before him. Lilly, her blonde pigtails slightly ruffled, and Gus' black hair damp and matted, they looked like they hadn't slept well in several days.

Fletcher folded his arms judgementally. "Well? Care to explain yourselves?"

"No," Gus replied tersely. Lilly smacked him.

"Mrs. Carp usually lets us have breakfast there in exchange for cleaning the kitchens after the morning rush," she explained, "but she's been closed for a few days on account of Mrs. Carp scheming to open the box at the park."

"And everyone else being too angry to eat, which is weird," Gus added. "I've never been too *anything* to eat."

Fletcher inhaled patiently. "Why didn't you talk to me? You think I wouldn't feed you if you said you had nothing to eat?"

Lilly continued, "Oh, you were so busy with the whole Ertha thing, we wanted to figure this one out on our own."

Ah, yes, the we - didn't - want - to - bother - you - so - we - committed - larceny defense.

He gestured for the two delinquents to join him behind the counter so he could put one of his giant hands on each of their shoulders. "Gus and Lilly, you could never bother me," he told them, his bushy mustache covering his smile. "You've had a lot happen to you, and none of it your fault. I'm able to help, and it brings me great joy to help you out and see you grow up into good people who don't rob family diners. Understood?"

Looking beyond the two faces nodding and struggling to hold back tears, through the window, Fletcher saw Ertha and a gang of four marching down the street, each clutching baseball bats.

"Speaking of robbing things..." Fletcher said. Gus and Lilly turned around and saw the mob coming.

"What's she doing?" Lilly asked.

"I dunno," Fletcher replied, "but at least she warned me."

"What do you want us to do?" asked Gus.

"I dunno either, but judging by the looks of those bats, I'd say don't get in the way."

Ertha threw open the door and the gang burst in. Fletcher quickly stood up, threw his hands in the air, and shouted, "Oh, no, is this a robbery?" with all the acting skill of a mousy accountant. Even Ertha struggled to hide the, *"What are you doing?"* look from her face in front of the impatient flannel-clad gang that couldn't wait to try ransacking a store for the first time.

Fletcher recognized two of Ertha's tough-as-tissue-paper gang and was more scared *for* them than scared *of* them. Mr. Blake Moaire is an accountant at the boat factory; and Mr. Dawson Crum was a part-time novelist, and a substitute teacher when his books weren't selling (which made him, in effect, a full-time substitute teacher). The only bruising about to take place, Fletcher suspected, was likely to be them hitting themselves in the back while winding up to take a swing.

"This sure is a robbery!" Blake announced, gripping his bat, as if unsure if he were doing it right.

"We're gonna mess you up!" Crum added on, doing his best to hide that he learned how to sound like a tough guy from watching low-budget Westerns.

"Stop!" Ertha commanded. "I get the first swing."

While holding his hands in the air, Fletcher checked his watch. *10:27.* "Can you wait a minute?" he asked, raising an eyebrow.

Crum stepped forward, bat held at the ready. "Unless you want to help us open that box, Fletcher, this store's gonna have to close!"

Ertha extended a hand to stop him. "Or..." she said, calmingly, "He can cave to our demands, right?"

The two bubbly bruisers looked disappointed, and simply nodded. Ertha stepped toward the counter with an envelope. In Ertha's own, unique, stylish cursive, the envelope simply said *Demands.* She placed it on the counter, looking Fletcher in the eye. One could forgive Crum and Blake for missing the subtle nod Ertha gave Fletcher, but Fletcher sure didn't. Nor did Gus and Lilly.

And, at that precise moment, Officer Pierce parked his squad car - no lights on - outside the store. "We should go," Ertha instructed, and then pointed with her bat, "Out the back."

Disappointed, the other two failed to even give Fletcher a menacing look as they followed Ertha out the back door. Pierce, meanwhile, popped his head in the front.

"Everything okay here?" he asked.

Fletcher nodded. "Think so. Just hang around outside for a few, will you?"

With a head tilt of acceptance, and relief that he wasn't stepping into a physical altercation, Pierce went back to the solitude of his car. Fletcher opened Ertha's envelope, to find only a note.

Shipley's Restaurant, back room, 9pm tonight. Someone knows what's in the box.

His brow furrowed together in thought as he closed the envelope. Lilly's sweet, innocent voice interrupted his thoughts over what to do next.

"What's happening, Fletcher?"

"Yeah," Gus added. "Open the box, don't open the box, who's right?"

Fletcher sighed. "It's not about the box, guys. It's about control. The fight over the box is just a way to get it."

"Yeah," Gus pressed on, "But, who's right?"

"The ones fighting hardest?" Lilly asked.

"Or with the most to lose?" Gus added.

Fletcher took a breath. This moment, right here, he knew, somehow, was going to shape the rest of their lives. He didn't know why he knew this. It was as if all the atoms in his body aligned to make sure he *knew* he had to say the right thing to these two children in this moment.

But what?

Once more, he gripped them by the shoulders. "Gus, Lilly..." He still didn't know what to say. Instead, he just...

stopped trying, and in that moment, some sort of deep, inner truth took over.

"Gus, Lilly... a bully is never right. If you have to fight for your cause through evil, that cause is never right. For thousands of years, people have fought and died for evils they thought were right.

"Look at the little guy. Find the weak and powerless. Look out for *their* best interest. *That's* what's right. *Really* listen to everyone. Listen to who truly wants to help everyone, and separate them from those who only *sound* like they want to help everyone but only want to help themselves."

But, instead of looking inspired, Gus and Lilly just looked confused. With eyes squinting and his concentration scrunching his face, Gus asked, "But what does this have to do with the box?"

Fletcher shrugged. "I dunno. But it does. That's what this fight is about." He felt the envelope again in his hand. *Shipley's Restaurant, back room, 9pm tonight. Someone knows what's in the box.*

Though it was not quite eleven, Fletcher stood up and flipped the sign on the door over to "Closed." No one was shopping today, anyway. He'd take Gus and Lilly back to his house and pack some meals. Then, it was off to figure out his next steps: Work with Ertha, rescue Cat, wait for Jasper.

Somehow, this would all come together.

***

From the hills overlooking Newhaven Bay, Hayalet looked with muted glee through his spyglass at the chaos erupting on the streets. Cat lay on the floor of the cave behind him, asleep. After tonight's meeting at Shipley's Restaurant, he could safely allow her to be rescued. It would give his adversaries a false sense of accomplishment and progress, and it would not disrupt his plan in the least.

Chapter 27

Eko, 1750

Seagulls swarmed Eko harbor with their ever-present squawking. They circled the sky, eyes trained on the ground looking for single bites of their next meal. Jasper, Gizmo, and his guards ran down the docks, ignoring the seagulls with the same ignorance as they ignored the air they breathed.

From the moment they left the hill, Jasper's eyes never left the tall masts of the *Rogue Wave*. Captain Moxie was sure to be surprised to see him again, although Jasper knew he could use this surprise to show his guards he was telling the truth. The *Rogue Wave* had sailed into Eko harbor carrying Catalina Sanchez, his woman of science.

He had his plan. Get Cat, help Adekunle redirect his river, get out. That is, if his crystal would recover by then. But, he was sure it would! *What replenishes him replenishes his crystal*, or something like that, is what Hassan told him. Accomplish this mission, go home. That's the plan.

Like busy bugs working their hive, the vessel's crew worked in perfect union to pull in her sails. Jasper and Gizmo watched from the end of the docks, and with a keen eye, they could make out the figure of Captain Moxie at the helm, looking for an open berth where he could slip in his ship. Finally, sailing slowly by a pier, the crew tossed off ropes to catch the bollards on the dock.

The *Rogue Wave* has arrived.

With their guards behind them, standing silent, but strong and domineering, Jasper and Gizmo approached the ship. On the top deck, Captain Moxie stood watch, monitoring how his crew laid out the gangplanks, took in all the sails, and prepared barrels of cargo for unloading.

"Captain Moxie!" Jasper called from the dock below, and the surprised captain turned to find the source of his voice. His eyes widened when he looked over his railing. Jasper couldn't help but wonder if they would invite him aboard the ship, whether he would immediately sail the ship away, or whether he would load his pistol with silver bullets and shoot Jasper as if he were a vampire.

"Hello! Captain Moxie!" Jasper waved politely and excitedly, while the captain still stood, stunned. He turned around to the guards. "See," he smiled, "he recognizes me. We're friends!"

"Moxie, old friend, care to invite me aboard?" Jasper sounded as if he and Moxie enjoyed regular tea parties.

"Not really!" Moxie called back out over the railing.

"Set your gangway and invite me up, or I'll have my men here throw me over your railing," he shouted, motioning to the guards, who were surely pleased to hear themselves called *his* men.

"Must we?" Moxie shouted. "Can't you see we're unloading cargo?"

"It looks like your crew is unloading cargo while you're just watching. Surely you can talk and watch at the same time!" Jasper couldn't help but notice a few crewmen nod with begrudging agreement.

Moxie reluctantly waved him on. "Come aboard."

Jasper liked the extra threat the three guards provided, so he motioned for them to follow along, and headed to the walkway from the dock to the ship. Gizmo dutifully led the way up, as if he were somehow an old hand at boarding ships. The crew didn't stop their labor, and worked around Jasper as they walked across the deck to meet the captain.

Captain Moxie stood at the helm, as if he were using the giant wheel as an extra layer of protection between him and Jasper. Jasper studied Moxie's face, and became slightly unnerved by how he seemed, somehow, to recognize Gizmo. How could that have been possible? Gizmo, too, seemed to recognize the captain. He didn't try to sniff him out at first sight, which was odd for a dog. Instead, Gizmo sat dutifully at Jasper's feet, eyes locked on Moxie.

Finally, Moxie spoke first. "I thought we were through with each other. I expected to see Hayalet here, not you." Gizmo's ears perked at hearing "Hayalet."

What Moxie said next crushed Jasper. He felt the weight of the sky collapse on him, and the seagulls became deafening for the first time in days.

"Hayalet told me to continue on to Eko after you took the prisoner."

What? Did he hear him right? Jasper's face blanked, and he stood for what must have been ages, before one guard pressed on his shoulder.

"What is he talking about?" the guard asked. "You already took the prisoner?"

"Huh?" Jasper's voice said, with no command from his brain. And then, without thinking, Jasper bolted. He dashed to the mid-deck, threw the woven cover off the hatch to the cargo hold, and sailed down the ladder, barely touching any rungs. His guards followed, and the ship rocked back and forth with their weight. After Moxie climbed down the ladder, Gizmo stood on the top deck, looking down and whining, unable to follow.

Down another deck, Jasper ran while the others chased behind. Gizmo paced back and forth around the hatch on the top deck. Jasper ran down the length of the ship, toward the rear, and threw open the door to the locked cargo hold. He didn't even notice the broken lock, where Hayalet previously burst through the door in pursuit of him.

Only a few wooden barrels dotted the empty cargo hold, and an empty pair of shackles swinging from the wall.

"Where's Cat?" Jasper exclaimed, breathlessly.

"You're looking for a cat?" the guard asked before bouncing his head off a ceiling rafter.

Moxie stomped into the room behind them. "You mean you don't remember?" he said.

Of course Jasper remembered. He just didn't believe he could be so stupid.

"Off the coast of Maine," Moxie explained, "You boarded, found the girl, and used your green flash to disappear with her. I thought Hayalet was going to have me executed. Instead, he just told me to continue on to Eko. I was supposed to be selling her here... so, I'm not even really sure why we're here now."

The sound of the seagulls outside grew to a deafening roar in Jasper's ears.

"You mean to say there is no woman of science aboard this ship?" a guard asked, angrily.

Moxie answered, "Were you the ones who were intending to buy her?"

How could Jasper have been so stupid? *Of course* Cat was gone! He himself had taken her! *Of course* the *Rogue Wave* was going to arrive without her!

The guards started closing in as Moxie interrupted his panic. "Are you not in league with Hayalet?" he asked, tilting his head to the side, trying to understand the situation.

Without saying a word, Jasper simply stared at the pair of empty shackles, and shook his head. He couldn't comprehend his next moments, and they passed by as nothing more than wet paint dripping down a canvas. The guards whisked him out of the ship, and Gizmo chased them all the way back, out of Eko harbor, through the forest, and back to Adekunle's settlement.

The only thing that stuck in Jasper's stunned brain were Captain Moxie's final words of warning:

"Your fight is feeble. Hayalet always wins."

Chapter 28

Newhaven Bay

Shipley's Restaurant is a relic of Newhaven Bay's happier times of ten days ago. Like most everyone in Newhaven Bay, the "Shipleys" had few options at which to purchase interior decorations than the various nautical supply stores. So, by default, and in no way connected to their name, Shipley's Restaurant's oak-paneled interior was draped in fish netting, adorned with weathered life buoys, festooned with antique ship wheels, and the servers used sextants to navigate guests to their tables (although a true sailor would know they're acting, one can't use a sextant for navigating without a clear view of the horizon, and either the sun or the North Star).

The back room, the "Captain's Quarters," as they called it, was entirely too large for the tall-masted sailing ships it attempted to emulate. It was more like a fourth-in-line prince who liked ships was given a large budget to keep him happy. The Shipleys built the biggest room possible, lit it with skylights, built railings where no one risked falling overboard, and hung life rings in case they did.

No light shone through the skylights as a group of a dozen sat at two separate tables in the center of the Captain's Quarters. On one side, a small group gathered around Henry Hoffner as the self-appointed duly elected representative for the "Don't open the box" side. Mayor

Nygaard made her grand entrance into the room, a silk bonnet covering her wispy red hair as she gracefully made her way to an opposing table. Hereto, it seemed nobody even knew what side the mayor was on, but if Henry Hoffner was on the "Don't open the box" side, the mayor took the lead on the opposite.

And then, not at the tables, but hidden in the bushes outside peering in through a window, Ertha crouched next to Fletcher.

"Can you hear inside?" Fletcher asked.

"If you don't stop jabbering," Ertha quipped back, pointing at the cracked-open window, "they can hear you!"

And so they waited, in awkward silence, until it happened. Ertha gasped.

Hayalet himself burst forward, through the swinging doors, into the Captain's Quarters. Ertha knew Hayalet was behind the chaos in Newhaven Bay, but she didn't expect it was him, personally, overseeing the operation. Fletcher, alarmed at Ertha's covered panic, conveyed worry with his eyes.

Ertha simply mouthed, "Hayalet," and pointed through the window. Fletcher observed.

He tamed his appearance, so as not to startle people. He simply wore a smart blue business suit, and a velvet fedora with a feather covered the scars on his bald head. Tonight, he didn't need the scars; his impressive height and strength were all he needed to command his audience's attention. Plus, like a magician saving his best trick for last, he planned an impressive exit that would silence any doubters of the outlandish story he was about to tell.

"Who are you?" Henry Hoffner asked, trying to be the first to show strength against this mysterious stranger.

"Mister Hoffner," Hayalet replied, stride unbroken, hands clasped behind his back, and not looking at Henry, "I have a few important details to share that are worth concerning yourself with; my name is not one of them."

Taking center stage in the room, in his low monotone, Hayalet continued, "And besides, Mister Hoffner, you're far too concerned with raising your stature above Mayor Nygaard. I wouldn't want to add any more worries than needed."

Mayor Nygaard held back a snicker, pleased at this mysterious stranger's snide takedown of her new nemesis. But Hayalet, not content to let her sit with that, turned toward her.

"What I offer today is not a task well-suited to those who lead for their own vanity." At his pointed insult, the mayor resisted shrinking into her own chair, though her soul certainly shrunk a tiny bit.

Hayalet owned this room. Any room shared by those used to owning a room is bound to be engulfed in conflict. But conflict only exists where Hayalet wants it to exist, and in this room, Hayalet is in charge.

So this is the mysterious Hayalet, Fletcher thought, looking through the window. "If we follow him back, we might find Cat," he whispered to Ertha.

Ertha said nothing, just continued observing through the window. Hayalet subdued his audience, and his commanding voice held their attention, briefly dimming the conflict between the two sides.

"I know who brought the box in the square, and I know what's in it."

This statement should have been a welcome relief to everyone in town, and it certainly was to those in the room; but it was also a lie. So convincing and practiced a liar is Hayalet, no one had the slightest inclination. From the looks in their faces, Hayalet knew he had the room's attention, and so he continued.

"Who is worthy of leading Newhaven Bay?" he asked. He gave them a few moments to think, as he saw their faces contorting into a number of positions, as they thought through the various ways they could say, "being me" without using those exact words. Before they had a chance to reason why only *they* should be the town's leaders, he continued, "Who in this town is most capable of seeing the most lowly, least powerful citizen, and acting in *their* best interest?"

Ertha's eyes widened. Not because she didn't expect to hear those words out of someone as evil and power-hungry as Hayalet, but because she had heard those words before...

...from the person crouching next to her. That was Fletcher's philosophy, a way of thinking he constantly imbued into her. A way of thinking she heard from few others who rose into leadership, certainly not as naturally as Fletcher seemed to.

And now, the evil, monstrous Hayalet stood feet away, preaching Fletcher's own prayer. Somehow, her gaze turned to Fletcher, who didn't notice. He simply continued listening.

"Are you familiar with the story of King Arthur's sword?" Hayalet asked the room.

Everyone in the room nodded. Mayor Nygaard, eager to show both her interest and her perceived intelligence, filled everyone in with one raised finger. "A magic sword was embedded in a stone, and only a worthy knight could remove the sword and become king. Though many tried, only Arthur was able, and he became King of the Britons."

"Yes," Hayalet replied, not acknowledging the mayor's contribution. "This box is your own stone, and within it, your own sword."

"And who are you then, Merlin?" asked a skeptical Henry Hoffner. Hayalet ignored him and continued undisturbed.

"And in this town, only one person is capable of opening the box. Only one person is worthy. And that person is due to be the leader of this town..." With a small twist of his head and the tiniest raising of an eyebrow, he leaned in and added, "...and more."

"How do we know you're telling the truth?" Mayor Nygaard asked, desperately hoping to find some way to dispel the notion that *someone else* may be destined to rule Newhaven Bay *and more.*

Through the window, Ertha saw a small grin come across Hayalet's face. She clutched Fletcher's arm. "Watch this," she whispered.

"Because," Hayalet explained, reaching into his breast pocket, "some truths are so self-evident that they reveal themselves to be true without relying on the identity of the prophet."

And then, he removed from his pocket a sparkling green crystal, and instantly vaporized into a cloud of green sparks.

Both the invitees in the room and the onlookers through the window sat, stunned. Yet, they wasted no time. It was Henry Hoffner who made the first move.

"I'm gonna go open that box!" he announced, springing from his chair, unable to comprehend that anyone but him may be worthy of leading Newhaven Bay. His crowd jumped up and followed his sprint from the restaurant, and the mayor's crowd quickly joined, hoping they could outrun their opponents (although no one realized that, if only the worthy one could open the box, the speed with which they reached the box wouldn't matter).

"So, that's Hayalet?" Fletcher asked, retreating from the window and leaning against the brick wall.

"Fletcher," Ertha asked, "why would Hayalet say the same thing you always tell me?"

Fletcher brushed his mustache. "Come to think about it, that did seem pretty similar, didn't it?"

"Similar! It was like he was quoting scripture! The *Book of Fletcher!*"

"It wouldn't be that hard to quote a book as short as the *Book of Fletcher*," Fletcher chuckled.

Ertha wasn't amused. "Are you working with him?" she accused, arms crossed.

"Hey now..."

"I've never heard anybody say that but you."

"Ertha, I've never seen that man before in my life!"

But Ertha took a step back. "He has an entire network..."

"Aren't you a part of it?"

For moments, an eternity, they said nothing. Ertha contemplated her next move. Jasper's mission notwithstanding, she was estranged from Fletcher for a reason. This may have added to it.

But their consternation between each other was interrupted. In the distance, up the hills on the outskirts of town, a small but brilliant green flash of light interrupted the darkness.

Even though she now realized Newhaven Bay's purpose for Hayalet, she had to put that aside, for now. Ertha also had to leave behind her new suspicions on Fletcher. Now, it was most important that she had an idea on where to find Cat.

Chapter 29

Eko, 1750

The guards plopped Jasper down on a stool, under the thatched roof of the open-walled hut in Adekunle's village. Gizmo, dutifully, stayed by his side, peacefully not attacking the guards so as to not endanger his own life. They stood around him in formation as Adekunle, slowly with age, but purposefully made his way over. As he approached, he heard Adekunle address his guards in a language he did not recognize. Studying their faces, he saw the guards' expressions change from anger and frustration to worry and subdued panic. He pointed, and the guards ran off.

Now, his full attention turned to Jasper, he sat down on a stool across from him, the beads of his tunic rubbing against each other as they swished with their own weight. He rubbed sweat off his bald head.

"While you were gone, someone came here looking for you," Adekunle revealed.

Jasper squinted, confused. "Looking for me?"

Adekunle nodded.

"Looking for me like they wanted to help me, or for something worse?"

Adekunle shrugged. "He promised he would be back, and if you were here, he would help us with our water problem."

"Was he tall, white, bald, and scary-looking?" Jasper asked.

Adekunle shook his head, no. So it wasn't Hayalet.

"Was he a funny man, from Eko?"

Again, no. So it wasn't Hassan. Who else would be looking for Jasper?

Adekunle added, "The man mentioned someone else, that he worked for Krylios, who could reward us."

That name. *Krylios*. The one who wants Jasper dead. He couldn't hide anymore. He didn't know what good this might do, but he had to explain everything to Adekunle.

In what seemed like a single, continuous breath, Jasper explained the whole situation - how Fletcher rescued him in the middle of the night, that Krylios is an evil man who uses time travel for his own benefit, that Jasper apparently grows up to be the one who stops him, for which Krylios came to kill Jasper as a boy before his time travel adventures even started.

He walked Adekunle through everything, how he arrived here in Eko.

"Why don't you just leave, escape?" Adekunle asked.

From the pouch hanging from his neck, Jasper withdrew his crystal. It had changed little - clear, with a faint green hue. "It's supposed to be a brilliant, bright green," he explained. "It's empty. I wore it out, and I don't know how to replenish it. I'm stuck here until I do."

"Well, that's a problem," Adekunle explained, "Because that man will be back."

Jasper realized in that moment that, if that man wasn't Hayalet, and Krylios himself cannot time travel, someone *else* was now out looking for him. Likely, the same person who came for him at Waveland Mansion. Was Hayalet even looking for him, or were they just having unfortunate run-ins together along the way?

Adekunle leaned in. "I have a problem, Jasper. We need water. I'm sure that man saw that we are not strong right now."

"That's why you wanted me to redirect the underground river that goes to Oladipo's well?"

Adekunle nodded.

"But, you know that would ruin Oladipo and his people, right?"

A stern look grew on Adekunle's face. "You do not live in the jungle, Jasper. Everything out here is a fight. The jungle itself fights against us, and we must fight back," he explained in anger, and he pointed to the corner of the hut, in which a tiger skull, long teeth showing, hung from the ceiling.

Jasper took a deep breath and looked around. Adekunle was right. He didn't know the ways of the jungle. But he thought back to his time at Waveland Mansion. In a home of twenty boys, conflict was inevitable. He didn't long to be back among the testosterone and hormone-driven gang of boys unaware of the foulness of their own sweat.

But, one thing he *could* do was solve the other boys' problems for them before anyone got hurt. How he wished he could do the same between Adekunle and Oladipo. His pure hatred of conflict drove him to this. It was his instinct.

"We used to be friends," Adekunle interrupted, "until our water dried up. Water is everything out here, Jasper. It's too bad, really. Oladipo is a talented metalworker, and we deeply miss their tools here."

Metal workers? A memory popped into Jasper's mind. A book, by his bedside, at Waveland Mansion. *How Things Work* the book was called. Quickly, his memory evolved into an idea.

"Adekunle, what if there didn't have to be a winner or loser?" Jasper asked.

"I don't see how that is possible."

"What if there were enough water for both of you?"

"Are you saying you can create water?"

Jasper shook his head. "No, but what if we can get it from the well faster?"

Adekunle raised an eyebrow as he contemplated Jasper's idea.

Inside the leather pouch hanging from his neck, unbeknownst to Jasper, his crystal grew ever so slightly more green.

Chapter 30

What Jasper didn't know was that his idea was impossible unless you like to die. Even if you like to die, his idea is still impossible, because you will die before you accomplish it. Even if you say, "I'm not afraid of death," you are afraid of death. Fear of death keeps people alive. People who are not afraid of death are already dead, and thus unable to help Jasper with his idea.

The biggest problem with Jasper's idea was that tensions between Adekunle and Oladipo were so strained, so terrible, that any member of one clan killed any member of the other clan on sight. So, Jasper's plan of asking the Oladipo to use their metalworking talents to forge a corkscrew-style Archimedes Pump to extract plentiful water from the well was likely to die with the messenger who tried to ask the Oladipo.

Jasper lay on a rolled-out reed floor mat, thinking, but barely, after an exhausting late-night brainstorming session around a campfire with Adekunle. The two of them tried, until the flames of the campfire shrank into red-hot coals, and then until the coals themselves put themselves out, to come up with any idea for approaching the Oladipo.

For a time, they considered some disguised donkey diplomacy. Jasper would disguise himself as a donkey, hoping to sneak into the Oladipo camp unnoticed. Of course, he'd have to contend with the minor inconvenience that the Oladipo had a fondness for roast donkey. They didn't care for roast python, but they couldn't convincingly dress Jasper as a python.

Yet, Adekunle showed a remarkable sense of trust and welcome to Jasper the outsider. He got his own tent, tightly sealed off from the mosquitos that dominated the nighttime. Now, listening to the cooing of the native birds, the rustling of the trees in the wind, and the weirdly calming insect chatter, his eyes drooped nearly shut. Having Gizmo nuzzled up against his side calmed him further.

"What do you think, Gizmo?" Jasper asked, softly. "There has to be *some* way, doesn't there?"

Gizmo just sighed and rested his head on Jasper's leg. Jasper sighed as well and kept thinking while scratching Gizmo's fluffy coat. There had to be some way… *some* way to get through to the Oladipo without being killed. Could he send Gizmo with a note?

No. He still didn't quite know how he acquired Gizmo, but he wasn't about to put him in harm's way now.

His body was tired, but his mind raced. Sometimes, he cursed the way his mind would attack problems with unrelenting force. Often, this came at the expense of his own sleep and sanity. Yet, way after way, time after time, idea after idea, Adekunle assured him it would not work. In the jungle, *survival* was everything. Every outside approach to the Oladipo was a threat. In this time of scarce water, threats were not investigated.

Only killed.

As his eyes finally closed and his brain nearly ground to a stop, he suddenly felt Gizmo jerk. Though dark, he faintly saw Gizmo's head jolt upward and his ears stick out. He heard something.

Then, Jasper heard it too. Footsteps, the crack of a twig beneath a sandal. With the quick jolt of his heart rate,

Jasper instantly understood why they treated threats so unkindly.

Someone came asking about you, Adekunle told him earlier. Have they come back?

As the footsteps grew closer, Gizmo stood and stepped over Jasper, standing over him, protecting him. If there were more light in the tent, he would see Gizmo's bared teeth.

Just outside the tent, the footsteps stopped. Gizmo stayed, perched over Jasper, listening. Jasper waited anxiously, desperately trying to hear the happenings outside his tent over the deafening beating of his own heart.

"Jasper..."

The soft female voice that said his name did nothing to quell his racing heart, nor did Gizmo stand down.

"Jasper..." she said again. "Are you awake?"

Jasper gulped. "I am now," he whispered back.

The threat of death in the forest caused many to jump to misunderstandings that would lead, unfortunately, also to death. This woman understood the jungle and the nature of humankind, and jumped to continue speaking before anyone could get too much further in assuming she was up to no good.

"My name's Ajoke," she whispered, pronouncing it *Ah-joh-kay,* "Can I come in?"

Gizmo growled a low growl that Jasper could feel vibrate his own body, but no one could hear outside the tent. Gizmo clearly didn't like that idea.

"Why?" Jasper asked.

"I know how to talk to the Oladipo."

Jasper sighed, reached around Gizmo, and squeezed in an enormous hug. After all Gizmo had done to comfort him, he wanted Gizmo to know this was going to be alright.

"Shhhhh…" he reassured his friend, "She'll be okay." But, no matter what Jasper said, Gizmo was most certainly going to stand guard until this stranger left the tent.

Jasper reached out and unlatched the tent flap and poked his head out. Moonlight threw soft beams through the thick jungle canopy. In the soft glow, Ajoke crouched low.

Their eyes met. She wasn't much older than Jasper. Her soft brown eyes betrayed her; in a clan of warriors, they could never compel her to take up a sword or spear. Slowly, they stood up together. Her thick, beaded hair swayed behind her broad shoulders.

It took a few moments before either of them figured out what to say next. He was certain Ajoke had seen him in the camp, but he was meeting her for the first time. "I'm Jasper," he nervously spit out.

"I know," she replied, seeming nervous, wondering if she were doing the right thing.

"You have a solution to my problem with the Oladipo?"

Ajoke looked down and hesitated. "Can you hold on to your dog?" she asked.

Strangely trusting and not asking why, Jasper kneeled down, put his arms around Gizmo, and held onto his collar with a firm grasp. "Okay," he said, "now what?"

The moonlight bounced off Ajoke's arm as she waved at a nearby tree. From behind it, the shadow of another man slowly stepped out, and walked toward them. Gizmo *did not* like this and immediately started growling. Sensing their fear, and knowing what fearful creatures did in the jungle, Ajoke quickly explained.

"This is my brother, Femi. Before the water crisis, he left the Adekunle and married a woman from the Oladipo."

Femi approached with cautious steps. He was taller than Ajoke, and they both wore cloth tunics that made little noise when they moved around. "My sister says you can bring us peace?" Femi asked, his voice deep and resonant.

"I said he can bring us water," Ajoke corrected. "Peace is up to us."

Still kneeling, Jasper hugged Gizmo once more, and gave him a few friendly pats for good measure. Seeing that the strangers didn't immediately try to kill them, Gizmo calmed slightly, and sat, though kept his ears poked out.

How could he explain what he needed? It was unlikely Femi nor Ajoke had ever heard of an "Archimedes Screw," and Jasper was no artist. Jasper searched around the moonlit Jungle clearing. "Find me a stick," he instructed, "perfectly straight. Like a walking stick."

Quietly and carefully, Femi and Ajoke searched for a walking stick, while Jasper peeled a few palm leaves off the roof of his tent. When they returned, Ajoke held out a perfectly straight fallen branch, about half Jasper's height.

"Is this what you're looking for?" she asked, hopefully.

Jasper nodded, took it, and then wrapped his palm leaf around it. He let the ridge of the leaf stick out from the branch, and left a gap about two finger-widths between each winding of the leaf. In the end, Jasper handed Femi back a screw made of stick and palm leaf.

"I need this," he explained, "twice as tall as me. The ridges need to be the length of your foot."

Femi grasped the stick, carefully studying it, and nodding.

"You can do this?" Ajoke asked, hopefully.

Femi nodded. "I can do this. I don't know how I'll explain what it's for, but I can do this."

"You better go before anyone else sees you here," Ajoke warned, beginning to push him away.

Femi looked back at Jasper. "I'll be back once I have it." Then, with feet moving lightly and silently, he swiftly ran away from their camp and disappeared into the jungle.

Jasper studied Ajoke's face as her eyes followed Femi off into the distance. "Thank you," he said, breaking her longing.

"You're sure you can bring us enough water for all of us?" she asked.

Jasper nodded. "There's plenty of water down there. You just need a better way of getting it out. You'll all have enough."

Ajoke remained motionless. Staring off into the distance, she simply said, "I fear, at this point, we may need more than water to heal our differences."

Chapter 31

Newhaven Bay

In the hidden cave secretly overlooking Newhaven Bay, it still bothered Cat that she was alive. Grateful, to be sure, yes, but she knew she shouldn't be. Across centuries, she had chased Hayalet, trying to undo his work, trying to give out for free the information for which he charged the most desperate of people. As good and fearsome as he is, Hayalet must know about Cat's exploits. And yet, having now captured her, she's still alive.

Leaving her alive after interfering with his carefully scripted plan is highly out of character for him. She's grateful to be alive, but exceptionally confused by it.

When the green flash reappeared to signal Hayalet's return, she closed her eyes, hoping again to fool him into believing she's asleep. But he never entered the cave; he never came to taunt her. Instead, she heard him outside, wrestling with some tools, and then walk off again.

She exhaled and then squinted her dark eyes. Hayalet is a planner. What are his plans for her? She shuddered. Knowing Hayalet, he will save the threat of death for later, at the right time to force someone to choose to save her over defeating Hayalet.

She's his escape plan.

A quick distraction ended her spinning. A noise in the brush outside - twigs snapping, leaves rustling, and the sound of branches being pushed aside. In the darkness, only a shadow whispered from the forest.

"Cat?"

Her heart skipped. "Ertha?" she whispered.

Ertha checked to make sure the cave was clear and unguarded. Certain that she saw neither Hayalet nor anyone else, she dashed from the woods to the cave entrance. "Where are you, Cat? I can't see anything!"

"Over here! Tied against the wall."

Stumbling in the dark, Ertha ran to Cat's side, found the knot in the rope binding her arms together, and untied her as quickly as possible.

"How'd you find me?" Cat gasped, gratefully.

"I spied on Hayalet. He had a meeting in town. He flashed out of the meeting and I just happened to see him flash in up here!"

Cat checked her arms, and cautiously stood, careful to check for any injuries. "Is Fletcher with you?"

"No," she added. "I'm worried about him... I think he knows Hayalet somehow."

Cat pulled Ertha out of the cave and into the moonlight, where she could see the worry in Ertha's face. "What? How could that be?"

Ertha looked at the ground. "There's a phrase. Fletcher uses it all the time. Hayalet used it in his meeting."

Cat studied Ertha for a moment. She didn't want an explanation. She wanted comfort.

"I'm sure there's plenty of good reasons for that," Cat tried to reassure her. "Don't look too much into it."

Ertha wiped her face, as if she needed a physical gesture to move her off of the topic of Fletcher. "We need to get to the library and figure out what's in store for Newhaven Bay."

Cat froze. "The library?" she sputtered. "For real? The library?"

The time travel archeologists' library is *sacred,* and secret. Only Krylios' archeologists are allowed to enter. Since archeologists can't time travel themselves, only *they* are trusted not to remove artifacts and hide them across time. Time travelers themselves are *not* allowed inside... especially time travelers not a part of the Krylios group.

The library itself was a creation of Krylios I, to give a place for archeologists to store the resources they use to help his time travelers. But access is tightly restricted.

"Are you going to take *me* into the library?" Cat asked, in a bit of shock.

"It'll be faster if we work together," Ertha explained. "I'll find a way to sneak you in."

The two of them ran down the hillside, and Cat's heart fluttered. Since learning to time travel, she had only dreamed of being able to access the archeologists' library for herself. Oh, the things she could learn! The questions she could answer! The Krylios group held back all the knowledge that Cat had to learn for herself, the hard way.

And even so, she always thought the library was a bit of a myth - a computer program or an internet. But now, no! It's an actual, physical place, and Ertha is about to sneak her in.

She knows it's Jasper who grows up to destroy the Krylios group. But now that Ertha's bringing her into their secret library... maybe Cat can do it herself.

Chapter 32

Eko, 1750

"Total Disaster" is a phrase best used to describe events that fail so spectacularly they attract onlookers who come for the entertainment. Participants in the immediate area get drawn in like a black hole, the calamity acting as a gravitational force on the morbidly curious.

As it would happen, it is also the phrase Jasper would someday use to describe the events of Eko, 1750. These events, set in place by Jasper himself and intended to heal the great rift between the Adekunle and Oladipo, served only to aggravate them.

It wasn't supposed to happen this way. Then again, total disasters are never *supposed* to happen the way they happen. The only ones who intend for total disasters are circus promoters from the late 1800s who intentionally run train engines into each other in front of paying crowds (which, ironically, are not disasters at all if the train engines run into each other at full speed as planned).

Simple enough, his plan seemed: the two clans fought because they lacked enough water. If he could give them enough water, they no longer needed to fight. And all he needed to give them enough water was a pump to get the water out of the ground faster. So, how did he and Gizmo wind up prisoners of the Oladipo? How did the Adekunle and Oladipo wind up in an all-out battle over the water over which Jasper had just ensured they would never again need to fight?

Water. Simple. The Archimedes Screw Ajoke and Femi built for them worked perfectly. With the Adekunle's bricks laid perfectly and Oladipo's human-sized screw inserted and spinning, endless fresh, cool water poured out, enough for everybody. It was time for a glorious celebration!

Each side did celebrate... until they saw the other side drinking. Then the battle ensued.

Why did they think Jasper even built this pump in the first place? Even when he screamed and shouted that they didn't need to fight anymore, no one seemed to hear, or even understand.

Total disaster. Now, things are even worse.

And yet, something curious: as Jasper sat, guarded in a straw hut, with Gizmo by his side (thankfully), he withdrew his time crystal from his pouch.

Green.

He blinked. Though he was under guard and risked being speared if he made any sudden noises, he wanted to shout with joy! It wasn't dead! His time crystal is alive! It's not quite all the way there yet, but it's alive!

Seeing the faded green, he wanted so badly to close his eyes, imagine Newhaven Bay, and escape. But, it still wasn't the brilliant, bright emerald green it was when he first received it. It's faded. Thankfully, not translucent nor white, but he thought it better not to tempt fate. Perhaps if he attempted time travel without a fully charged crystal, would he wind up only halfway back to his destination? Somewhere in the mid-Atlantic in the mid-1800s?

He didn't know. And in that moment, he wished someone could teach him. Hassan. Ertha. Cat. His parents. There is still so much he doesn't know.

And why was it that his crystal turned green in the first place? How had he restored it? Hassan's lesson popped back into his mind.

What rejuvenates you, what gives you purpose, will rejuvenate the crystal and give it purpose.

Thinking back, he felt fantastic about building the pump. Coming up with the idea, designing it, putting it all together... and that feeling when he stood back and saw it working for the first time... he could've stood and stared at it for hours. That feeling is the most proud he felt on this entire journey.

"So what do I do next?" he actually asked his crystal out loud. If it wants to be his partner, he may as well ask, though Gizmo thought the question was for him, and he just sighed, as if to tell Jasper, "How would I know?" Something inside Jasper swore that's what the crystal said, too.

The sound of an argument in a language he didn't understand outside his hut interrupted his thought. After a few moments of what was very clearly shouting between the guards and a woman, Ajoke shoved her way through the guards and into the hut with Jasper. Gizmo swung around and stood between them.

"Get me out of here!" Jasper begged, leaning forward, desperately. The straw walls of his hut may well have been an iron fortress. "I have to fix this!"

"You've done enough to fix this," said Ajoke, though not in anger. "I told you it would take more than water to heal us."

"So what is it? What will it take?" Jasper clutched his crystal, partially asking Ajoke, partially asking the crystal. *If I fix this,* he thought, *then I can go home. Home. Find Fletcher, Cat, Ertha... my parents.*

"You can't leave this hut, Jasper," Ajoke warned. "Someone's looking for you. The guards... they're also protecting you."

Jasper sighed. "I gave you water. Why is everyone still fighting?"

Ajoke looked off into the distance, unable to determine how to explain years of history into a few moments. "It's not just the water, Jasper. We've both done horrible things to each other trying to get the water. There's a lot of hurt, anger, frustration... the water is here, but the memories are also here."

"So what?" Jasper shrugged it off. "Enjoy your water. Work on fixing it!"

"You assume everyone wants to fix it."

"Why wouldn't they?"

Sometimes, questions that are impossible to answer remain unanswered, as would this one. For no logical reason, no reason that could make sense to anyone, especially Jasper, the two clans would remain fighting.

But somehow, while clutching his crystal and staring at its dull green glow while trying to think, he knew... he *knew* he had to do something. He *must* help these two clans resolve their differences. *That* is what will recharge his crystal.

Ajoke interrupted his thoughts. "There is a way. Femi and I know..."

"What!?" Jasper interrupted, excitedly, ready to help.

But Ajoke glared at him. "If you want to let me finish?" Jasper nodded, reluctantly, and she continued. "Femi and I have been working on a plan for some time. If you're patient, if you can trust us, I think now is the time for us to get to work."

Patience. Trust. Jasper's two least favorite words. It's hard to trust, well, *anyone*, when your parents and protectors drop you off unceremoniously at an orphanage without even a reason or explanation. Someday, he would learn that reason. But, right now... all he knows is it must be *him* who helps reunite the Oladipo and Adekunle in order to rejuvenate his crystal.

"What's your plan?" He asked, trying not to sound like he was begging.

Ajoke shook her head. "I know people like you," she explained. "There's a difference between being *smart* and *knowledgeable*. You're smart enough to help, but not knowledgeable enough to help without doing more harm."

Then, making none of the typical goodbye gestures, she simply stood to leave. "Give it a few days... it'll all be over." She walked through the straw walls, and they swished and swayed behind her.

Jasper put his crystal back in his pouch. *A few days*, he thought. That would not work. He's still in danger and to trust *someone else* with his safety? With completing his mission?

No. If he learned more about this conflict between the Adekunle and Oladipo, if he understood it, if he understood the people, he could come up with a solution. He could learn, he could study, and armed with knowledge, he *could* fix this... and quickly.

"Gizmo?" he whispered, as his dog's ears shot up. "Distract the guards, I have an idea."

***

Jasper barely had enough time to process the outline of his shadow in the green flash that came from behind him in the jungle between the homes of the two clans. Before he knew it, before he could react, before he could fight, before he could regret leaving the safety of his prison hut, they had him. The brush was too thick, his knowledge of the jungle too shallow for him to keep running. And, in his imagination he was much larger and more powerful, but he was only twelve. They got him. Easily. As they got him, he struggled to know where their arms ended and where the branches and vines of the jungle began. It was as if they had gotten the jungle itself as their ally.

He didn't know who "they" were, but he was quickly unconscious and unable to fight back.

Hunger was his first feeling as he came to. As he became aware of his surroundings, the hunger surprised him, as if he hadn't eaten in days. He slowly, and only slightly opened his eyes. Something told him he needed to appear as though he were still out.

He couldn't move his arms. They were bound behind him, and he was tied to a tree, ten feet or so above the ground. He didn't recognize the men below him, but their leather trench coats betrayed them as not being from the Oladipo or Adekunle. Their accents as they spoke were clearly not from Eko, 1750.

"Did it surprise you, how much the kid is like him?" One man asked the other.

"When do we get to kill him?" The other asked.

Jasper's heart leapt into his throat. *Kill?* It was funny: in his mind, he imagined cold-hearted killers as gruff, deep-voiced, and unruly. But the silhouettes of these men stood tall and straight, and their voices sounded... *crisp?* And definitely... *professional.*

"Wait until we have the go-ahead," the first man said.

"We did that the first time, and he escaped the orphanage!" complained the second.

The first man pointed upward. "He will not be escaping now."

"Krylios wants him dead!" the second man pointed in stubborn persistence.

The first man turned and pointed into his companion's chest, slowly, and serious. "First, Krylios has to make sure taking him out of the picture doesn't change any of the important stuff."

The second man backed down, not liking the answer, but understanding its truth. Staring off into the horizon, he changed the subject. "Any idea what happened to his dog?"

The first man simply shook his head.

"I hate that dog," continued the second.

The realization startled him, though with his hands tied behind him, he had nothing to do with his startle. These were the men who came for him that night at Waveland Mansion. Somehow, they tracked him, through Liverpool, and now into Eko, across time and distance. He kept his eyes closed. He didn't know how he would handle this, but for now, he couldn't let them know he was awake.

And the men below him stood watch. Soon, they knew, the boy in the tree would meet their boss, courtesy of his long-lost parents.

Chapter 33

The Library

Ertha's house, tucked away in the hills just outside Newhaven Bay, looked on the outside to be nothing special. The small, three-room brick cottage aptly looked like the owner was a young person with neither the skills nor money to maintain it properly. The slate roof still held, though just barely, and when the wind blew right, smoke from the fireplace poured out the side of the chimney instead of the top. A few dirty bricks lay strewn against the wall from which they fell. A back window would have a picturesque view of the majestic farmland below if it weren't boarded with a sheet of plywood.

Ertha led Cat up the crumbling front steps, unlocked the door, and ushered her inside. The inside looked just as good as the outside: a dirty kitchen with only a wood-burning stove, a bedroom with only a mattress on the floor, and a bathroom that seemed, perhaps, like it may work. But, dirty as it was, Ertha didn't need this house for living; she only needed it for hiding her secret entrance to the library.

"Go to the bedroom and find some clothes that fit," Ertha instructed. Cat, after all, was still wearing her clothes borrowed from Fletcher, soiled from the days of laying in Hayalet's cave.

"Ertha," Cat asked, digging through piles of clothes in the bedroom, "Why are you an archeologist?"

From the kitchen, Cat heard Ertha pick up an iron tool for working the fire in the oven. "Time-sensitivity isn't magic," she explained while she worked. "It's science. It's a recessive gene. You can only time travel if *both* of your parents had the time-sensitivity gene. For me, it was only my mom, I think, and she couldn't time travel either. But, because I have the gene, I can *sense* time waves, I just can't travel along them."

"But that still means someone from Krylios would have had to find you and recruit you, right? How did that happen?"

Cat heard a scraping sound, like the fire iron was scraping against a brick wall, as Ertha explained, "It was funny. When I was sixteen, I found a really old book in a bookstore, an autobiography of a man named William Culpepper, a governor of Connecticut in the 1780s. But then, when I tried to talk about him in history class, my teacher got mad at me, and told me no man by that name had ever been governor.

"I thought that was weird, so I went to find my book, and I couldn't find it. It had just disappeared! So, I went back to the bookstore, and the man who sold it to me thought he remembered me, but he didn't remember the book, and he had no record of ever having that book or selling it to me... or that the book even existed!

"And I thought it was crazy, like I had dreamed the whole thing. Or hallucinated it, or something. Most people would keep that a secret, but I'm, you know, me, so I started telling people at school, trying to figure out what happened. Then, one day, there was a note in my locker, with a key and an address, telling me that's where I could find that book. It was a key to the library."

By now, Cat had found a cute pair of jeans and a knit purple sweatshirt that was a bit big for her, but she wrapped up the side into a knot and made it work. She ripped a swath of fabric off her old, white dress and used it to tie her hair back. Then, she joined Ertha in the kitchen to see that she had cut a brick away from the wall, and removed from within it an old skeleton key.

"William Culpepper?" Cat asked, as if the name vaguely rang a bell.

"Quickly," Ertha quipped, "How many signers were there of the Declaration of Independence?"

"Fifty-six!" Cat chimed, then squinted and turned her head. "No, fifty-seven."

Ertha smiled a bit as she saw Cat churning through information in her head. "No, it was fifty-six, but why... why is fifty-seven popping up in there?"

"Because," Ertha explained, "It was fifty-seven. But then, someone from Krylios killed William Culpepper in 1770."

"But the Declaration of Independence was signed in 1776."

"Exactly. He did sign it in 1776, but then he was killed in 1770."

Cat huffed and rolled her eyes. "Try explaining that to someone who doesn't know about time travel."

Ertha chuckled. "Sometime after I read that book, someone killed Culpepper in 1770, and the book ceased to exist. *But I still remembered* the book, because I can sense time distortions."

Cat's eyes widened. "And that's why I can still remember fifty-seven, and the rest of the world thinks it's fifty-six."

"Exactly," Ertha nodded, proudly displaying her skeleton key and smiling. "Let's go to the library."

In the bedroom, Ertha pushed aside her mattress, revealing a trapdoor in the floor. She pulled the latch and opened the door. Inside, a flight of stairs led down to a solid oak door that glowed, very faintly, a shade of light green.

After a decade of traveling all over the centuries, very little surprised Cat. But, this was the first she had ever seen anything such as this. "Is that..."

Before Cat could finish her sentence, Ertha interrupted. "It's time crystal dust, yes. Only you and I can see it. If you don't have the time gene, you can't see it at all."

The door glowed enough they needed no light to descend down the stairway. At the bottom, Ertha inserted her key into the lock, and turned it until it clicked. But then, she stopped, and turned back toward Cat.

"There shouldn't be anyone here right now," Ertha warned, "but if someone comes, you'll have to hide."

Cat just nodded, willing to do whatever it took to be the only known time traveler to have been invited inside the archeologists' library. Ertha turned the door handle and gave a firm push to the heavy door. A sucking sound followed, and a gust of wind pulled their hair toward the room.

When her eyes adjusted to the light of the room, she couldn't believe what she saw...

***

Cat and Ertha entered at the top of a ten-story cavern, lit overhead with a giant domed skylight. A huge open space in the middle let them see all the way up to the bottom. The grand domed skylight high above filled the place with warm, natural light. It was like being inside a massive, endless treasure chest of books.

Radiating out from the central atrium like rays from the sun, five floors stretched outward. Each floor had twenty rows of bookshelves extending back from the center, disappearing into the distance as far as the eye could see.

Lavishness decorated the library in a style that made you feel you were stepping into a glamorous past. Shiny, golden patterns lined the walls, with sleek, geometric designs that seemed to sparkle. The floors were polished and smooth, and there were fancy, colorful tiles arranged in eye-catching shapes. Even the light fixtures were special—elegant lamps with sharp angles and brilliant, stained glass that cast a warm, inviting glow. Bronze-plated electric scooters and elevators zipped up and down the floors of shelves, providing quick access to any book.

It was a place that felt both old and new, like a hidden gem filled with endless stories waiting to be discovered. A visitor could be forgiven if their brain automatically added jazz music to the room's atmosphere.

"Art déco!" Cat blurted, first recognizing the artistic style of the interior decorating.

Ertha nodded. "Krylios I was a fan of the 1920s," she explained.

Cat was again confused, a feeling she didn't like at all. "Didn't Krylios I live in the mid-1800s?"

Ertha smiled, reveling in her opportunity to be the one to teach someone else - especially someone as experienced as Cat - about time travel. "He loved the pictures people gave him," she explained.

She motioned for Cat to follow, and they descended an ornate, wooden staircase that spiraled around the center atrium. "We all have our own entrance. There's probably a bunch of other archeologists in here right now, but I can't see them because they're from other time periods. *We* can't travel through time, so, in this time, at this moment, we're alone."

Cat had to shift her mind from a state of amazement into getting to work. "Alright," she asked, "what do we need to do here?"

"We need to find every reference we can to Newhaven Bay and see if we can find out what Hayalet does to it."

Cat looked around, studying. "And how do we do that?"

"Archeologists and time travelers work together to try to get copies of the same books and documents across time. Once a volume is brought into the library, it's shielded from time wave interference, and can't be changed no matter what happens on the outside."

"So your book on William Culpepper still exists... in here!" Cat quipped, putting the pieces together of why this library worked.

"Exactly."

Cat noticed something further: many of the books seemed to be informal, more like notebooks, not bound and printed by publishers with titles embossed in the spine.

"What kind of books are these?" Cat asked, still admiring them.

"History books are always second-hand information," Ertha explained. "If we want to know what was really going on, we have to go back to the source. Most of these books are journals and diaries, notes and letters. They come right from the people who directly experienced history."

Cat nodded. "Anything from Newhaven Bay?"

"That's what we're looking for. If we can find references to Newhaven Bay, and see how they change across changes to time, we might be able to figure out what Hayalet's up to. The catalog system's down there... let's go."

As they jogged down the spiral staircase, a spy at the end of a distant shelf watched their every move.

Chapter 34

Eko, 1750

"Boy, I have some advice for you," warned menacingly the dark-suited captor who climbed a vine up to Jasper's level. He leaned in. "Tuck and roll."

Then, without warning, the man unveiled a long, sharp, curved knife, and swiftly cut the rope holding Jasper up in the tree. He fell (obviously), and hit the ground with a *thud* before he could even process the meaning of the phrase, "tuck and roll." He was not tucked, and he did not roll, but years of built-up twigs and leaves saved him from injury, though not pain.

Groaning, he winced as the other captor yanked the collar of his blue tunic and sat him up before he could figure out which parts of his body may be injured. The captor from the tree descended his vine much more slowly and gracefully, bragging that he had concern over the health of his body *and* the freedom to do something about it. For the first time, Jasper studied the faces of his captors.

The one who released him from the tree seemed to be in charge. He wore a black jumpsuit as if he dabbled in burglary on the side but didn't want his protective uniform to hide the unnatural muscles he most certainly spent years building. Behind his well-kept, trimmed, brown beard was a tightly wrinkled face. This man knew what work was like.

The other, younger. He had not taken the time to custom-tailor his jumpsuit, and it hung loosely. Bright and unbearded, olive-skinned and shorter, he was the bull to his partner's racehorse.

Those were his two captors: the bull and the racehorse.

The bull ripped the satchel off Jasper's neck, dug inside, and removed his translucent crystal. He held it out between his thumb and index finger, and the two studied it.

The racehorse smiled. "He wore it out."

"Can he still talk to Krylios?" the bull asked, furrowing his brow.

The racehorse now grinned an evil grin, revealing a row of perfectly cleaned but never straightened teeth. "He can." He grabbed the crystal away from the bull and held it to the small space of bare sky through the jungle canopy, studying it. "It has enough."

The racehorse then looked Jasper in the eye. "Do you remember your parents?" he asked, menacingly.

Jasper nodded. Without intention, an image of his parents, happy, in their home, before leaving to go to Waveland Mansion, popped into his head.

Exactly what Mr. Racehorse wanted. "Good," he taunted, and then reached out his arms and slammed Jasper on both sides of his head to grip him firmly between his hands, the crystal pressed between the man's palm and Jasper's temple.

Instantly, Jasper's vision blanked. But, he wasn't unconscious. He was fully aware - fully aware that he no longer felt his body, fully aware that he no longer needed to breathe, fully aware of the green fog that enshrouded his vision.

The sounds came before the sight. Clanging. The sound of glassware and silverware. The hum of a fan. Something industrial. A laboratory.

He knew what it would be before his vision came to. His vision restored and perfectly matched the memory of his previous accidental visit to what seemed to be a laboratory of his parents. But, before, it was trashed. Now, it was clean, pristine, and active.

And two scientists in lab coats stood, hunched over equipment, on the far side. A man and a woman.

His parents.

He tried to shout, but he couldn't. He was nothing but a visitor, a silent observer. Did they even know he was there?

He quickly got his answer.

"They can't see you, Jasper. They don't know you're there."

The ominous voice echoed from what sounded like his own head. But it wasn't his voice. And yet, without ever having heard this voice before, somehow he knew: *Krylios*.

Krylios. The boss of Hayalet. The man who Jasper would someday kill... or nearly kill. If you come for the king, you best not miss. The very fact that Jasper was on this journey was evidence that he had destroyed the kingdom, but not killed the king.

"You made a mess for me," Krylios' deep voice echoed. "How do you become what you become?"

From across the lab, smoke rose from a test tube. Jasper's mom, holding a crystal with a pair of tweezers, dropped it in. The smoke instantly stopped.

"Do you even know what your parents are working on? Why they disappeared?" Krylios paused, awaiting an answer from the boy who couldn't speak. "It is true that you can't travel into your own future, but that's only an obstacle of science. It's not an unbreakable law of the universe.. That's what they're working on. And they're nearly done, too... if only we could've seen you coming."

What was Jasper seeing right now? An illusion? Was he actually there? Had his spirit become separated from his body, transported across from space, to wind up in his parents' lab only to remain unseen by them? Did they know he was there?

Why couldn't they work on their project without leaving him at Waveland Mansion?

"I suppose at this point it doesn't matter if I reveal anything to you or not," Krylios taunted. "I would go back and end *their* journey before you even came into being," he slowly explained, referring of course to Jasper's parents. "But I need them."

Watching his parents work their tools, mix chemicals in their test tubes, and examine crystals under a microscope, they seemed... happy. Were they working for Krylios?

No, Jasper thought. They couldn't be. No, he's just... he's just... he's just using them.

"Before I end your story for good, I need to know..." if a voice inside your head could squeeze every part of your being, Krylios' voice was doing it. "I need to know… even at your age, do you know where my weapon is?"

His weapon? Truthfully, he had no idea, and Krylios sensed this. "Very good, then. Goodbye, Jasper Berry."

The green cloud surrounding his vision swirled, crystalized, glowed and zoomed. The feeling of his stomach was back, and it was the feeling of flying through space. Without warning, he slammed full force back into reality and landed at the feet of his captors.

And into the middle of an all-out war.

Chapter 35

The Library

Hours upon hours they searched the shelves under the geometric ceiling that should have been echoing with big band jazz. They split up, and darted back and forth, from the center on out, looking for book after book after book.

First, volumes on Rhode Island History. Ertha taught Cat their special labeling system - they found three copies of the 1945 volume of <u>Rhode Islanders</u>, whose labels noted that time travelers retrieved them from 1950, 1970, and 1990. The 1950 copy looked brand new, and the 1990 copy looked forty-five years old. It was printed in 1945, but retrieved by a time traveler in 1990, and thus labeled, <u>1945.R1990</u>. And, though they were the same book, technically printed at the same time… each had subtle differences.

Towns and places that existed in <u>R1950</u> did not exist in <u>R1990</u>. Sometime between 1950 and 1990, a time traveler went back to before 1945 and changed history, or so Ertha explained to Cat. That's why a town could be present in <u>R1950</u> but not in <u>R1990</u>.

"Sometimes," Ertha explained, "A time traveler needs to know *what* has changed, and *when*, and *why*. And so, I need to compare these books to piece together the story."

Cat nodded, quickly understanding Ertha's job. "Or, after your time traveler does whatever it is they're doing, you need to update your books."

"Exactly."

As they worked, they pulled volume after volume. <u>Rhode Islanders</u>, books about lakes, books about fishing clubs, books about native settlements, travel guides depicting quaint New England towns. They worked more and more frantic as they discovered that exactly zero of these books even mentioned Newhaven Bay.

At Cat's suggestion, they tried maps. Dozens of maps, and dozens of variants across time, all showed Newhaven Bay where they expected to be, nothing else. Finally, exasperated, Cat lay on the ground, staring blankly at the dome ten stories above her.

"There's no census records?" she asked.

Ertha shook her head, "No." She slumped over her table beside Cat, her frizzy hair bouncing over her face. "It's like they've been..."

"Taken."

They both knew. *Hayalet*. Though he had removed every reference in the library to the town he was about to victimize, Ertha knew there was still a large, outside world.

"I have an idea," Ertha nearly shouted, jumping into action. Cat looked on, surprised the force of her own hair did not throw Ertha to the ground when she threw her head backward. "Follow me!"

They jumped on a scooter and raced toward the far end of one of the rays from the center. Here, the library transformed into some sort of post office, where hundreds of individual mailboxes lined the walls. Too quickly for Cat to see what she was writing, Ertha scribbled a note on a piece of paper and slipped it into a box.

Cat studied the mailbox. "Who's *I. Hassan?*" she asked.

"He's a time traveler I work with, and he has a way of getting around."

"Wouldn't he be a part of Krylios?"

"We can trust him."

An ornate 1950s tube TV flickered to life beside the mailboxes. In grainy black-and-white, an image of a well-dressed African blinked a few times before it steadied.

"Ertha?" Hassan's voice sounded distorted, like from a radio too far away. "Ertha, are you there?"

Ertha ran to the TV, clearly excited. "Hassan! You got my letter!"

"What letter?"

"The letter I sent you?"

"I didn't get a letter."

"Then how did you know to call me?"

"I just wanted to talk!"

Ertha exhaled in frustration. "Well, then I need to fill you in."

"About Cat and your struggle to find anything about Newhaven Bay?"

"How did you know about that?"

Hassan burst out laughing. "Because I got your letter!" He roared, holding Ertha's letter up to the TV screen. Cat smiled, and she didn't care whether or not that annoyed Ertha. She liked this Hassan.

"Is this Cat?" Hassan asked.

"Catalina Rodriguez," Cat replied, nodding her head in the best over the air greeting she could muster.

"Idrissi Hassan, pleasure to meet you."

Ertha interrupted. "Hassan, we need your help. But first, how's Jasper?"

That caught Cat off guard, and she looked quizzically at Ertha.

"Don't ask questions you don't want to know the answer to, Ertha," he warned.

"But you *are* watching over him, right?" Ertha pressed on, seriously.

Hassan paused for a moment. "I... *was*."

"Hassan!"

"He's *fine*, Ertha. He's negotiating with some locals and doing a fine job at it."

Ertha sighed in relief, only for Hassan to continue being himself. "I know this," he added, "because they haven't killed him yet... although they have tried."

Ertha nearly screamed at the TV, "Hassan, I swear to you, I'll march right up to Hayalet and tell him right where to find you!"

"He's okay, Ertha, I promise," Hassan did his best to reassure her in his most calming, serious voice. "Now, what do you need my help for?"

At this point, Cat figured she should step in, and give Ertha a few precious moments to become less murderous. "We need you to find artifacts about Newhaven Bay, in Rhode Island. It's important to Hayalet's plan, and he's removed every reference to it in the library."

Hassan nodded. "Huh, right. I'll do what I can and let you know when I find anything."

"And, Hassan," Ertha continued. "Cat needs a crystal. Can you get me one?"

Hassan froze and his face twisted and contorted. Happy Hassan left. This Hassan was the one seen by his enemies. "Do you know what you're asking of me?" he grumbled.

"I do," Ertha returned with equal seriousness. "It's important."

Hassan said nothing, only nodded. And with that, the TV went blank, illuminating their corner of the room with only black and white static.

Ertha breathed heavily, clearly worked up by Hassan's antics.

"He seems fun," Cat quipped. "Do you think he'll find anything?"

Before Ertha could answer, the TV flashed back to life. It was Hassan again, but different. Instead of the happy comedian, this Hassan was running... quickly... and away from something.

"Ertha, Ertha, are you there?" Hassan shouted, between breaths.

"What?" Ertha gasped.

"First of all, your crystal's in my mailbox, he wheezed, still running. "Secondly, I didn't find out much about Newhaven Bay."

Cat listened as she ran to *I. Hassan*'s mailbox. She stared in awe as she opened it to find a single, glowing, green crystal. *Time travel is truly amazing*, she thought.

"It's okay, you only just started looking," Ertha tried to reassure him.

"I've been looking for ten years!" Hassan huffed.

"But you just left!" Cat sputtered, confused.

"Time travel!" he shouted, as if it should be obvious to all of them by now.

Cat and Ertha looked at each other in frustration, unsure of their next move.

"Nothing?" Ertha asked, desperate.

"No, but I do have one question: Why is it called Newhaven Bay?"

Ertha shrugged. "I don't know. What else would you call it?"

Hassan still ran, checking over his shoulder every few seconds. "But, it doesn't have a bay," he exclaimed.

"By the lake!" Ertha yelped.

"What lake?" a puzzled and exhausted Hassan shouted back.

Cat jumped. Her brain cells clicked. She knew what was happening! "Hassan, I got it," she shouted, "Go back to running from whatever you're running from! We got this!" She slipped her crystal in her pocket as she bolted away.

"Thank you!" Hassan shouted back. "This will be a lot easier when I'm not..."

The transmission cut again. Ertha nodded sharply. "He's okay," she tried to assure them both. "What's your idea?"

Cat raced off. Ertha followed and jumped on the back of her scooter. They flew past the rows of books on the shelves as if Cat needed to make it back to the atrium before she forgot her idea. She slammed on the brakes and stepped off the scooter without breaking her stride.

At the table, Cat unfurled all the maps they found earlier. She stacked them on top of each other. "Newhaven Bay, Newhaven Bay, Newhaven Bay," she said, pointing them out one by one.

"Right," Ertha said, "they're all there."

"We missed something important." Cat pulled out two maps in particular. One of the faded, fragile, yellowed maps was labeled <u>R1945</u>, and the other <u>R1970</u>. She pointed to the town, one with each hand. "What do you see?"

Ertha instantly saw it. How she missed it earlier, she didn't know, but there it was, clearly and plainly, as if it were mocking her inattentiveness. Running her fingers over the faded yellow fibers and delicate creases in the folds, she stopped over the label, *Newhaven Bay.*

The two of them locked eyes and said it at the same time: "The lake!"

While <u>R1945</u> showed Newhaven Bay nestled up against the familiar lake Ertha had grown up boating, <u>R1970</u> showed no lake. That's why Hassan couldn't find anything - without a lake, Newhaven Bay was nothing remarkable nor historical.

Ertha gulped. "The dam. Hayalet is going to blow the dam and drain the lake."

"And kill the town in the process," Cat added.

"But why?"

Cat threw her head back and covered her face with her hands. She knew.

"Krylios is after something and Hayalet is trying to get it. He's making a huge time wave in order to draw someone's attention to Newhaven Bay. It's a trap, of sorts."

"Who?"

"I don't know *exactly*, but us resistors, time travelers not part of Krylios, we have an idea."

"Okay... what?"

Cat puckered her lips, trying to think of where to begin. "I'll tell you on the way. We have to warn Fletcher. It has to do something with King Arthur's sword."

As they ran off, the spy who had been watching them the entire time knew Hayalet had a problem on his hands. As they went to warn Fletcher, he had to go warn Hayalet.

Chapter 36

Eko, 1750

"Gizmo, distract the guards, I have an idea." Like most of Jasper's ideas since the two of them met in Liverpool, Gizmo knew this one was poorly thought out, likely to fail, and stupid. And yet, as a dog, Gizmo's only loyalty was to his master. And so, as he had always done, he obeyed his master's instructions, burst forth from their tent, ran in circles to attract the guards' attention, lept up onto one of them to snatch a satchel off his belt, and then dashed off into the jungle.

The guards chased clumsily, bewildered at how this dog could navigate their jungle better than they could. Gizmo vaulted over logs that tripped them, ducked under vines that caught them, and scurried up hills that exhausted them. Once free of his would-be captors, he dropped the satchel, unconcerned with its contents, and went back to helping Jasper who, by this point, certainly needed his help.

But he knew he would be no help by himself.

Jasper's well was key. He ran to the well, a brick tunnel buried in the hillside with the long, metallic screw turning, dumping water into a newly formed pond. He bolted to the pond, barking and snarling with a ferocious attitude that would scare off even the most fearsome lion. As Gizmo danced and barked, women and children from Adekunle's clan scurried back from the pond. A crowd of onlookers came about, also too to encroach upon the enraged Australian Shepherd.

Gizmo needed this commotion to draw a crowd of more than just Adekunle, and it did. Femi and a group of Oladipo men emerged from hiding among the jungle's trees, and slowly made their way toward the pond, opposite the side of the Adekunle. And yet, it didn't seem at first as though Gizmo was on their side. The dog's energy doubled to keep darting around the pond, barking and holding everyone back.

Through the Adekunle crowd, Adekunle himself stepped forward, his elegant blue-beaded tunic swishing with his purposeful walk. "How dare you show yourselves at this water," he shouted over Gizmo's incessant barking.

From the other side of the pond, Femi shouted back, "We were going to steal it."

"It's ours," Adekunle rebuked him.

Then, from the Adekunle side, Ajoke stepped forward, and rebuked her own leader. She approached him, and with no hesitation, looked directly into his eyes. "No, it's not," she asserted, slowly, stubbornly.

Then, with a nod across the pond to her brother, Femi the Oladipo, they walked toward each other. With outstretched hands, they stepped toward the pond, crouched down, and drank from it... completely unbothered by the raging dog, still holding everyone back from the lake.

"Jasper built this for all of us," Ajoke stood and rebuked the crowd. "Not you, you, or you, but *all* of us."

Femi continued as Gizmo quieted down, "We only fought because we tried to claim it as our own. But Jasper showed, there's more than enough for all of us!"

"And there always was!" Ajoke shouted. "It was there the whole time! We never needed to fight, we just needed to be smarter about it."

"This dog will let you drink if you come to the water, together, peacefully."

But no one in the crowd moved. On both sides of the pond, men, women, and children stood, staring, arms crossed, still glaring at their foes in anger. The crowd hushed further by the sight of Oladipo himself stepping through his crowd, joining the gathering by the pond at last. Only the chirping of the birds in the canopy far overhead and the ever-present bubbling of water falling from Jasper's pump made any sound as the two sides stood off against each other.

Adekunle reached out, silently demanding a spear from the man next to him. At this sight, Oladipo did the same. The two of them together marched along the banks of the pond, slowly, purposefully toward each other in complete silence from the crowd.

Then, they stood. Femi and Ajoke stepped back from the banks and allowed the crowd's full attention to center on their leaders. Gizmo, however, just sat. He didn't bark, snarl, or whine. Adekunle and Oladipo stood across from each other, staring, saying nothing. The crowd breathed more quickly, and in unison.

Oladipo raised his spear. Adekunle mirrored his movements. And then, in perfect unison, they tossed their spears into the pond and embraced each other in a long, tight hug. The surrounding crowd exhaled all at once, and Gizmo could see their shoulders relax. Even the chirping of the birds seemed to celebrate!

Immediately, years of built-up unnecessary tension evaporated, and the two sides, who secretly craved to no longer be two separate people, joined as one and drank from the pond together. The joyous crowd hugged, screamed, laughed, shouted, and danced around the pond banks. Some ran back to their homes and returned with water jars, joyously filling them to the brim with water that was plentiful for everyone.

The first half of his plan complete, Gizmo once again caught everyone's attention. He jumped to the top of the brick wall housing Jasper's pump and barked at the top of his lungs. Slowly, the celebration stopped. When Gizmo had everyone's attention, he jumped off the wall and ran back into the jungle.

But this time, warriors of both sides grabbed their spears and followed.

***

Jasper fell back to the ground. They hadn't meant for his vision to be over. The Krylios agents had more in store for him. The attack from behind distracted them, but only for a moment. They weren't about to let an attack by who they saw as primitive natives from 400 years ago be anything more than a temporary distraction.

Learning to survive in the jungles surrounding Eko made the Oladipo and Adekunle ruthless and unforgiving against enemies, and now the Krylios enforcers who threatened their new friend bore the full force of a spear attack by dozens of warriors. Spears flew through the air as missiles guided by the hands of skilled throwers. Jasper, with a moment's freedom, ducked behind the tree he hung from moments ago.

With the sound of shouts and the crack of spear tips planting into trees around him, he was surprised to find himself all wet on the side of his face!

Gizmo!

There was Gizmo, who rushed through the battle, to his side, to lick him on the side of his face and make sure he knew everything was going to be alright. *I've got this all under control,* Gizmo tried to tell him. *It may look like chaos, but it's controlled chaos and I'm the one controlling it!*

Yet, somehow, the Krylios agents avoided injury! Peeking around the tree, Jasper saw both Bull and Racehorse remained crouched in their positions! And then, to his horror, Jasper watched as a spear flew straight at Bull and promptly bounced off him! *That suit!* Jasper knew, *That's an armored suit!* How would they defeat these men?

From a bag at his feet, Racehorse reached in and pulled out a shiny, metallic silver box. Jasper instantly recognized the green crystal protruding out of the top as a time crystal, similar to Jasper's own. As Racehorse pressed the crystal into the box, suddenly, like a movie projector, an image appeared in the clearing between the Krylios agents and the battling warriors.

The image stunned them. Shining as a bright cloud, Bull stood up and pointed to the very well and pump over which the Adekunle and Oladipo had just united. With a deep and gravelly voice, Bull pointed at Jasper's pump.

"He made this for you?" Bull asked the crowd, who had stopped in stunned silence at the vision. "He, Jasper, the kid who magically solved all your problems?"

He spread his arms broadly, gesturing, questioning, almost sarcastically asking, "Can it really be that easy?"

Then, into the vision, appeared a man. Dressed in the clear blue of the Adekunle, he snuck in and cautiously peered around, ensuring no one had followed him nor seen him. Then, with something like a sledgehammer, he quickly smashed the pump and pummeled the brick well in on itself, collapsing the opening back closed until it was nothing more than the remnants of a hole in the ground.

"Or are your rifts really that healed?" The Bull taunted the crowd, which grew more and more agitated. "A hundred years of fighting and suddenly, on this boy's word, you can trust the other side not to betray you?"

"Can it really be that easy?" Bull had just finished asking the crowd. But, for him, it was, and the crowd instantly turned from fighting he and Racehorse to, once again, fighting each other. The warriors ran up, reclaimed their spears from the tree trunks, and began a fresh round

of what had become familiar hand-to-hand combat. With a nod to Racehorse, Bull stepped back from their projection.

Jasper felt something cold in his hand. During the distraction, Gizmo quietly retrieved his crystal from where Bull and Racehorse had dropped it. Gizmo pressed it into Jasper's palm and then pointed upward with his nose. Thinking quickly, Jasper grabbed a vine and climbed.

He didn't know how he knew how to climb a vine, but he knew. As the two clans fought, to the delight of Bull and Racehorse, Jasper climbed. Twenty feet up, above the arcs of the spears, he reached a branch that extended over the battlefield and the still glowing projection of his sabotaged well pump. Straddling the branch, he stared at his crystal.

"Somehow, they can use you to communicate to everyone," he begged the crystal. "Show me how!"

When nothing happened, he looked down and saw Femi shoving Ajoke backward to protect her from the flying battle debris. Ajoke's face and heavy breathing gave away her fear and confusion. After their beautiful reunion, how could this still be happening?

Clutching his crystal, Jasper remembered Ajoke's warning. Generations of horrible deeds made trust difficult. Bull and Racehorse knew this. It was easy for them to use these divisions for their own benefit.

Jasper couldn't let that stand. Closing his eyes and clutching his crystal one more time, he whispered, "Help me."

Then, he shouted. When he shouted, his voice boomed and echoed a deafening roar, bouncing off the trees. "Hey!" Jasper shouted, and the battle instantly stopped. He didn't stop to ponder how strange it was that people can so quickly go from trying to kill each other to having their full attention on him. Seeing the anger on Bull and Racehorse's faces, he knew he had to get to his point quickly.

What was his point? He didn't even know. He just clutched his crystal and kept talking.

"It's a trick! They're showing you the future of you continuing to act as enemies! But it doesn't have to be that way!"

Below him, Racehorse ran to the tree, grabbed a vine, and began climbing. Quickly, Gizmo bit down on his pants leg, and pulled him down with all his might.

"They're showing you nothing more than what *could* be your future! But that's all they'll ever be able to show you! What *could* happen!"

He didn't know where these words were coming from. In all the books he read back at Waveland Mansion, he read nothing remotely related to time travel. He never read science fiction. The wisdom of a time traveler much older and wiser than he was coming from a place he didn't recognize nor know. But it *was* coming through him.

"You can't avoid evil. You can't shut yourself off from it. The voices of evil may always seem louder! The only way to avoid a future like this is to teach yourself to look directly at it and say, 'That's not me. That's not what I do.'"

As the crowd stood stunned, Bull saw Racehorse's fight with Gizmo and took matters into his own hands. He reached out and took a discarded spear from one of the warriors, picked it up, and aimed it toward Jasper in the tree.

As his wind up reached full power, Bull suddenly found the spear snatched from his hands. Ajoke caught the spear, and a group of blue-suited Adekunle pulled Bull down to the ground, as orange-suited Oladipo rushed to Gizmo's aid to yank Racehorse off the tree.

Jasper looked down, and to his relief, exhaled. His head drooped as his tension melted away. And then, from the corner of his eye… a green sparkle flew from his hand.

His crystal glowed a bright, full, luminous green. It was back, restored.

He knew exactly what he had to do. He crawled quickly down the branch, shimmied down the vine, to Gizmo, smiling happily with his tongue hanging from his mouth. He hugged Gizmo around his shaggy neck. In the distance, Ajoke and Femi stood with both Adekunle and Oladipo.

With a smile and a nod, they knew this would be the last time they saw each other. Adekunle waved, and Jasper knew they could go. He and Gizmo raced off through the jungle. They had one more stop to make before heading back to Newhaven Bay.

***

The evening sun in the empty windows gleamed off the tile mosaic lining the inside of Idrissi Hassan majestic house. A ray of sunlight bounced off the wall and glimmered at Jasper's fully green crystal on the table. Something in the house seemed off, and it bothered him.

"Thanks for your help," Jasper joked. "We were both almost killed!"

Hassan smiled. "You know what they say - what doesn't kill you, makes you stronger!"

"Yes, but what *does* kill us makes us *dead!*"

"I wouldn't have let that happen."

"Were you watching us the whole time?"

Hassan turned away from them. "No. I was busy. But," he tapped his temples, "time travel."

Jasper shook his head in amazement as he patted Gizmo's neck.

"So you didn't find your girl?" asked Hassan.

"No," answered Jasper. "But you knew she would not be there, didn't you?"

Hassan just shrugged. Jasper needed to learn that he didn't need to ask questions to know answers.

Something still bothered Jasper about the house, but he had more questions for Hassan. "The Oladipo and the Adekunle - they're so... so... *similar*. Why fight?"

"Sometimes it's hard to outgrow the jungle," Hassan explained. "In the jungle, even the slightest threat can be a threat to your life. We, as humans, unfortunately evolved to see others as threats much quicker and easier than seeing them as friends."

Hassan looked out his window, deep in thought, and took a deep breath. "In the eternal battle between good and evil, *that's* what evil uses to take hold. Fighting it takes..." he sighed. "...takes... work and... I don't know..."

"Imagination," Jasper jumped in.

Hassan smiled. "Yes. Work and imagination. We have a bias toward negativity. Most of human history, we have had to fight to survive. Survival means protecting our group! But today, and especially in your time, *all of humanity* is our group. We can only survive by fighting *for* each other, not against each other. But to do that, sometimes we must first fight our own brains, and our own instincts.

"Not all battles can be won by picking up a sword and fighting. Some take cooperation."

Jasper nodded, but kept looking around, unable to figure out what bothered him. As he exhaled, and the usually talkative Hassan struggled to find the words to say next, Jasper thought back to his past few days. *I actually talked to Krylios,* he thought. *But I still don't know how I fit into all of this.*

"I talked to Krylios," he blurted to Hassan.

Hassan's eyebrows raised in fear. "You talked to Krylios? Himself?"

"The agents who captured me. They held my crystal to the side of my head and I saw a vision of some sort. It wasn't a trick, was it?"

Hassan shook his head. "Unlikely. What was it he said?"

"He asked me about a weapon." Jasper thought that seemed like the most important piece of their brief chat.

Hassan crossed his arms and grunted a long, drawn-out, contemplative rumble from deep within his throat. "King Arthur's sword," Hassan explained as he stared blankly out the window. "Excalibur."

The mention of the ancient British legend confused him, and he had to ask, "Krylios is after Excalibur? That doesn't seem... well... I don't know..."

"Smart?" Hassan surmised.

"Sure."

"He's not after *Excalibur*, exactly. But, around the world, nearly every culture has a myth just like it. In almost every culture, there's a myth of a weapon, placed by a wise wizard, that only the one worthy ruler can wield. Because this myth is all over the world, Krylios believes it was a time traveler who spread it."

Only a few days ago, Bull and Racehorse came to Waveland Mansion to kill him. Was it all because their insane ruler believed in an ancient myth? That didn't make sense.

"So?" Jasper fumed, a bit angry and still confused.

Sensing his anger, Hassan kept explaining. "Krylios believes, if he can find the time traveler who spread the myth, he can reveal the location of the *true* weapon, the *real*

Excalibur. If he can wield the weapon himself, he can lay claim to being the rightful ruler of the world."

"Is it real?" Jasper asked.

Hassan shrugged. "Four generations of Krylios leaders have tried to find it. I guess someday, we'll find out... or not."

Finally, Jasper figured out what was bothering him. The cooking area sat empty, and no fire burned in the firepit. "Why aren't you cooking?" he asked.

"I have to leave here, permanently," Hassan explained, looking longingly out the window.

"Because of me?"

Hassan nodded. "I don't regret helping you. But once you leave, Krylios will stop at nothing to find you. That includes coming here for me. So, I have to leave, too."

Jasper winced. "I'm sorry."

"Don't be," Hassan sat at the table for the last time and reassured him. Assertively, he looked into Jasper's innocent eyes. "You *will* defeat Krylios."

Jasper remembered the wisdom he had given the Adekunle and Oladipo during the battle in the jungle. "Maybe."

Hassan knew what he meant and nodded. Then, looking outside, he saw the sun lowering toward the horizon, over the ocean in the distance. "We should go before it's dark enough they can see your flash."

When Gizmo whined, Hassan smiled. "Take your dog with you."

Jasper nodded. As they stood, he reached down, emptied a canteen of water into his hands, and let Gizmo slurp a much-needed drink.

"Hey," he asked, "before we go, I think I learned more about listening to my crystal, but it's still weird to me."

"How is that?"

"Well, I don't..." How could he describe it? "I don't hear anything."

Hassan looked down at Gizmo, still slurping water from Jasper's cupped hands. "How did you know your dog needed water?" he asked.

Jasper shrugged. "I don't know. I just, sorta, *knew*."

Hassan nodded kindly. "And *that*, Jasper, is listening."

They stood up, and with a kind smile, they shook hands. Jasper studied for a moment as Hassan clutched his own crystal, closed his eyes, and disappeared in a green flash. Then, he looked down at the shaggy Australian shepherd sitting obediently at his feet.

"Gizmo, let me tell you about Newhaven Bay." As he closed his eyes and clutched his crystal, he stopped for just one more moment.

"And don't bark at Fletcher when you meet him."

Chapter 37

The lab. His parent's familiar laboratory, one again shaded in a light green fog. For the first time, Jasper finally got a good look at his parents' faces. His mom, her long blonde hair tied back, looking frayed, as if she hadn't had the energy to maintain it in some time. His dad, tall, studied scribbles on a blackboard while repeatedly running his hands through his graying and thinning hair.

"I just don't understand," his mom sighed, dejected, sitting at a counter and gazing at a picture frame. "How could he betray us like that?"

He? Jasper thought. Who is "he?" Then, a quite unpleasant thought hit him. Hayalet? Krylios? They are working for Krylios, aren't they? He did say he needed them.

"We could've done it, just the two of us," his dad warned ominously, still staring at the blackboard. "Now, we have to protect all this from falling into the wrong hands."

They both startled at the sound of a bang on the door.

"But that means-" his mom started, urgently. But his dad cut her off.

"Now!"

Quickly, with the sound of the door shaking in its frame, they tossed all their vials and beakers onto the floor, violently shattering with deafening noise. He watched his dad hoist a bucket of liquid and throw it at the whiteboard, which not only erased it, the surface dissolved and dripped down to the floor.

The door slammed open. They turned, facing the door, throwing their hands in the air.

Then, Jasper's green vision dissolved away, revealing in front of him the majestic view of Newhaven Bay, from Fletcher's back deck.

***

Jasper would have liked to relish in the friendly feeling of having everyone back together again, of having Ertha, Cat, himself, and Fletcher, all in Fletcher's living room, with the lake out the window and Gizmo at his feet. He would have liked to take joy in Fletcher not minding Gizmo's hair all over the furniture. Instead, his latest vision haunted him.

"Everybody here has gone nuts," Fletcher announced, as he paced behind the couch. "They're lining up at the box, fighting over who gets to go first, every trying to open the blasted thing! And then you have that Henry Hoffner character, insisting that 'all he's waiting for is the right moment.'

"The mayor, however, is pleased, because as long as no one opens the box, she gets to stay in charge!"

But Jasper sat, distracted, everyone's voices echoing around him. Their words bounced off his ears, ringing around inside but not absorbing into his brain. Gizmo noticed and pressed harder up against his leg.

"And now, you're telling me we're gonna lose our lake?!" Fletcher grumbled, exasperated.

"Not if we can help it," Cat answered, turning around on the couch to face him. "But I need to know more about this dam. Is there a way inside or anything?"

Fletcher popped down on the couch. "We have the whole town all in arms ready to kill each other. I don't even know who to ask that we can trust at this point."

"We know a way," a young, soft, tentative voice sang out from over the balcony. Gus and Lilly, apparently unsafe in the town alone, had taken over Jasper's bedroom in his absence. The group turned toward them.

Gus, clearly unsure whether or not this was knowledge he should have, looked at Lilly and trusted her with how best to continue. Lilly looked back at him and then took a deep breath. Perhaps their years of being a public nuisance were about to pay off.

"There's a secret entrance at the base, hidden under the spillway overhang. I think it's left over by the builders. If you're not afraid to get wet, it's a good place to hide..." she looked at Gus, unsure, "...things."

"We don't wanna get in trouble," Gus added, "we just wanna help."

"How could he destroy the dam?" Ertha asked.

"It wouldn't take much," Cat explained, thinking through the problem. "Explosives, maybe. Or, he could just weaken it, but then the timing is less precise."

Jasper wanted to contribute. He wanted to help. But all he could think of were his parents, and that they clearly trusted someone they shouldn't. Was he capable of making the same mistake? Could he really trust everyone sitting in the room right now? They seemed nice, yes, but... how would they handle the moment of trial?

A familiar thought reappeared: he didn't want to *grow up* to defeat Hayalet and Krylios. Perhaps, he had a chance to do it *now* and save decades of frustration... and perhaps his parents from the clutches of whoever had them in his visions. Hayalet was here *now*. He defeated Bull and Racehorse in Eko, he could defeat Hayalet now.

"Let's go see it," Jasper jumped up. "You can get us there? I'm not afraid to get wet!"

Gus and Lilly looked at each other and nodded. "Yes, we can get you there."

Fletcher shook his head. "No," he insisted. "It's too dangerous for them."

Jasper argued back, "You thought things were too dangerous for me, and I just stared down two warring African clans."

He pointed at Ertha, who really did not want to be brought into this. "You thought things were too dangerous for her, so she left."

He paused, just briefly, to see Fletcher wince before he finished his point. "And look at what she's become!"

Fletcher held his breath, as did the rest of the room. He knew Jasper was right, but he didn't have time to admit it before Jasper made up his mind.

"We're going… or, at least, *I'm* going. If you don't let them go, I'll find it myself." He looked up at Gus and Lilly. "You said it's under the spillway overhang?"

They nodded quickly and then looked to Fletcher for guidance.

Fletcher slapped his knees and then stood up, staring beyond the lake to the dam in the distance through his picture window. A light wind whipped up small whitecaps on the lake. A few fishing boats bounced, but not enough to stop their work.

"Alright then," he announced, "It's settled. After dark, we'll all get flashlights, and I'll drive us to the dam. Until then, let's rest up."

Rest, then, is something they would all try, but fail, to achieve.

Chapter 38

Under the cover of darkness, the six of them plus one dog piled into Fletcher's car. Jasper, once again, couldn't help but notice this would be the same car that rescues him from Waveland Mansion forty years in the future. The girls squeezed into the back seat, and Jasper insisted on straddling the gearshift in the front bench. There wasn't room for Gizmo on the front bench, but he squeezed himself up between Jasper and Gus; he would not be content to just lay on the floor without being able to watch where they were going. If they didn't make room for the dog, they weren't going anywhere.

Without turning on his headlights, Fletcher eased the car off his property, and didn't turn on his lights until they had blended onto the road. Everyone sat in silence, listening only to the sound of the tires on the pavement and the rumble of the engine as Fletcher navigated the winding roads on the far side of the lake. Following Cat's advice, everyone but Fletcher closed their eyes the entire ride to let their eyes adjust to the darkness.

Twenty minutes later, Fletcher pulled off the road and into a tall grass field surrounded by bushes. He switched off the lights, and then the engine. "I don't think I can get us any further driving," he said. "Gus and Lilly, can you lead us there?"

They nodded.

"Fletcher, since your eyes haven't adjusted, you take Ertha's hand and go in back," Cat advised. "Don't use our flashlights unless we absolutely need to. As soon as we turn them on, we'll lose our night vision."

"And we'll attract attention from across the lake," Jasper warned. "Gus and Lilly, take us in. We'll follow."

Single file, following Lilly, they marched through the tall grass below the trees bordering the lake. Silently, they heard nothing but the crunch of the grass below them and the wildlife in the nature around them. When they emerged from the trees, they saw the beautiful lake to their right, reflecting the night sky in the still water. To their left, a sharp drop off into a valley below.

"That's the levee," Lilly whispered. "It's not here naturally. It's part of the dam that holds back the lake."

A short walk further, guided by the light of fireflies milling about, they came to a footbridge, and heard the sound of water rushing below their feet. High concrete walls contained the water between them, as it rushed down an artificial waterfall into the river and the valley below.

"This is the spillway," Gus explained. "If we climb down this hill a bit, right behind the waterfall is the doorway to inside the dam."

By now, Fletcher's eyes had adjusted to the darkness, and he didn't need Ertha's guidance. Gingerly, and still single file, the group trod off the trail, guided by the moonlight and the sound of the rushing water. Slowly and carefully, they took just one step at a time, until Gus' feet hit concrete. In front of them, the tall wall of the spillway waterfall.

Gus and Lilly held hands and looked back at the group. They shrugged and said, "Just run through it!"

Then, without warning, they did. They ran toward the waterfall until it swallowed them whole. It was everything Fletcher could do not to turn on his flashlight and search the river below, where he expected to see his two juvenile delinquents floating away. But, before he could warn them to find another plan, Jasper and Gizmo ran into the waterfall, followed by Cat and Ertha.

With nothing left but himself and his own courage, which was quickly draining, Fletcher, too, ran through the water.

Behind the water, a sight few in Newhaven Bay knew existed: they stood on a slimy concrete walkway, with an iron door at the end.

"It's not locked," Lilly said. "But we'll need our flashlights now."

"Wait, hold on!" Cat warned, before anyone could turn on their lights. She pulled a small bag from her pocket. "Everybody wear these."

Jasper smiled as she passed them out: pirate eye patches.

"Eye patches?" Fletcher asked.

"Cover one eye, and you'll keep it adjusted to the darkness," Cat explained. "When we need to come back, uncover that eye, and you'll see just fine."

They all took a moment to don their eye patches and then, with a collective, silent nod, put them on. Jasper even put one on Gizmo, who cooperated gleefully, happy to be one of the group. One at a time, with a click and a flash, they turned on their flashlights and pointed them at the iron door at the end of the ramp.

"Let's go," Jasper said, and pushed past everyone. He reached the door, and with a loud, rumbling groan of the wet, rusty hinges, swung the heavy door open.

When everyone pointed their flashlights inside, they couldn't believe what they saw.

Chapter 39

The dark, narrow, concrete walls of the arched tunnel extended straight back under the levee. For one hundred yards back into the darkness, anyone who entered would need to bring their own light. Jasper studied the layout and pictured the dam's design: this concrete tunnel shaped and held up layers and layers of clay, mud, dirt, and grass that held back the force of the lake's water.

He watched Cat as together, they carefully stepped forward, inspecting the concrete walls with their lights, running their hands over the damp surface. He knew she, too, quickly put together a stunning mental image of the dam's structure.

But the problem wasn't the darkness. Along the entire length of the tunnel, cracks traversed the walls, and water streamed through. Each drop of water, now free from the bounds of the lake, burst through the walls, creating a light but powerful shower all along the tunnel.

The group walked in, already wet from the waterfall, and bravely inched forward, shining their flashlights up, down, and sideways, studying. Gus and Lilly stayed together, stunned that the whole town might soon be grateful for their illegally obtained knowledge.

"It wasn't like this before," Lilly said, perplexed. "It's always been dry."

Gus chimed in. "We've slept here sometimes."

Cat waved Jasper over. The two of them shined their flashlights at a single point on the wall in front of her. "Look," she said, astonished. "Chisel marks."

Jasper studied the scrapings that surrounded the crack. Indeed, the crack wasn't natural. Someone had pounded on the wall with a hammer and chisel until the crack spread from its point. That *someone* wasn't a mystery. Instantly, they all knew: it was Hayalet.

Ertha found her own crack in the wall and, as she moved closer, it too had grown from very clear chisel markings in the wall. As she ran her finger over it and studied, it suddenly widened and a new stream of water burst forth and struck her in the face! The force and surprise knocked her backwards, and she collided with the back wall before falling to the wet floor.

"Ertha, you okay?" shouted Fletcher, who ran to her side to help her up.

"I'm fine," she said, shaking off the shock. "It surprised me more than it hurt."

"It's growing," Jasper explained, in awe of the size and scale of the damage. "Eventually, the wall won't be strong enough to hold back the lake, and it'll crumble."

Fletcher couldn't believe it. This dam had been here his whole life! It was sturdy, immovable, a part of the very earth itself! It's not possible that this dam, even with some help to get started, could just fall apart.

"Are you *sure* the dam fails?" Fletcher pleaded. "It's just... it's just... I don't believe it."

Jasper suddenly found himself overwhelmed with a realization, a lightbulb moment that felt more like a supernova explosion than a simple flick of a switch. Overcome by dizziness and barely breathing, he stumbled, and nearly fell before Cat propped him up. Gizmo rushed to his side and whined.

Jasper knows what's happening, but he removed his crystal from its pouch, held it, and tried to listen, just to be sure. After a moment, he was certain.

"Fletcher," he explained, "remember how I first arrived here in the middle of the lake?"

"Yeah?"

"In the future, future you brought me to the middle of an open field before you gave me my crystal and taught me how to time travel. I think the middle of the field is the same spot as the middle of the lake."

Fletcher huffed. "No, it can't be!"

"I've lived in Newhaven Bay my whole life, and in the future, there's no lake. And it's been gone long enough, no one talks about it anymore."

With Fletcher in a state of shock, struggling to make himself comprehend what was happening, Ertha stepped forward. "Cat, how do we fix this?" she asked, hoping there even was a fix.

Cat wandered up and down the tunnel, running her light across the various cracks, formulating a plan in her head. The group looked on as she mumbled incoherently, dashing from one wall to the next, sometimes shaking her head, rapidly flipping through and rejecting what seemed like hundreds of ideas.

"We have to fill in the tunnel," she explained. "Drill a hole in the top, every ten feet or so. Fill it to the top with gravel and cement powder. The water will turn it into concrete, and it will harden and strengthen over time."

Ertha nodded, able to see Cat's plan. "It'll take the whole town's help, though. We can't do this alone."

"But the whole town's fighting!" Lilly chimed in.

"That's the point," Jasper warned, ominously. "Hayalet plunged the town into a crisis. He made everyone fight each other so that when a *real* crisis comes about, we're too broken to fight it."

He pointed to the walls. "And here's the real crisis."

"How do you know that?" Fletcher asked.

Jasper closed his eyes, clutched his crystal, and sighed with the weight of reluctant assurance. "Because," he said, "that's what I would do." Jasper knew, in that moment, that idea wasn't just his own; it came from him and his crystal working together, as partners.

Clutching his crystal, he listened to it, just as Hassan had taught him. He didn't "hear" anything, not like you can hear someone talking to you, but he realized he knew, in his heart, it was true. He took a breath, nodded, and stored his crystal back securely in the pouch around his neck.

"Guys," he announced, confidently. "I gotta do something. You start working on how to get this plan in action, quickly. I'm gonna put the town back together."

He nodded to Gizmo, and before Fletcher nor anyone else in the tunnel could protest or stop them, the two of them took off running, and disappeared back through the waterfall.

Chapter 40

The box still sat in the middle of Fisherman's Park, taunting the town with its mystery and its inability to be opened nor moved. Everyone in the town heard the legend that only one was worthy of opening the box, and everyone had tried. Some tried twice. Now, few thought it worthwhile to try again in the wee hours of the morning, and the park was quiet.

Under a lamppost, Deputy Street rested his plump feet. The expected light duty of the evening made him the perfect guard. Though the crumbs of a previous pastry decorated the front of his uniform, he opened a paper bag and removed yet another. Pastries, it seemed, were the only thing that got him through a long, boring night of guarding the box.

In an instant, Street, who was not hard to surprise in the first place, spit all over himself when Gizmo leaped onto the bench, stole the chocolate bearclaw from his hands and took off running. He stopped ten feet away and taunted Street to ensure the deputy gave chase. Then, he kept running, at a pace that bored him, slow enough that Street could keep up, but fast enough that he couldn't catch him.

Once sure that Street was distracted enough chasing his second dessert, Jasper crept in swiftly. He approached the copper-walled box. The riveted leather seams bore scars of people attempting and failing to pry it open. In the side, Jasper eyed the single hole.

Slowly, with his right eye, he leaned in closer. What happened next would have shocked anyone lucky enough to look on.

A green light flashed from the hole. A narrow green beam scanned up and down, reading Jasper's eyeball. After two wipes, it retracted back into the hole. Then, with a quiet popping noise, the rivets each popped out, one by one, until nothing held the sides together. A click from inside unlocked the contraption, and the sides of the box slowly fell open.

There was no steam, no rays of light, no organ music, and no magic aura. The sides now lay flat on the ground. And in the middle: nothing.

Nothing.

No weapon. No magic wand. No *Excalibur*. No book of wisdom nor messages from the future. The mysterious box that had ripped apart the sleepy town of Newhaven Bay was just an empty box.

The myth of the box contained more power than the box itself.

Jasper tilted his head in puzzlement. First of all, that meant they were right: the only purpose of the box was to cause conflict. Maybe now that he had opened it and revealed it to be a ruse, could the town go back to normal? Could they get everyone to help repair the dam?

He wrapped his fingers around his crystal's pouch. If they could bring together two warring African clans, they could bring together this town. Together, they could unite Newhaven Bay.

He looked off to the edge of the park to see Deputy Street still chasing Gizmo in futility, and then ran back down to the road. Once Gizmo saw Jasper safely away from the park, he dropped the pastry and ran full-tilt away from Deputy Street, who crouched down, retrieved his snack, and wobbled back to the bench.

Jasper and Gizmo jogged side-by-side, through the empty streets, back up the hills to Fletcher's house. They had work to do.

Chapter 41

When the morning crowd gathered at the park, the surprise was not that someone opened the box. The hushed whispers and gawking of those who gathered, from both sides of the conflict, centered on just *who* had opened the box. It was not someone they expected. They expected either a powerful leader, or a meek peasant, in the style of the story of King Arthur. Instead, who did they get?

Henry Hoffner.

With his hair perfectly styled, wearing his best suit, and resisting his clear temptation to sport a cape, Henry Hoffner stood on the picnic table near the platform containing the now-open box. High above his head, he held a dagger. Long and sharp, the shiny blade protruded from a leather-wrapped hilt, styled in the same leather-and-rivet styling that once adorned the edges of the box.

"Henry Hoffner opened the box," the edges of the crowd told the new onlookers that rushed in from the outskirts of town. Hoffner himself said nothing. He just stood proudly in the center of the crowd, wishing he had a cape billowing in the wind behind him.

Fletcher, Jasper, Ertha, and Cat drove up and dashed into the park to join the crowd. Early this morning, when Jasper burst into Fletcher's house and replayed the story of how the box opened to reveal nothing, Fletcher innocently hoped that meant their whole ordeal was over. But, perhaps, now that the town had divided itself, it could never heal.

"Did anyone actually *see* you open the box?" shouted a skeptical voice from the front of the crowd.

From next to Hoffner, Deputy Street seized his moment. "I did!" he gleefully shouted. "It was magnificent! The hole in the side, it was a button. He pressed the button, and the box just fell open, revealing the dagger!"

"The Dagger of Democracy," Hoffner exclaimed, his voice deeper than normal. "Signifying that I have been deemed worthy of leading the town of Newhaven Bay into the future!"

"The *Dagger of Democracy?*" Ertha mocked to Fletcher. "It's not democracy if a magic box appoints you leader!"

"Right," rebuked Jasper. "And that cop saw nothing. He was chasing Gizmo!"

Hoffner interrupted them, beginning a new speech. "I would like everyone to extend a hand of thanks and gratitude to Mayor Nygaard for leading us so elegantly and wisely these past few years. I look forward to the brave challenge of assuming the mantle, and I hope to be worthy of the praise and adoration you will all show me!"

"Alright," Fletcher calmed the group. "Maybe it's not that bad. Sure, he's a lying thief... but, *maybe* he can bring the town back together again."

"Don't trust a liar," Cat admonished him.

"You can't trust a liar," Jasper corrected her, "but you can *use* one."

Cat glared at him. "Are you serious?"

Jasper shrugged. He is right, after all.

"How do we tell him about the dam?" Ertha asked.

But, her question was not soon to be answered. An argument erupted, showing the rift between the two sides of the town was still alive and well.

"Screw you, Hoffner!" shouted a voice in the crowd.

"Hey, that's our leader!" shouted another.

"Mayor Nygaard's our leader!"

"She couldn't open the box!"

"What did that guy say? That only the one *worthy* of leading could open the box?"

"Why didn't you open it in broad daylight where more people could see you?"

"He's a coward who didn't want to risk failing in front of everyone!"

"Who is some random guy to tell us how our town gets to work, anyway?"

And then, the shouts of the crowd grew too loud and too quick to be distinguished, as the entire crowd erupted into a giant brawl. Punches flew and teeth flew out, and bruises spread around. Polite schoolgirls finally got their chance to use their suppressed anger and surprised the schoolboys with the might of their rage-powered fists.

Fletcher stood tall above the crowd, not joining in, but studying Hoffner. The town's "leader" took a few moments, but he found a way to use the fight to his benefit and try to further legitimize his power.

"Yes, yes!" Hoffner shouted, holding his dagger up high. "The strong will win, and we will move forward together!"

***

Fletcher, Jasper, Ertha, and Cat retreated to the safety of the car. While the battle raged on in the distance, they fretted over what to do next.

"You're right, Jasper," Fletcher lamented. "They are too broken to repair the dam. Tell me it's not useless?"

"It's Hayalet," Jasper asserted. "He's the one doing this. If we can get him out of here, if we can get him to leave us alone, things might go back to normal."

"But how do we do that?" asked Fletcher. "And can it be fast enough?"

Jasper clutched his crystal. *Talk to me,* he thought. *Let's do this together.*

"If I can talk to Hoffner, I think I might have a way of using him to get everyone to work on the dam," declared Ertha. "But you'll have to trust me to do it while you take care of Hayalet. Can you do that, Jasper?"

Through the leather pouch holding his crystal, the crystal nearly burned his hand! He quickly let go of the pouch with a silent *ouch.* If that wasn't a sign from the crystal, he didn't know what was.

"Alright," he said. "I trust you."

"You can get Hayalet to leave us alone?" Fletcher asked, skeptically.

Jasper nodded. "I'll need Cat, and Gizmo." He glanced at Cat. "We can do it."

Cat nodded, ready to help.

Fletcher inhaled apprehensively. Deep down, he knew the town's future, good or bad, would be decided today.

Chapter 42

Outside his cave, hidden in the hills high above town, Hayalet relished what he saw through his looking glass. Finally, he caused the trouble he needed to cause. But one thing troubled him: that box was never supposed to open. He had placed nothing inside of it.

Being able to open that box and convincingly brandish the weapon he supposedly "found" inside showed Hayalet that Henry Hoffner was an even more useful liar than they expected. All he needed now - and what he expected to get - was for Hoffner to dig into his deception, further fracturing the town. The town stood perilously close to the point of no return, where the dam would break, and the lake would drain. Once the town of Newhaven Bay finally died, the original creator of the "King Arthur" story would arrive to investigate why a town destroyed itself over a version of the story he did not plant.

Hayalet uncharacteristically jumped backward at the sight in front of him when he lowered his spyglass. Jasper stood casually, hands in his pockets, leaning against the cave entrance, staring at him with a hint of a smile.

"You!" Hayalet grunted.

"We need to talk," the kid announced. "You got any clothes that don't make you look like a cartoon villain?"

***

The hundreds of young and old, men and women, boys and girls battling in the park dispersed into the streets, and Henry Hoffner remained on his picnic table, dagger in hand. He looked on, casually nodding his head, trying not to show he was actually just too afraid to move off the table.

"Good, good!" he shouted. "I can't wait for the strongest of you to emerge! Imagine all the great things we can accomplish together!"

Fletcher ran up and startled him from behind, and he jumped, assuming that Fletcher was there to pick a fight that Fletcher would surely win. Even without a dagger, Fletcher was at least four times his size. His dagger and devilish good looks were no match Fletcher's muscle and mustache.

"Henry," Fletcher pleaded, much to Henry's relief, "Something's happened with Ertha. I think you're the only one who can help!"

This shot an injection of pride into Henry. *Of course* he was the only one who could help. He is the chosen one, after all. Chosen by himself, yes, but chosen nonetheless. He relished this chance to prove his worth!

He followed Fletcher and ran through the park, wielding his dagger overhead because something told him that's what he needed to do. At Fletcher's car, Fletcher opened the passenger door for him, and he tried to pass it off as being helpful when it seemed like Fletcher shoved him into the passenger seat.

His assumption of good intention vanished, however, when Ertha popped up from the back seat, snatched his dagger, and wrapped her arm around his neck.

"We know you didn't open the box, Henry," she taunted him.

He tried to cover for himself. "But, the prophecy said only one person was worthy. How could I have the dagger if it wasn't me?"

"Because, we *know* who really did."

Henry gulped. "You do?"

"Yes, and we know you didn't get that dagger because that's not what was in the box."

"What *was* in the box?"

Ertha pressed his neck harder. "It doesn't matter," she threatened. "You're still the only one who can save the town."

It wasn't just the pressure of Ertha's bicep against his neck that made his eyes pop. "Really?" he beamed.

Fletcher plopped himself into the driver's seat. "Fletcher's going to take us on a little trip," Ertha continued. "You'll go willingly, every step of the way."

Henry attempted to nod. "Of course! Where we going?"

"Fletcher," Ertha instructed. "To the dam."

Chapter 43

At Jasper's insistence, Hayalet re-familiarized himself with his powder blue suit. The two of them used their time crystals to transport themselves from the cave onto the deserted Main Street, where the fighting crowds had not yet swarmed in. After arriving and retrieving the awaiting Gizmo, Jasper quickly checked his crystal: still bright green. The quick jaunt from the cave hadn't drained it in the slightest.

He sighed, relieved. Now, could he convincingly dupe Hayalet?

"I'm still trying to understand time travel," Jasper said, as the three of them casually strolled past empty storefronts. "You've been chasing me. First, on the *Rogue Wave* when I rescued Cat, then on the *Rogue Wave* again in Liverpool, when I escaped right out from under your nose and went to Lagos, or Eko, as they called it.

"Do you remember those things, or have they not happened yet, in your timeline?"

"They happened," Hayalet acknowledged. "I know who you are."

"And you're not going to try to kill me right now?"

Hayalet shook his head. "My job right now doesn't involve you. I only succeed because I stay focused."

They turned a corner, walking between two brick buildings, toward the lakefront. Normally teeming with activity, all the boats had their sails stowed while their owners battled for supremacy around town.

"I know you're going to destroy the dam," Jasper said. "What do you have against this town?"

The more they walked, the more Hayalet seemed peaceful, at ease, and unarmed. "I have nothing against this town," he explained. "I serve Krylios IV unemotionally."

In silence, they marched another block, to a bench overlooking the water. The beach, again, looked strange to be empty. The voices normally on the beach now echoed, shouting in anger, from the hills above. On the beach, only the gentle swish of the waves in and out harmonized their conversation.

They sat, facing forward and not looking at each other. A temporary truce between two enemies, driven by their curiosity about each other.

Hidden around corners, behind boxes, and through windows, Cat followed at a distance. With a camera and a long lens, she snapped photos. By the time they reached the bench, she had a dozen, though that would be more than she needed. Evidence for a future deception.

She wrapped her fingers around her new time crystal, and for the first time since she tried to stop Hayalet in Liverpool, dissolved away to her next destination.

***

Seagulls comically stumbled about the beach, looking for scraps normally left by the now-absent beachgoers. Above them, Jasper and Hayalet remained on the bench, Gizmo dutifully sitting by Jasper's side, listening intently to the conversation.

"I'm quite busy, Jasper Berry," Hayalet warned. "I'll afford you the ability to talk, but get to it."

Jasper nodded. "You're going to leave this town alone."

"Am I?"

Jasper took a breath, hoping to suck in confidence. "I know I grow up to be the one who brings down Krylios, and I think you do, too."

Hayalet said nothing, but slowly nodded in agreement. Jasper continued.

"Right now, Catalina Rodriguez is waiting to meet Krylios, right after my future self attacks him."

"What makes you think he'll take the meeting?"

"She has something he wants."

Hayalet raised an eyebrow. "And what is that?"

Jasper smiled. "Her. He knows her talents. He's been trying to get her for years. That's why you tracked her down and held her hostage on the *Rogue Wave*."

"Smart of you, to figure that out."

"I know you were planning to have her build a well for the highest bidder, either Adekunle or Oladipo, to have one of them win and give their allegiance to Krylios. I'll have you know *I* solved their problem *and* united them."

Now, Hayalet tried to hide a frown. "You did?" he answered, skeptically.

"I did. Now, you wanted me to get to it, here we go: if you don't leave the dam alone, and leave the town alone, Cat will approach Krylios with pictures of the two of us having a friendly walk and conversation, practically holding hands. I'm sure you don't want him to see that."

Hayalet leaned back and smiled. "Why would I be concerned about some pictures?"

"Because," Jasper leaned in. "You know that I nearly end him. That makes me an enemy. And here you are, spending a great deal of time with me and not doing anything about it."

"I see."

"Keeping me alive could only mean you're planning to double-cross Krylios," Jasper taunted him, "Or at least that's what Cat will tell him."

Hayalet leaned back and took a deep, contemplative breath. But Jasper wouldn't let him have his moment. Taking advantage of a quickly growing avalanche of courage, he pressed in further.

"Cat's monitoring the history books. If she sees that this lake disappears, she approaches Krylios. And you know how badly Krylios wants to meet her."

Hayalet put his elbows up on the back of the bench and crossed his ankle over his knee. He stared at the horizon, a slight smile on his face, undisturbed.

"Jasper Berry," he said, calm and undisturbed. "You have no idea what your future holds."

He removed from his breast pocket his own green time crystal, remarkably similar to Jasper's own. He wrapped his fingers around it, still looking out at the dam on the far side of the lake.

"Fletcher and Ertha are out there at the dam, aren't they?" he asked, already knowing the answer. Then, he turned his glare to Jasper. "You grow up to be the one who destroys Krylios. But, you don't want to *grow up* to do it, do you? You want to do it now! Why wait on Fletcher and Ertha? Why wait on Cat? Why wait for them to do their jobs when you could do yours now?"

Jasper's heart lurched. He wasn't wrong. Before he could say anything, Hayalet reached into his breast pocket again, returned the crystal, and withdrew... a medical syringe and needle? Inside the syringe, a strange, green liquid swirled. At the sight of the syringe, Gizmo whined.

"You've seen your parents the past few days, haven't you?"

Jasper nodded.

"And you know they've been working on a way to let people travel into their own future. Well, here it is," he handed the syringe over to Jasper. "This is it. It's extracted from time crystals brought back from the future... thousands of years into the future. Inject yourself with that, and you can go see your parents *right now*."

Jasper struggled to grasp what he said. Could it be true? Could he see his parents *right now*?

"But," Jasper asked breathlessly, "What about visualization? Don't I need to see where I'm going first? How do I visualize something in the future I've never seen?"

Hayalet leaned in and grinned. "But you *have* seen the future, haven't you?"

His visions. His parents' lab. It was true. He knew where they were; he knew what they looked like. Roughly, he knew where he was going.

Hayalet pressed on. "In the future, you *almost* defeat Krylios. By yourself. Imagine what you could do, together, with your intellect and their science? You're ready, and you have the tools, if you have the will."

Jasper took the syringe and held it delicately between his fingers. The glowing green sloshed and swirled in the chamber. Jasper was used to out-thinking his opponents. And now, with this strange, cruel new twist, Hayalet had out-thought him by reaching deep into the darkest desires of his own mind.

Hayalet stood and stretched. "Truth is, Jasper, I don't need to do anything more. The dam is - pardon the pun - the dam is history."

He reached down and selected a smooth, blue stone from the sand beneath his feet. Effortlessly, he tossed it into the water, where ripples floated out from where the stone plopped in. "I've begun the ripple effect. But where you fall... well, I guess we don't really know yet, do we?"

Before Jasper could say anything, Hayalet nodded at Gizmo, then disappeared in a green cloud and flash. Jasper didn't need to look back up the hill toward the cave. Hayalet was gone, his time in Newhaven Bay complete. There could be no defeating this villain in this time and place.

Only in the future, a place he could now go.

He knew Fletcher, Ertha, and Cat were at their stations, playing their part. He knew they were capable. All he had to do was wait.

Gizmo put his paw on Jasper's wrist and tried to direct his attention away from the syringe. But, as he twirled the glowing green syringe between his fingers, he couldn't help but wonder: what if that didn't matter anymore?

Chapter 44

Henry Hoffner shook off the water from the spillway waterfall and instinctively searched for a mirror with which to reset his hair. Unable to find one, he did the best he could with only his hands, and decided that this is the way he wanted it in the first place.

Ertha led him to the iron door to the tunnel, as Fletcher followed. Henry held his ears to hold back the deafening groan as Ertha strained to open the door. Once open, she and Fletcher shined their flashlights to reveal the rapidly growing cracks in the concrete walls and the thousands of jets of water rushing through.

Henry's eyes widened at the sight. Though he had only just discovered this place existed, and he was barely willing to admit he didn't know how it worked, he knew it didn't look good.

"It's falling apart," Ertha stressed, "and it's been sabotaged."

"Sabotaged?" Henry exclaimed. "What do you mean?"

Ertha pulled him into the tunnel and showed him the chisel marks around the cracks. "Someone *made* these cracks," she explained, shining her flashlight to point out more and more cracks down the length of the tunnel. "Someone is trying to destroy the dam."

"Destroy the dam!" Henry chuckled in obvious denial. "This dam's never going anywhere. You can't destroy this thing!" He pounded on the wall with his fist to gain false reassurance from its satisfactory *thud*.

"It can and it will," Fletcher ducked and joined them, towering over Henry. "Minute by minute, more cracks form. This is already worse than it was yesterday!

"And think about it: This town *depends* on this lake. Without this dam, the lake dries up. When the lake dries up, we lose everything. We lose the fishing business, the shipping business, boat builders, tourism... our view... our *bay*...

"What is Newhaven Bay without the bay?"

"Everything in this town looks like a sea captain decorated it," Ertha pressed on. "It'll look pretty stupid without a body of water in sight."

Henry stuttered and struggled for words. "I... I... I... I mean... well... wh... what do you want me to do?"

Ertha pressed a finger into his chest. "*You're* the only one who can unite the town!"

"Me?" he recoiled. "I... it can't be me."

"You have the dagger!" she kept poking him.

"I made it up! I'm not the chosen one!"

Fletcher grabbed his shoulders. "And that's why it has to be you."

Henry still didn't get it. "But how?" he exclaimed.

"Tell the truth," Ertha told him, as clear as she could make it. "*If* you tell the truth, *if* you tell them what you did, that the box was already open, that you're not the chosen one, they'll know you're not their leader... but you *will* have their attention."

"Then," continued Fletcher, "you tell them about the dam, what's at stake, and how to fix it."

A new crack opened overhead and more water rained down on them. With the lake dripping down his face, Henry shook his head.

"What if they don't listen to me?"

Fletcher and Ertha looked at each other, and shrugged.

"Then we're done for," Fletcher warned, glum and deflated. "If saving the lake doesn't bring the town back together, nothing will."

Henry turned away from them, and stared further down the tunnel, running his fingers through his slick, wet hair. From behind him, Ertha looked on, and tried to reassure him.

"You wanted to be the greatest man in Newhaven Bay," she assured him, softly. "Maybe, admitting you lied is the best way to do that? Maybe that's the true path to becoming the greatest man in Newhaven Bay?"

"How do we fix it?" Henry asked, still studying the cracks.

"We fill it in," explained Fletcher. "It'll take trucks, shovels, and lots and lots of people. We can only do it if they stop fighting."

Henry huffed, and then pivoted, marching back toward the tunnel entrance. "Let's go," he ordered. "We don't have much time."

Chapter 45

The Future

The sidewalk cafe in Belgium hardly looked like it had been through battle. Cat sat at her tiny table, a mug of coffee in hand, with the crumbs of a finished biscuit on a plate to her side. The yellow stone walls of the old, tall apartments kept the cafe in a cool, constant shadow, though with the sun always nearby to keep the mood bright.

The world seemed almost blind to the great battle that had dismantled the Krylios Organization. A mafia, really, Cat considered it, and Krylios IV the boss. Everyone involved did only one thing: they researched innocent people, discovered horrifying events in their future, and promised to protect them from the oncoming horror for the small price of everything they had.

And it's a price they would gladly pay to prevent the death of a loved one.

It was horrible, and that's why Cat refused to join. She's glad they're nearly gone, and she wants to do her part to help Jasper finish the job.

But first, she has a job of her own. In an envelope on the tabletop, a dozen pictures of Hayalet and Jasper practically holding hands on a moonlit walk through Newhaven Bay, the type of friendly chat that would enrage Krylios. In her own hand, a map of Newhaven Bay. As soon as the lake appeared on the map, she would know Ertha, Fletcher, and Jasper had succeeded, and that Hayalet would leave their town alone. And, if that didn't happen soon, she knew how to get a meeting with Krylios.

She sipped her coffee. Waiting to meet with Krylios wasn't her only goal. Jasper didn't know about this one, and she hoped to never have to tell him.

She recognized the two figures walking up the sidewalk, who just caught sight of her at the end of the cafe.

Tall and middle-aged, a peppered-gray black-haired man with glasses, and a tall woman with graying blonde hair.

Jasper's parents.

They joined her at the table with pleasant smiles, finally adjusting to life freed from Krylios' grasp... but under the constant threat it might return. Cat stood to greet them.

"Irma, Marvin," she smiled and excitedly took their hands. "Thanks for coming. I wasn't sure you would!"

Marvin pulled out a chair to gentlemanly assist Irma in sitting and then sat down himself. "No, it's our pleasure," he said. "Truth is, we were hoping you might show up."

"Really?" Cat seemed a bit taken aback. Actually, something else bothered her, too. Though they had never met, Irma and Marvin seemed a bit... familiar. But she shook it off. That couldn't be.

"Well," Cat explained, "I really just wanted to reassure you that your plan to save Jasper worked. He's alive, well, and happy back in Newhaven Bay with Fletcher."

"Young Fletcher?" Irma asked. She strangely didn't seem all that enthused by the news.

"Yes. Why? Is there a problem?"

Irma leaned over and quietly whispered something to Marvin. She couldn't quite hear it all, but she thought she heard, "the backup plan." What did that mean?

Marvin seemed to hesitate before he answered. "Well, you see, that plan... the plan to rescue him from Waveland Mansion... it wasn't a plan of ours."

"We're delighted that he's safe, of course," Irma chimed in.

"Yes, absolutely. You have pictures?" Marvin asked.

Cat nodded and took out the pictures of Jasper and Hayalet. Irma and Marvin shuddered looking at them, far from the happy, joyful parents she expected.

"I'm sorry," Cat pleaded, suddenly changing her mood. "Truly, I didn't know."

"No, no," Irma interrupted, "This is wonderful." She turned to Marvin. "He's alive, and maybe this time he will... or he won't..."

Cat looked on, and with her eyes, pressed them to say more.

"It's just like we remember him from back then," Marvin added. "Cat, tell me, has the dam burst yet?"

Cat checked her map. Sure enough, right at Newhaven Bay, the lake reappeared. She smiled. Their plan worked! Somehow, Henry Hoffner led the town into repairing the dam! Somehow, mere mortals defeated Hayalet! But, looking at the two nearly distraught parents sitting across from her, she felt there was more to the story.

"The plan seems to have worked," she said. "But, how did you know?"

Irma nodded and mustered up the courage to push through her emotions. "Cat, this isn't the first time you've met us."

I knew it! She thought. I knew they looked familiar!

"We were there, in Newhaven Bay," Marvin added. "But we had different names."

Cat instantly knew. Her eyes exploded wider! It was as if all her brain cells had fired at once! She burst out of her chair, nearly shouting.

"You're Gus and Lilly!"

They nodded. Cat, embarrassed to have caused a scene at the normally tranquil cafe, regathered her chair and eased back down.

"When we wanted to go into science, our names had a record," Marvin explained. So, with Fletcher's help even, we changed them."

"And, Cat," Irma... or Lilly added... "There's really only one reason why we wanted to meet you today."

She closed her eyes and hesitated. After a moment, she found the strength to continue.

"There's something you don't know about Jasper. And now that you're involved, it's important that you know."

Chapter 46

Liverpool, 1750

Hayalet knew he had failed. His entire life, his one and only goal was to defeat evil. Day after day, year after year, he did nothing but look evil in the face so much that, by now, evil was all he could see.

Krylios IV would live, for now. Most of the organization was gone. Krylios would rebuild, of course, and this time without Hayalet. Quickly and swiftly, a plan Hayalet built over years, he destroyed every layer of the Krylios mafia… except the top. Somehow, some way, at precisely the last moment, Krylios had seen it coming.

After his narrow escape, Hayalet now sat alone, on the bare floor between the bare rock walls of his tiny cottage just outside Liverpool, 1750. By his side, the only partner he could count on: an intelligent brown Australian shepherd with a tag that said, "Gizmo" hanging from his neck.

Gizmo didn't think it strange in any way to feel a man as large, tough, powerful, and scarred as Hayalet reach down and give him one last hug around the neck. Hayalet's image as Krylios' tough enforcer was only an act, designed to earn him access to the very top. In the layers of his heart he shielded from the rest of the world, Hayalet loved this dog.

Gizmo, too, loved his master in return. The dog seemed to be the only other living creature on Earth and across time that saw through his master's heart.

"You know what to do, Gizmo," Hayalet whispered, holding his dog in one last embrace. "Find him." Then, he looked on in longing as Gizmo obediently leaped through the glassless window and began his long run toward the docks in Liverpool.

The sudden inward explosion of his door signaled that his current failure was complete. Krylios' two new henchmen had found him. His replacements. When they entered, they found Hayalet strangely smiling - smiling because he knew something they didn't.

They would kill him now, for sure. That was unavoidable. But, as a man who spent his entire life planning for every eventuality, he had also planned for this.

He knew, one day, he would attempt to destroy Krylios. He also knew Krylios was so formidable that his plan may fail. So, he'd also spent decades building a backup plan that spanned across centuries. If he failed to bring down Krylios, it would set in motion a series of events that gave him a chance to begin again, from the beginning. He would get another chance to learn what he had not learned the first time, a second chance to acquire the skills that would allow him to attack Krylios again, only this time, more intelligently.

And that plan began with an old friend of his parents: Fletcher.

Hayalet smiled at Krylios' two new henchmen, one with the stature of a bull and the other with the attitude of a racehorse.

"Did you know," he smiled as he told them, "when I was twelve years old, I lived in a boy's orphanage in Rhode Island? That's where my story began."

The weapon Racehorse pointed at him, shiny and metallic, was entircly out of place in 1750. As the weapon's hidden internal parts *whirred* into operation, he warned, "And tonight is where your story ends."

With his final thoughts, Hayalet rebuked them. "Krylios has already lost. He just doesn't know it yet."

***

Hiding between buildings just outside the docks at Liverpool, Gizmo saw a familiar green flash in the distance. He stood back and watched, ready to jump in and help his young master when the time came.

Chapter 47

Newhaven Bay

Fletcher never thought magic was real. Then again, he didn't think time travel was real, until a time traveler showed up in the middle of his lake and he found out his niece somehow worked for them. If time travel could be real, then so could magic, and that magic was on full display the past few days in Newhaven Bay.

Remarkable, Fletcher thought, as Henry Hoffner took the podium in the park and sang an admission of his own lie through a megaphone. For a moment, so aghast was the town, they forgot their fight against each other. They forgot just long enough to keep listening, as he implored them to marshall their resources for emergency repairs on the dam.

Near instantly, men and women dropped their fisticuffs, retrieved their wheelbarrows, started their trucks, and scrounged up enough gravel to fill dozens of dump trucks. Henry turned leadership over to Fletcher, who directed traffic atop the dam. One hole at a time, they drilled through the top, dumped in a load of concrete mixture (per Cat's instructions), and moved onto the next.

One day is all it took. They *weren't* too broken to fix what was most important. When they had no choice but to repair the dam that literally held their town together, they did it. Together.

They filled the next few days with apologies, some fast and some slow, some easy and some hard... but they would come. Slowly, the diners and cafes reopened. Officer Pierce and Deputy Street returned to their more comfortable roles of directing traffic. People walked down the streets and, once they got over the inertia of that first timid wave, smiles crept back into Newhaven Bay.

The crisis over, Gizmo chased rabbits in Fletcher's yard while Jasper sat below the majestic picture window overlooking the lake. Finally, he could turn his attention to something that truly interested him, the book he discovered his first morning at Fletcher's house: <u>Riverboats of the Mighty Mississippi</u>. He flipped through happily, looking at pictures, mostly, too tired to read.

The vial of green liquid with which Hayalet had tempted him earlier was now destroyed, crushed beneath his feet and dissolved into the lake. So badly, he wanted, to leap into the future, save his parents, and destroy Krylios right then and there. But, he now knew he would not be able to do this alone. He would need Cat, he would need Ertha and Fletcher, and he would need Gizmo. Hassan would be helpful, if he could find him again.

Some battles can't be won just by picking up a weapon and fighting, Hassan taught him. Really, it was his time in Eko, and his time here in Newhaven Bay that taught him this lesson. Hassan just tied it all up in a bow. Under the guise of being helpful, Hayalet had handed him a death sentence.

Now, Jasper knew better. But more time for learning would come later. At this moment, all he wanted to do was mindlessly flip through pictures of old steamers while his dog played outside.

How did that dog get so smart? He thought. *And where did he come from?* These thoughts, and more, he would save for later.

Ertha and Fletcher sat at the table behind him. Cat had not yet returned from the future, but they expected her shortly. Ertha's contacts in the library assured her Cat was still alive and well.

"I'm sorry for accusing you of being in league with Hayalet," Ertha apologized, recalling their spy operation on Hayalet's meeting at Shipley's. "I know you're not. I still don't know though, how Hayalet could repeat your words almost exactly."

Fletcher shrugged. "Maybe I'm famous in the future."

Ertha smiled and shook her head. "No."

"I've always wanted to write a novel."

"It doesn't sell."

Fletcher rolled his eyes.

"But write it anyway," Ertha urged him.

As they chatted behind him about nothing in particular, Jasper blankly flipped through the book as his thoughts drifted helplessly to the future. Eventually, he would take down Krylios, or *almost*. When should he start? Should he start planning? What does he need to learn?

Should he return to his own time, to Waveland Mansion? Or did he now belong here, with Fletcher, and Ertha? So many questions bothered him, he was glad he had this familiar book to distract him, at least a little.

As he flipped through the pages, he now landed on the familiar story of the *Natoma*. He once again studied the picture of the magnificent, three-deck steam-driven paddle-wheeler, ornately decorated in the best of 1890's riverboat styling. Like a long cake, with a black base and three white layers above, smoke billowed out the twin smokestacks protruding from the vessel's flat roof.

He gazed at the passengers casually walking up the gangway on the *Natoma's* final voyage, which ended in catastrophe, when her boilers exploded on a mile-wide section of the river outside St. Louis. He didn't need to read the book now to remember it: officially, it was an accident, but some thought it the result of nefarious dealings.

And then, something caught his eye. He held the book closer to his face.

It's remarkable how little detail one needs to make out a familiar face. Leaning against the railing on the top deck, as women in puffy dresses and men in top hats walked behind him, Jasper recognized a tall man in a powder blue suit gazing at the passengers boarding on the gangway. His heart leaped, and it was unmistakable.

Hayalet.

Instantly, Jasper knew: the *Natoma* sank from nefarious dealings, indeed.

He looked behind him, at Ertha and Fletcher still chatting away at the kitchen table. Now that the immediate crisis was over, they had a lot of work to do. But now, something more pressing ate at Jasper.

In the future, he *almost* defeats Krylios. Armed with this knowledge, he doesn't know how many years he has, but he *must* find a way to finish the job. He needed a teacher, and now he knows just where to find one that knows Krylios' darkest secrets. Hayalet had every reason to kill him, and yet, did not. Jasper smiled. He liked his chances in a second round.

Fletcher and Ertha didn't even notice Jasper roll off the couch, escape into the yard, call over Gizmo, and then disappear in a green flash.

***

In a flash, Catalina Rodriguez re-awoke in Ertha's old bed at Fletcher's house. This time, she paid no attention to the furnishings nor the paintings, but ran downstairs, as quickly as possible, her heart still pounding.

"Guys," she yelled, pounding down the steps from the upper level, skipping every second or third step. "Guys! Where's Jasper?"

Fletcher looked around and spotted the empty couch. "I dunno," he said, "He was just here."

"Are you okay?" Ertha asked, noticing Cat's flush face and rapid breath.

Cat huffed and wheezed, spitting words out between gasps of air. "We... could... have a... problem."

"What?" Ertha implored.

"I... just... got back... from the future... Jasper's parents." She took around to ensure Gus and Lilly weren't home. Ertha and Fletcher eagerly waited for her next words, hoping she would not pass out.

"What?" Fletcher implored. "What about Jasper's parents?"

"No, not them," she gasped. "It's Jasper." She paused. She didn't know if she could say it. Not to them, not after everything they just went through.

"What?" Ertha pleaded.

Cat slowed her breath and looked at them, her face overcome with panic and seriousness. Knowing she had to, she broke the news.

"They told me something about Jasper... something horrible."

Epilogue

The deafening roar of a steam whistle bellowed overhead. In the vested suit of a wealthy boy, Jasper led Gizmo down the third deck of the *Natoma*. Though the steward was reluctant to let the shaggy dog aboard, Jasper talked his way past, ensuring that since Gizmo had a ticket, there was no reason to deny him boarding.

He made his way down the deck, toward a tall man in a powder blue suit and a top hat to cover his baldness. He leaned against the railing, overlooking the last few passengers making their way up the gangway. His eyes widened when Jasper tapped him on the shoulder to get his attention.

"You!" Hayalet grunted. But he played calm, and didn't let this child disrupt his demeanor. "You're not supposed to be here."

"We have work to do," Jasper told him, confidently.

Moments later, the captain raised the gangway and blew the whistle once again. The *Natoma's* red paddlewheel churned the waters of the mighty Mississippi as they headed north, upstream, toward St. Louis.

The End.

Also by David Dubczak

For young readers:

Torpedoed! Surviving the Lusitania

Based on True Events

***

Passengers set sail aboard the RMS Lusitania after an ominous warning: submarines might sink her before she arrives in England!

It's the First World War, and Great Britain is at war with Germany. Despite the war, two thousand people dare to ignore the warning and travel anyway.

Seventeen-year-old deckhand Leo Masterson joins the crew of the RMS Lusitania at the last minute. He knows the Lusitania is fast enough to outrun any submarine! But the uncertainty of sailing into a warzone makes all the passengers and crew nervous.

The night before they reach the English coast, Captain Turner asks Leo to help get all the lifeboats ready for lowering. Should Leo be worried?

***

Chapter 24

Captain Turner stood on the starboard bridge wing. *The captain always goes down with the ship*, the saying goes. But Captain Turner knew the moral of the tale: the captain should not try to save himself until he knew everyone on board was safe.

The torpedo hit Lusitania at 1:50. His pocket watch now read 2:00. In less than ten minutes, Lusitania's bow had already disappeared under the water. He would *never* know if everyone was safe. He doubted any of Lusitania would be left by 2:10.

As he stood on the bridge wing, he also knew a horrible truth: no one would be coming to help. Last September, the HMS Aboukir of the British Navy was sunk by a submarine. The HMS Cressy and the HMS Hogue, sailing nearby, rushed to help.

Unfortunately, the U-9 that sank the Aboukir waited for her rescuers to arrive, and then sank the Cressy and Hogue as well. In one day, one ghostly submarine sank three of Britain's finest warships.

Captain Turner knew the British Royal Navy's new orders: no ocean-going vessels could come to the rescue of a submarine attack. All he could do now was stand on his bridge and watch the lifeboats struggle to get away in time.

Captain Turner had never been a war captain. He had never sailed on a warship. But he knew, until this war, warships always saw their enemy coming.

Before steam, it was sails. You could see the enemy's sails for miles, and be ready when they caught you. To fight you, they would have to get close enough to see your face.

But that was before.

Lusitania was not a warship, and Turner was not a war captain. And now, his ship was the victim of war, sunk by an enemy he didn't see coming. He couldn't see their faces. He never even saw their ship!

The rules of war didn't just change; they vanished.

Like the ship that sunk him.

He remained standing on the bridge wing as the deck sank from under him, and the wash from the water carried him away into the open sea.

He wondered if his enemy could see his face.

Torpedoed! Surviving the Lusitania
is available through:
Amazon
Barnes and Noble
Direct from Author at www.DavidDWriter.com
and usually available to order through your favorite
local bookstore.

About the Author

David Dubczak is an educator, author, and playwright. His writing interests include history and comedy. Originally from Holmen, Wisconsin, he lives in Iowa with his wife Laura and dog Avila, whom they affectionately refer to as "Noodle."

You can read his plays and check out his other writings, with more to come, at DavidDWriter.com.

Look for "David Dubczak – Writer" on social media.

Like this book? Amazon and GoodReads reviews are essential to helping independent authors grow their brand. Please share how much you enjoyed this book!